**Levels of**

(The sequel of

**P N Tho**

## _Acknowledgements_

### _Cover Creation_

Jake J Thompson

### _Proof reading_

Eve Vangeline

### _Createspace & Amazon_

Leon Gray

### _Dark blue trainers donated by_

Sammy Wills

### _Editing_

Sherri Weber

**Thank you again gang**

# Levels of Deception

*The things that we see in front of us are not always as they first appear to be….*

*The mind often tells the eye what it chooses to see….*

## Level One
## Wednesday January 3rd 2001

It was just after nine on a very cold morning when thirty three year old autistic genius David Stringer scrutinised files inside Jane Chapman's computer at Glade road Watford.

He viewed them however from one of his own computer monitors at Tranton road Bermondsey south east London.

He scanned for information that his complex mind recalled from some point in the past during one of his many clandestine visits to Chapman's computer files.

Although Jane Chapman was something of an expert in this particular field even she had absolutely no idea that her own computer system was being routinely invaded by David Stringer.

Chapman was by now largely responsible for the abduction sale and transportation of more than a thousand people from the streets of London England although she wasn't solely responsible.

She had considerable help from a few of her friends.

The auction site that was buried deep inside a bogus online dating website was however her personal concept and creation.

David Stringer continued to stare at the screen in front of him.

"I know you're in here somewhere because I've seen you before." He quietly uttered to himself.

In fact he was actually talking to Jane Chapman's files as he stared at them.

As he carefully scrutinised the monitor his heavily magnified eyes suddenly widened and appeared even larger than usual.

"There you are my skinny little friend." He quietly uttered with a grin.

Without removing his stare from the screen he reached across with his left hand and picked up his mobile phone.

"I knew I'd seen you in here."

Without removing that stare he started to press the international dialling code for Turkey from memory into the phone but suddenly his train of thought was interrupted by a faint knock from downstairs at his front door.

David sighed.

"Who the hell can that be?"

He kicked back his black office chair after he stood up.

He then headed out of the room and made his way down the burgundy threadbare carpeted staircase.

"I just got myself ready then!" He said with a sigh.

A few moments later down in the hall he opened the front door and an icy winter chill blew inside.

His over magnified eyes widened again as he now stared at an attractive woman that stood on his doorstep.

She stared back at him.

She had long straight blonde hair and bright blue eyes and he correctly judged that she was in her mid to late twenties.

"Hello." David nervously said.

As he continued to stare into her blue eyes she smiled back at him.

"Hi, are you David?" She asked.

Stringer didn't nod or shake his head to confirm or deny anything and he wasn't going to until he at least knew who she was and what she wanted.

Something was however just beginning to manifest at the back of his mind.

He couldn't quite recall what that was or who she was for that matter but something was there.

David's medical conditions dictated that he sometimes developed limited short term memory issues and with the tasks that he had set himself today, he had completely forgotten that she was due to arrive.

All that mattered to him right now was that she was quite hot.

She was quite tall at around five feet eight or five feet nine and her long straight blonde hair was pulled back into a ponytail.

She did somehow look vaguely familiar to David.

"Have we met before?" He nervously asked her.

It was freezing outside and David didn't know it yet but she had just travelled up to London by train from her home at Ashford Kent in the south east of England.

She was dressed in a fully fastened thick black padded jacket and figure hugging faded blue denim jeans with dark blue training shoes on her feet and she carried a completely empty dark blue canvas holdall bag.

"I'm Jaz." She informed him.

"Are you David?" She asked again.

"You did know I was coming here today, didn't you?"

She still stared as David continued to stare back at her.

The atmosphere was more than a little uncomfortable but he wasn't about to give anything away just in case.

Her question was followed by another uncomfortable pause of silence from both of them as they continued to stare at each other.

Jaz waited to be invited inside as David slowly allowed all of the relevant information to sink in.

It was from a vague conversation that he had on New Year's Eve and this woman was very slowly becoming that relevance.

Eventually he managed a half smile before he ushered this still quite vague recollection of a woman into his house.

He finally concluded that she wasn't a result of one of his many failed online dating conquests and as soon as he closed the front door behind the mystery blonde everything suddenly cascaded into place.

"Oh crap I know who you are!" He blurted.

"You've come for the wig and the eyes haven't you?"

She continued to stare at him.

"That has to be the single most random question that I've ever been asked." She replied.

Jaz then smiled at him again.

"Were you expecting somebody else?" She asked.

David now displayed a wry smile of his own.

"Well obviously lots of women do come here but no." He replied.

"Oh obviously they do." She sarcastically uttered.

She continued to stare into his over magnified eyes and they blinked back at her in slow motion.

"Come upstairs." David finally said.

Jaz took in a long deep breath and then sighed.

"Wow I didn't even get offered coffee first."

David ushered Jaz up the threadbare carpeted staircase and eventually into his converted office bedroom where she slowly scanned the room before she turned to face him.

"Do you launch rockets from here or something?" She asked.

She started to slowly turn full circle until she eventually faced him again.

David displayed a grin partly due to her quite comical question.

He also now recalled exactly why she was here.

"Yes I do." He eventually replied.

Jaz stared at him and his grin disappeared but then it reappeared some ten seconds later.

She then picked up an orange handled electronic screwdriver from the table to examine it.

David immediately took it from her hand with a fake smile.

*'You might be quite hot but don't touch my stuff!'* He thought to himself.

He didn't however say it out loud.

"So what's this?" Jaz asked.

She walked toward the monitor that displayed the data from inside Jane Chapman's computer at Watford.

David followed her and promptly minimised the information to reveal his personalised screensaver which was a bikini clad brunette on a beach.

He just as promptly returned to the contents of Chapman's less revealing data to the screen.

"Your stuff is over here." He announced.

He pointed to a large white cardboard box as he walked toward it and Jaz followed him.

From on top of the table beneath the closed window Jaz reached forward and removed the lid from the large square white box and stared into it.

She then reached inside and pulled out a long wavy blonde wig that was actually not unlike her own natural straight blonde hair.

"There are coloured contact lenses inside this." David informed her.

He displayed in his hand a small black plastic tube that had a grey sealable cap and then he scrutinised her pale blue eyes for a brief moment.

"There are two green pairs and two blue pairs." He added.

Jaz nodded with acknowledgement as she briefly studied the small black tube.

She opened up her large blue canvas holdall bag and stuffed the wig inside it before she placed the black tube that contained four pairs of coloured contact lenses into a small side pocket.

David now reached into the opened white box and removed a small sealed plastic bag that he opened while Jaz watched.

"Are those the moles?" She asked.

David nodded as he placed one of them onto the tip of his right forefinger and then carefully and very gently pressed it onto the left side of her bare neck.

"Won't they get picked up by some kind of detecting device at the airport?" She asked.

She pulled her long straight blonde hair out of the way as David carefully pressed the mole onto her neck and then he very gently blew onto it.

"These aren't transmitters or receivers." He informed her in a very quiet tone.

"So there's nothing inside them to pick up."

He then gently stroked the small dark brown mole that was now firmly stuck onto her neck before he moved to the right side.

"So these ones are just for decoration then?" Jaz asked.

David started to gently press down the second identical mole but a little lower and this time on the right side of her neck.

"Yes one is to use and the other is a spare in case the first one somehow gets lost." He replied.

Jaz suddenly displayed a playful grin.

"So which is the first one?" She asked.

There was a tease in her tone but it completely bypassed David's current train of thought.

"That one is." He eventually replied.

He pointed to the mole on the other side of her neck.

"That's why I put it on first."

There was absolutely no difference between the two fake moles.

For a few moments the slightly startled blonde stared into his over magnified eyes with disbelief.

She eventually leaned her head to the left so that David could finish sticking down the second mole onto the right side of her neck.

She then felt another cool breeze as he gently blew onto it.

"Does that blowing help the glue to dry quicker?" She asked.

In his own little world David thoughtlessly shook his head.

"There is no glue." He replied.

"They positively react to body heat, don't worry they can't just fall off." He added.

He continued to gently blow.

Jaz stared up at the window for a few moments as she digested this new information.

Eventually however she just had to ask the next question.

"If there's no glue why are you blowing onto my neck?" She finally asked.

She turned to face him and stared into his over magnified eyes.

David immediately stopped blowing and stared back at her but still with pursed lips.

"So that's everything!" He eventually announced.

Jaz could see that his face was now slightly reddened.

"When do you fly out?" He asked.

She watched him walk toward the right side of the room purely to avoid eye contact with her.

"At ten o'clock on Saturday morning and if there's no glue why were you blowing onto my neck you little shit?" She asked.

Of course she already knew the answer to her own question.

The remainder of her time inside David Stringer's house was a time of quite uncomfortable silence.

She decided to make an excuse about train timetables and that she needed to head back to her home at Ashford Kent.

David was the first to meet her and he definitely made quite an impression.

## Level Two
### Wednesday January 3rd 2001

There were four connected computers on top of the work surface on the left side of the room and David Stringer's complex mind always seemed to use them in sequence from left to right.

He re-read the international telephone dialling code that he earlier memorized that was buried deep inside Jane Chapman's computer files.

He dialled it and the accompanying private telephone number into his own phone but he still didn't press the green button to make the call.

David used the computer monitor to the right of the first to locate a German spy satellite that was about to pass over western Turkey from some sixty miles high in the sky.

He then used the third computer to activate a series of codes.

Within a matter of two minutes the corrugated steel roof of the shed that stood outside in his concealed back garden slowly started to electronically slide open.

"Euston we don't have a problem." He chuckled.

David was more than a little nervous about what he was about to do.

Suddenly on that same third monitor a vague overhead projection came into view and he grinned again.

"German technology is bloody marvellous." He quietly uttered.

He started to use the additional functions of the overhead German satellite and the image on the monitor systematically closed in on its target.

As David watched the process he pressed the green button on his phone and listened to the long number as it dialled and he waited for the slightly distorted image to clear.

The recipient of the call picked up and David broke into another broad smile.

"Good morning Mr Sanchez." He chirped with an element of sarcasm in his tone.

David received no reply from the forty three year old Spanish trafficker on the other end of the line.

"Before you hang up the call Mr Sanchez I think you should listen very carefully to what I have to say." David continued.

"My name is Dave and I've been watching every single move that you've made for the past six months." He informed Sanchez.

"Like this morning when you went out and bought a newspaper." He added.

"And I can always watch you wherever you are in the world." He continued.

"Like right now as I'm staring at your hotel at Manisa in Turkey."

Miguel Sanchez stared across the spacious hotel room at his wife Theresa.

She also listened to the call via the inbuilt loudspeaker device.

Theresa stared back at her husband in complete silence.

She watched Miguel walk toward a closed sliding glass door that led out onto the balcony of their luxurious fourth floor hotel apartment.

Miguel pulled open the glass door and stepped out onto the balcony where his narrow squint-like eyes carefully scanned the area outside where he paid particular attention to the parked cars below.

"Can you see me yet?" David asked him.

He then bit into a cold triangular slice of last night's delivered pizza.

"You're looking in the wrong direction." He added with a mouthful of food.

Sanchez spun around and glanced back into his hotel room at his wife.

"I'm definitely not in there." David chuckled.

That remark showed Sanchez that David really could see him right now.

It wasn't a bluff.

He continued to toy with Miguel before Theresa Sanchez also appeared on the balcony.

"And there's the lovely Mrs Sanchez!" David said.

He zoomed in just a little closer before he covered the mouthpiece of the phone with his hand.

"Actually she's not that lovely is she?" He very quietly uttered.

"Now as you can see I really am watching you Mr Sanchez." David eventually continued.

There was another lengthy pause before Miguel Sanchez finally responded for the very first time.

"What is it that you want?" He quietly asked.

He continued to search for this caller within the immediate vicinity of the hotel.

'They never look up.' David thought to himself.

"I have a friend of a friend of a friend that wants to meet with you in Turkey Mr Sanchez."

He continued to watch both Miguel and Theresa search for him in the full car park below.

"I am sorry but I must leave Turkey today for a business trip." Sanchez lied.

Miguel and Theresa continued to search.

David sat back in his black leather office chair.

"Mr Sanchez if you return to the Indigo before you meet with my associate we'll inform the authorities about your activities within ten minutes of you boarding it." David assured him.

"And yes I also know that the captain is your cousin Louis Fernandez." He revealed.

The image started to distort because from sixty six miles above the German spy satellite gradually started to move out of range.

"Stay at that same hotel until you hear from me again Mr Sanchez." David calmly instructed.

"If you move at all the authorities will know about that ship before you even reach it." He added.

"And we both know what they'll find inside some of those big containers don't we?"

He then glanced down at his phone and used his thumb to press onto the red button and abruptly ended the call.

There was a momentary pause before he glanced back at his computer screens and took in a long deep breath.

David then chuckled.

He logged off from everything connected in front of him so that the call could never be traced back.

"How was that Richard?" He asked.

"It scared the bloody life out of me!" He added.

Richard Willows had listened to the entire one sided conversation.

"Dave that was brilliant." He replied.

"Keep an eye on him to make sure that he stays at the hotel." He added.

"Call him again in a couple of hours to arrange the meet."

David nodded as he stared at one of the computer monitors in particular.

"Miguel Sanchez is on his phone right now to his cousin Louis Fernandez on the Indigo."

## Level Three
**Friday January 5th 2001**

It was just after nine on a grey wet morning when a silver Ford car pulled up in a narrow alleyway beside a disused Chinese restaurant just five minutes walking distance from the bustling Charing Cross railway station London.

The recently appointed substitute boss of the task force initially assembled to tackle the case of the missing homeless back in July of last year, sat in the passenger seat.

Fifty three year old Chief Inspector Keith Curtis now temporarily transferred from New Scotland Yard, stared across at the driver of the car.

"Are you sure you're going to be ok with this?" He asked.

Forty seven year old Detective Inspector Sam Henning glanced back at him and took in a long deep breath before he blew it out.

He nodded his head in silence but the truth was that Sam didn't really know how he felt right now.

"Just try to remember that he isn't your boss anymore." Curtis said.

"He's now our prime suspect."

The permanently closed Chinese restaurant at Henrietta Street wasn't and had never been a genuine restaurant of any description.

It was and always had been a New Scotland Yard disguised safe house front.

The shop was actually the face of an undisclosed holding facility that was owned and in continuous use by undercover officers.

Curtis figured that if the abductors were bold enough to send Roberts into an interview room to hand a suicide pill to the captured foreign abductor, they could be bold enough to attempt a rescue or assassination of the former Chief Inspector too.

He wasn't about to take any chances.

As much as Curtis disliked Roberts he was one of just two inside links to the case and the other, a Romanian former soldier wasn't talking at all.

They had no idea that Emil Hagi was even Romanian and there was absolutely no clue leading to his identity.

Right now the suspended Chief Inspector Martin Roberts was their best, in fact only realistic option.

Curtis and Henning climbed out from the car and closed the doors behind them before they walked to the front of the shop where Curtis knocked on a badly painted red door on the left side of the disused shop itself.

"I was expecting a top secret holding facility to be a little more glamorous." Sam quietly chuckled.

Curtis shook his head.

"We're hiding Roberts in plain sight." He replied.

"And whoever they are will probably also be looking for something a little more glamorous." He added.

When the red door slowly opened Sam Henning saw a tall and broad plain clothed police officer that immediately stepped aside as Chief Inspector Curtis stepped inside.

Sam could see that the two men knew each other well.

Thirty one year old Daryl Rickets from New Scotland Yard nodded to Sam as he followed Curtis inside.

"Rickets this is DI Henning from the task force headquarters." Curtis explained.

Rickets closed the red door behind them as Sam silently surveyed a darkened narrow hallway in front of him.

They both waited for Rickets to lock and double bolt the inside of the red reinforced door.

As he bent down to slide across the lower bolt Sam spotted a holstered 9mm pistol beneath his black suit jacket.

Eventually Rickets walked along the narrow dusty darkened corridor where at the far end Sam saw on both sides closed brown wooden doors.

He would later learn that the door on the right led to a narrow flight of stairs that in turn led up to a three bedroom apartment where the rotating off duty officers could rest between shifts.

The closed door on the left side however led to something completely different.

Curtis and Henning watched Rickets as he unlocked and then opened the door before Curtis started to climb down an even more dimly lit narrow stone staircase.

Sam raised his eyebrows with surprise before he followed and then the door was closed and locked behind them by Rickets.

When they reached the bottom of the stone steps Sam stood behind Curtis in a just as dimly lit corridor that had no doors other than one at the far end.

A second fully armed plain clothed police officer stood in front of it and silently stared back at them.

"We go down another floor yet before we get to Roberts." Curtis quietly informed Sam.

Halfway down the corridor the fifty three year old Chief Inspector stopped and turned to Sam again.

"He'll have a duly appointed lawyer sitting in with him." He explained just as quietly.

"But don't worry about the lawyer because what Roberts doesn't know is that he's a fully qualified lawyer but he's also one of our detectives." He added.

**Level Four**
**Saturday January 6th 2001**

Twenty seven year old chartered accountant Edward 'Eddie' Harris celebrated the birth of his first child at St Georges hospital Tooting south London.

The date was June 16th 1971.

His wife Linda gave birth to a daughter weighing a healthy eight pounds seven ounces and Eddie already knew the baby's name before she was even born.

He planned this day and another soon to follow with valid reason for his choice of names.

The baby was later christened *Jade Louise Harris.*

But baby Jade in the June of 1971 was the beginning of Eddie's very, very closely guarded secret.

A little more than three months later on Friday September 24th 1971 his secret love Melissa Stiles gave birth to his second daughter.

On Eddie's insistence his second child in three months by two different women was purposely named Jasmine.

She was later christened *Jasmine Louise Stiles.*

Her friends and now David Stringer knew her as Jaz.

Much later in the July of 1979 Eddie's wife, Jade's mother Linda died from cancer but he continued to keep his closely guarded secret mainly because at just nine years of age Jade was still very young.

She was simply too young to understand the truth.

Again much later in the April of 1992 when his daughters were both twenty one Eddie Harris suffered the first of two massive and near fatal heart attacks.

Right up until that year not only had the half-sisters never met but neither still even knew of the other's existence.

But now Eddie was determined to repair the damage before it was too late.

On Monday May 4th 1992 at his hospital bedside he finally revealed his long hidden secret to his twenty one year old daughter Jade.

He finally told her that she was not in fact an only child.

Eddie had maintained constant contact with his other twenty one year old daughter Jasmine Stiles for her entire life and yet Jade had no idea that she even existed.

The news obviously came as something of a shock to her.

On Wednesday May 6th Eddie finally revealed to Jasmine during her pre-arranged visit that she had a half-sister named Jade.

He made the arrangements for them to finally meet at his hospital bedside on Friday May 8th 1992.

Edward 'Eddie' Harris passed away at 9:42am on Friday May 8th 1992.

His two daughters that had never met Jade Harris and Jasmine Stiles both arrived around forty five minutes later as arranged.

Eddie never saw the two daughters that he loved and adored equally finally standing side by side.

Jade Harris and her sister Jasmine Stiles finally did meet for the very first time at their father's empty bedside when they were both twenty one years of age.

Instead of malice and resentment toward each other the two daughters of Eddie Harris would form an incredibly close unbreakable sisterly bond.

In fact, just four days before her abduction on Wednesday November 1st 2000 Jade Harris stared up at her completed purple shop front facia at New Kent road Walworth south London.

### *Jasmine Fashions.*

"Just wait until you see this Missy." She uttered.

She stared up at the new gold signwriting on purple facia with a beaming grin and she was in fact referring to the person that her new shop was named after.

It was her half-sister Jasmine Stiles.


There was an unexpected break in the weather on the Greek Ionian island of Kefalonia.

At eleven o'clock in the morning a privately rented Leer jet approached and landed on the wet runway until it taxied to a stop right outside the small glass airport terminal building.

Eventually twenty nine year old Jasmine Stiles climbed out from the jet and stepped inside the building where she handed over her flight ticket and passport.

The two small dark brown non-functioning adhesive moles were still firmly attached on either side of her neck and she wore the long wavy blonde wig over her almost identical long straight blonde hair.

She also wore a pair of blue coloured contact lenses over her already natural blue eyes.

Jasmine still looked exactly like her passport photograph.

The two pairs of green coloured contact lenses that she brought with her were lightly glued to her earlobes over the spare blue pair and appeared like shiny pale green almost see-through stone studs.

Jasmine casually strolled through the almost desolate customs area at Kefalonia airport without question or suspicion and now everything that she needed to bring, was on the island and completely without detection.

She was dressed in an old faded blue denim jacket over a pale peach coloured t shirt and figure hugging faded blue denim jeans with white training shoes on her feet.

Slung over her right shoulder was the same blue canvas holdall bag and in her left hand she carried a large dark brown leather suitcase.

Both were filled with more than enough clothing.

In fact she easily carried more than enough clothing for two people.

She stepped through the sliding glass doors out to the almost empty car parking area and glanced up at the grey clouded skies that looked to be full of yet more rain.

"It's odd how I never get invited here in the summer." She quietly uttered.

Her attention then turned to a row of four stationary local taxi cabs that were parked ahead on her right side.

She studied the four drivers that stood in front of their cars and they were all seemingly hoping to be chosen to take her fare.

At the front of the line was a silver Mercedes.

The driver in front of it grinned straight at her and she instinctively knew that this one was her ride.

Jasmine casually walked toward him as he continued to stare back at her with a cheeky grin.

"Do you know who I am?" She eventually asked.

His grin broadened.

Jasmine assessed that he was around six feet tall and he had short dark brown hair dark brown eyes and a Greek pale olive complexion.

"You are Jasmine I hope." He finally replied.

He spoke in perfect English but with his native Kefalonian accent just evident.

Jasmine nodded her head in response.

"And who are you?" She enquired.

When he opened the front passenger door for her he grinned again.

"I am Marinos Georgas!" He proudly announced.

Jasmine then opened the back door of the car and climbed inside leaving him standing there.

"I've heard all about you Marinos Georgas so stop talking, get into the car and take me to my sister." She curtly replied.

Marinos chuckled.

"You know who I am?" He asked.

He then closed the front passenger door that she hadn't used and he chuckled again.

"You are so very much like your sister!"

He then walked around the car and climbed into the driver seat.

As the Mercedes pulled away Jasmine stared out of the window at the beautiful scenery even though she had arrived during the season of rain.

After a short while she glanced to the front and made eye contact with Marinos via his rear view mirror.

"You have beautiful blue eyes." He told her with a flirtatious smile.

Jasmine nodded.

She pulled the long wavy blonde wig away from her long straight blonde hair.

"My sister told me loads of times what a flirt you are." She informed him.

"So if you don't try to flirt with me I won't kick you in the nuts when the car stops, ok?" She asked.

Again Marinos chuckled and shook his head.

"You really are so much like your sister."

He meant that in more ways than one.

A short while later while Jasmine stared out of the rear passenger window Marinos studied her again from his rear view mirror.

He could now see exactly what Carmen explained to Richard and himself when they first discussed this new plan.

Jasmine had long straight blonde hair whereas Jade's was shoulder length, straight and reddish brown in colour.

Jade had green eyes and her half-sister seated in the back of the Mercedes had blue.

Jade of course had an unmistakable dark brown mole just above her upper lip and Jasmine did not.

Their facial features however apart from those three obvious differences were almost identical.

Marinos couldn't possibly know it but they both looked just like Eddie Harris.

Even their noses were exactly the same shape.

"You can stop staring at me whenever you're ready." Jasmine informed him without looking ahead.


The journey from the airport to Carmen Richardson's eight bedroom house at Lourdatta south of the island took just a little longer than thirty minutes.

When the silver Mercedes turned into the side driveway Jasmine saw just one familiar face and it was that of thirty four year old Carmen Richardson.

Carmen stood outside the opened kitchen door beside a tall broad shouldered man with swept back blonde hair.

Jasmine had never met him before today but she knew that he was a former captain of the elite British army SAS regiment and that his name was Richard Willows.

She also knew that he was a friend of the idiot that she met at Bermondsey a few days ago.

The tears already started to well up in Jasmine's eyes as soon as she saw Carmen before the silver Mercedes even stopped.

The tough exterior that Marinos had endured for the past thirty minutes suddenly disappeared and she leapt out from the back seat of the car.

Carmen and Jasmine tightly hugged each other as tears started to roll down both of their faces.

"She's ok." Carmen quietly blurted.

"She's safe."

Jasmine could only nod her head as she also continued to sob.

Both Richard and Marinos watched in silence.

Eventually the two women broke off and as she began to wipe her tears Carmen introduced Jasmine to Richard Willows.

"This is the man that went to the auction and bought her back for us." She explained.

An emotional tremble remained in her tone as she continued to wipe her eyes.

Without uttering a single word Jasmine launched herself at Richard and tightly held onto him.

"Thank you so much." She eventually croaked in his ear.

Her tears started to flow again.

After a short while the still tearful Jasmine was properly introduced to Marinos Georgas.

"And this crazy arse was the one that actually met the abductors at the port in the middle of the night and took delivery of Jade from them." Carmen explained.

Carmen still tried to quite pointlessly dry her eyes as Jasmine just as suddenly launched herself at Marinos and now tightly hugged him.

"Well this is much better than kicking my nuts!" He quietly chuckled.

Eventually Jasmine broke off from him and she slowly turned to face Carmen.

"So where is the dopey bitch?" She asked with the same croak in her tone.

Jasmine and Carmen both attempted to stem the flow of ever running tears.

Eventually Carmen broke into a smile.

"Go through the kitchen and out to the hall and then open the first door on your left." She replied as she pointed.

Jasmine stepped inside the house.

Carmen turned to Richard.

"Well that was a little bit emotional." She quietly told him.

She continued to wipe her tear-filled eyes.

Jade Harris sat curled up in a large cream coloured armchair in the huge lounge where she watched Greek television of which she understood between very little and none.

Her face was still slightly swollen curtesy of her own solid wooden baseball bat at the hands of the leader of the Turkish group, forty seven year old Barak Yazici.

She suffered a fractured cheekbone and a fractured jaw and she had since had two of her back teeth removed on the island.

It was a farewell and thank you gift from the Turkish contingent back in London.

The attack was due to the fact that Jade killed his fellow countryman and friend forty year old Doruk Gezmen during her abduction at her flat at New Kent road at Walworth London.

That attack was two months ago and Jade was still healing up.

She was today dressed in a long white knitted pullover and a pair of blue denim shorts that were given to her by Adi Georgas, the younger sister of Marinos.

Outside the closed lounge door Jasmine momentarily closed her still tear-filled eyes and took in a long deep shuddering breath.

She finally pushed down on the handle and opened it.

When Jaz stepped inside Jade turned to see her sister standing in the open doorway with her hands placed on her hips.

"I can't leave you alone for five bloody minutes, can I?" Jasmine asked.

There was without a doubt a tremble in her tone.

Jade could see the tears welling in Jasmine's blue eyes regardless that her tough exterior momentarily reappeared.

Jasmine could clearly see the swelling around the right side of her sister's face as Jade mocked a grimace at the mere sight of her.

"You'll do anything for a free holiday won't you?" She eventually asked in response.

"In the summer you idiot, yes I would!" Jasmine replied.

There was a momentary pause as both sisters stared at each other.

Jade then suddenly leapt from the chair.

Jasmine suddenly ran toward her and they embraced in the centre of the lounge where many, many more tears started to flow.

"Will you stop getting yourself abducted you silly bitch?" Jasmine asked.

They hugged as if they were never going to let go.

"Will you stop following me?" Jade sobbed.

Carmen, Richard and Marinos appeared in the open doorway where even more tears ran down both of Carmen's cheeks as she watched the two girls.

"I'm so crap at this!" She quietly whispered to herself.

During all of this time Richard meticulously studied Jasmine's facial features and like Marinos had, he could clearly see the almost identical resemblance to her half-sister.

'They could be twins.' He thought to himself.

Carmen was right once again.

Eventually the last embrace broke off and both Jade and Jasmine attempted to stem the flow of tears as did Carmen Richardson.

"Get off me you silly bitch." Jasmine quietly blurted to Jade.

"Jasmine did you pick up the items?" Richard asked.

She turned to face him and nodded her head.

"I brought a blonde wig, two pairs of coloured contact lenses and these." She replied.

She used both forefingers to point to the two adhesive dark brown moles on either side of her neck.

Richard briefly glanced at Jade before he returned his gaze to Jasmine and then he nodded with a smile.

"That's perfect." He replied.

Carmen now interjected in an attempt to lighten the mood.

"So you met David Stringer then?" She asked.

Jasmine again turned to Richard.

"Exactly where the bloody hell did you find that man?" She asked.

Both Richard and Carmen immediately burst into laughter.

Richard of course had heard the entire conversation between Jasmine and David at Bermondsey three days ago.

**Level Five**
**Monday January 8th 2001**

It was just after nine in the morning when the newly appointed head at task force headquarters Chief Inspector Keith Curtis from New Scotland Yard sat behind his new desk.

Seated opposite him from left to right were Detective Sergeant Jacob Saunders, Detective Inspector Nicola Garwood and his personal friend Detective Inspector Sam Henning.

This meeting was primarily called to discuss the recent visit and interrogation of their former boss Chief Inspector Martin Roberts, currently held in police custody.

"What we're about to discuss does *not* leave this room!" Curtis adamantly insisted.

"I have a policy of nothing but the truth within our inner circle but it stays strictly between us." He added.

"This is how we realistically get jobs done."

His three subordinate officers sat and listened as he explained that the currently suspended Chief Inspector Martin Roberts was being held for questioning under very special conditions.

He went on to explain that there were specific reasons for those conditions.

"As bizarre as this sounds our biggest problem right now is that the abductions have suddenly stopped and everything has gone underground." Curtis informed them all.

"Roberts will be more than aware that if we don't get some kind of lead soon the powers that be will begin to wind this task force down to nothing but a skeleton crew purely to cut back on resources." He added.

"He was involved in setting the whole thing up in the early stages at Westminster so he knows just about everything involved with it."

He went on to explain that his predecessor was currently being held in a top secret location for at least the next six weeks because he was their only source of information as the other, a still unknown man wasn't talking at all.

He referred to the Romanian Emil Hagi but they still didn't even know his name.

"The next problem is that because Roberts knows that with no evidence available we have no case and that we're now battling against time." Curtis continued.

"And I doubt that anything that he does tell us will be even close to the truth." He explained.

"But in around six weeks if we're still where we are with this right now with no new leads we'll start to lose resources and I suspect they'll start with the safe houses." He added.

"They'll be the most cost effective."

He then motioned with his hand to the three senior officers in front of him.

"There's an open mouth policy in this office." He explained again.

Nicola Garwood was eventually the first to speak up.

"Sir on a slightly different note we definitely need to discuss Jade Harris." She began.

Curtis shook his head but not to dismiss her point.

"Drop the sir crap Nik I'm Misery guts Curtis not Roberts." He reminded her.

"Here's the problem that we face with the Jade Harris situation." He continued.

"Roberts named her during the interview two days ago and we know that he's playing for time so if he named her the chances are that she isn't involved." He informed particularly Nicola.

"Remember that he's playing for time and he'll send us on every single wild goose chase that he can think up and let's face it, at the moment he has plenty of time to think them up." He added.

"We have highly trained specialist officers that are dissecting the interview that Sam and I carried out two days ago." Curtis continued.

"But that's a painstakingly slow process so I'll keep you up to speed on it as it happens."

Garwood nodded with acknowledgement but she wasn't finished with the matter of Jade Harris.

"But there's also the evidence of the unknown blood sample and fragments of human skull that were discovered at her flat." She reminded him.

"I'm convinced that she murdered whoever that blood and those skull fragments belonged to before she fled the scene in a hurry." She explained.

"And she left all of her clothes and other items of some value behind." She added.

Again Curtis nodded his head.

"But with no corpse and no confession realistically we don't have a murder scene Nik." He reminded her.

"We have blood and fragments of skull and a suspected crime scene with no dead body."

There was a pause before Curtis continued.

"But you're right."

"But with all of that in mind if Jade Harris walked in here right now and said that she had no idea about any of it you've got nothing on her."

Again Nicola nodded her head.

"And if she did that with a valid reason for being missing and unavailable you have even less." Curtis added.

Again Nicola nodded with acknowledgement.

"That is unless you somehow manage to find a matching body to those samples and link it to her." He added.

"That would dramatically change things." He pointed out.

"I have to bloody well find her first." She very quietly uttered.

Keith Curtis quietly chuckled.

"Back to the matter of former Chief Inspector Martin Roberts," He continued.

"We're holding Roberts under highly illegal special conditions that have been secretly granted to me by the powers that be." He began again.

"Roberts has not been officially charged with anything as yet." He informed them.

"But he'll also know that what we're doing right now is against the law but we'll cross that bridge when we come to it."

Both Nicola Garwood and Detective Sergeant Jacob Saunders raised their eyebrows.

"He has no legal representation because nobody knows that we have him in custody." Curtis continued.

"We're fighting fire with fire but you three know none of this." He quietly uttered in his defence.

"His legal representation is in fact one of my Scotland Yard coppers and not the duly appointed brief that Roberts believes he is."

Curtis then glanced at Nicola Garwood again as he adjusted his train of thought and returned his attention to what was rapidly becoming her very personal matter at hand.

"I'm of the belief that your girl Jade Harris is out of the country." He told her.

"That anonymous phone call naming her as the ring leader was just far too timely and convenient." He added.

"Contact Interpol and have them put a flag up for her should she pop up at any air or sea port anywhere in Europe."

Jacob Saunders Nicola Garwood and then Sam Henning all climbed to their feet and headed toward the door.

Sam Henning stopped and turned to face Curtis again.

"I think I'll take a drive out to Mayfair and have a little chat with Carmen Richardson." He said.

Curtis raised his eyebrows.

"Do you know her Sam?" He asked.

Henning nodded his head.

"Not as one of her former clients though before you ask guv." He chuckled.

"I nicked her once or twice back in the old days." He revealed.

"Carmen's actually one of the good ones and if Jade Harris is involved with human trafficking I think Carmen would tell me that simply by refusing to have anything to do with her."

Curtis sat back in his chair and shrugged his shoulders.

"It might be a good move to give her chain a little tug to see if she tries to bite you." He suggested.

Sam nodded and then followed Garwood and Saunders out of the office.

## Level Six
**Friday January 12th 2001**

From his converted office bedroom at Tranton road Bermondsey David Stringer had meticulously planned to the second his involvement in the meeting that was about to take place some nineteen hundred miles away.

He knew exactly what needed to be done and what simply *had* to be achieved today.

Miguel and Theresa Sanchez were contacted twice over the past two days to ensure that they remained inside the hotel at Manisa Turkey and did not return to the giant cargo ship the Indigo.

The Spaniard yesterday telephoned his cousin the skipper of the giant Spanish vessel to inform him that there was still a delay.

This was the starting point of the deviation from Richard Willows original plan involving a team of unknown and therefore untrustworthy mercenaries.

This morning Richard and Carmen Richardson landed on a private chartered flight at the small airstrip just outside of the town of Manisa where Miguel and Theresa Sanchez were staying in Turkey.

Their pre-booked hotel was however some thirty five miles west at the insistence of David Stringer.

"The little town of Foca is the perfect place to meet them and it also sounds quite funny." Stringer explained with a chuckle.

During that conversation Richard shook his head but he didn't know what his friend David knew.

What Richard didn't and couldn't possibly consider was that every single overhead spy satellite that covered that particular region passed directly over the town of Foca western Turkey.

David would have continuous eyes on the ground from around sixty miles high in the sky.

It was just after six in the evening when thirty five year old Richard Willows and thirty four year old Carmen Richardson sat beside a large window that overlooked the beautiful flat calm bay from their hotel restaurant at Foca.

Richard's short wavy blonde hair was as usual swept back and he was dressed in a pale grey suit over a white open necked cotton shirt with highly polished dark brown Italian leather shoes.

The wealthy former high class prostitute Carmen sat opposite him with the view of the bay at Foca to her right.

Carmen was dressed in a short figure hugging sleeveless black dress with shiny black patent leather high heeled shoes on her feet.

She picked up her glass of white wine and sipped as she stared out at the beautiful lights on the slopes at the other side of the bay.

"I bet it's beautiful here in the summer." She quietly commented.

She turned and glanced at Richard but his mind seemed to be elsewhere and for very good reason.

For Richard tonight was the most important of nights.

It was all in or bust regarding the safe return of his twenty two year old sister Sasha and he was absolutely certain of this.

Carmen stared at him and half smiled before she reached across and gently squeezed his hand.

"Everything's going to be ok Richard." She assured him in her usual calm and quiet tone.

"When you told me that you had a new plan and a better way of getting your sister back I wasn't sure." She said.

"But I am now." She continued.

"This is a much safer and more fool proof way for all of us, including Sasha."

Richard half smiled back at her but his mind was clouded and filled with nothing but doubt.

Killing another man was easy for Richard Willows because he was trained to do that.

Negotiating with one was something completely different and in truth it was very much outside of his field of expertise.

Suddenly they both heard a familiar but this time chilling voice in their ears.

"Ok get your game faces on." David Stringer told them.

"The lovely little Mr Sanchez and his not so little and not very lovely wife have just left their hotel at Manisa." He announced.

Richard turned and raised his hand to get the attention of one of the waitresses and when she arrived at the table he ordered another drink.

Carmen carefully watched him.

She understood that it was now just short of a year since Richard had started this search for his sister and that this evening could quite easily get the better of him.

It was the reason that *she* had come to Turkey with an alternative plan should Richard's negotiations start to falter.

She also knew that this task of negotiating wasn't his speciality.

She glanced back out of the large window at the picturesque bay.

"David, did you get all of that information that I asked you for?" She quietly enquired.

From his office room in Bermondsey David Stringer simultaneously stared at multiple live images on several of his computer monitors and he nodded his head as his over magnified eyes continued to stare.

"It's all ready and available, guvnor." He replied in a mocking tone.

Twenty seven minutes later a shiny black hired car slowed to a stop at the hotel car park and forty three year old Miguel Sanchez climbed out from the driver seat and closed the door behind him.

The thin Spaniard was dressed in a light blue cotton open necked shirt that was tucked into the waistband of a pair of black neatly pressed trousers and he wore shiny black leather shoes.

Miguel used his thumb and forefinger to habitually smooth over his thick black bushy moustache as he stared across the roof of the shiny new black hire car and waited for his wife to emerge.

Eventually the passenger door opened and the considerably larger frame of thirty eight year old Theresa Sanchez slowly climbed out from the car.

Her long wavy black hair this evening was down and her make-up was impeccably applied.

She was dressed in a larger version of the exact same knee length black sleeveless designer dress that Carmen wore.

The Spanish husband and wife glanced at each other but no words were spoken before they both headed toward the hotel restaurant door.

"Blue shirt and black dress Dave?" Richard quietly asked.

David confirmed that he was correct.

Carmen calmly sipped white wine and waited in silence but she was prepared for just about any scenario this evening.

A few minutes later the thin Spaniard and his wife approached the oval shaped glass table beside the window overlooking the scenic bay.

Richard immediately climbed to his feet and politely ushered them both to a seat.

Nobody shook hands.

Carmen now sat with Richard directly opposite her, Theresa Sanchez to her right with her back to the large window and Miguel Sanchez on her left.

There was already an intense electrified atmosphere around the table.

Richard opened his mouth to speak but Theresa Sanchez immediately raised a single forefinger to prevent him from doing so.

"Before you speak Mr Handley I want you to know that we do not take threats or intimidation." She explained in English.

Her Spanish accent was clearly evident.

"Do not threaten us." She advised him.

"You have not made us fearful and we are here for curiosity only." She added.

She displayed a completely fake warm smile.

"I am curious only about how you found us at our hotel."

Theresa knew that she and Miguel held and dealt all of the playing cards around this table.

Richard smiled back at her but his smile was just as false.

Carmen and Theresa very briefly exchanged glances.

For that brief moment Carmen stared through Theresa's dark brown Spanish eyes and it was a look that only Carmen Richardson could give.

It was a look of nothing but utter contempt.

Richard reached into his inside jacket pocket and produced the most recent photograph of Sasha that he owned but before he handed it to Miguel he glanced up at the ceiling to compose his thoughts.

*'Don't do that.'* Carmen thought as she watched him.

*'Show them confidence!'*

Eventually he glanced back down and straight into the Spaniard's very narrow dark brown eyes.

"Mr Sanchez we're both businessmen." He began.

Already Miguel's thin eyes widened as he purposely displayed a wry grin and then chuckled.

"How did you find us Mr Handley?" Miguel enquired.

"We are not easy to find." He added.

"We are not easy to find because we do not wish to be found."

Carmen continued to observe the Spanish couple as they kept the momentum of the conversation on their side by purposely provoking Richard.

She quietly sipped more white wine.

Richard again smiled at Miguel Sanchez before he continued.

"We have good resources Mr Sanchez." He eventually replied.

Now he slid the photograph of Sasha across the glass table toward Miguel.

"We know that you took her and we know where you took her to." He began again.

"We know about the military base at Mamuju."

The Spaniard didn't even glance down at the photograph, not even for a second.

Carmen continued to watch in silence as Theresa Sanchez still showed that same smug confident grin.

"We want to buy this girl back from you and we want you to travel to Mamuju and get her for us." Richard continued.

Miguel quietly chuckled again as did his wife seated beside Carmen.

Carmen sipped more wine and she could clearly see that Richard's tactics were not going to work with these very arrogant Spaniards.

Theresa Sanchez suddenly interjected again.

"Mr Handley, first of all we do not ever return goods." She informed him with a chuckle of contempt in her tone.

"But also we definitely do not return damaged goods and if the girl that you seek is at Mamuju she is now very damaged goods." She added.

Her husband quietly chuckled at her remark as she provoked Richard again because of course they knew that they held and dealt all of those heavily stacked cards.

Carmen knew this too as she listened and sipped more white wine.

For a brief moment Richard considered shooting Theresa Sanchez in the face and right now but he somehow held his nerve.

Carmen's 'east end charm' as April Marsh often referred to it was however about to surface.

Together the Spanish couple continued to provoke something from Richard.

Carmen took another sip and then swallowed before she slowly shook her head and placed her glass back down onto the table and sighed.

"I've heard enough of this bullshit." She very quietly uttered.

"It's my turn."

She immediately turned her attention to the somewhat provocative Theresa Sanchez.

Carmen once again stared into her eyes and straight through as only she could.

She reached across with a smile and gently squeezed Theresa's hand no differently to how she did Richard's earlier.

"If you open that mouth of yours again I'm going to shove this wine glass so far down your throat that you'll piss vinegar for a month." She assured Theresa.

Carmen still displayed that same warm smile.

Suddenly that smile disappeared as Theresa Sanchez stared back at her with utter disbelief.

Carmen released her hand.

"I had no idea that they made this dress in family tent size so I'll be demanding a refund as soon as I've finished with you."

Theresa Sanchez sat with a stunned wide eyed expression with her mouth just as wide open.

'Let me give you a free lesson in how to provoke somebody you Spanish bitch.' Carmen thought to herself.

Her eyes again bore straight through Theresa.

Theresa's eyes remained widened and her mouth even wider from Carmen's sudden but very calm outburst.

Carmen was calm and she was always in control.

"Close your mouth and keep it closed or I swear I'll do what I just promised." She told Theresa.

That same Carmen Richardson stare bore straight through Theresa Sanchez once again and for some reason the Spanish woman chose not to test her.

Her mouth slowly closed.

There was something about Carmen that Theresa did not wish to test.

Carmen Richardson's *'east end charm'* was now in full swing and she turned her attention to Theresa's husband Miguel.

"Now for you super Mario." She began again.

She then picked up her wine glass and just as casually sipped before she returned it to the table as she was secretly fed information via her hidden earpiece.

"Your full name is Miguel Juan Sanchez and you're forty three years of age." She began again.

"Your little trafficking racket operates from a giant Spanish cargo vessel called the Indigo and your cousin Louis Edwardo Fernandez is the captain of that ship and that's how you travel around the world completely free of charge."

Carmen then went on to inform them both of when Theresa became ill and her diagnosis, the date that Miguel's mother died and all three vehicle registrations of his beloved battered old green military truck.

She went on to reveal to Miguel his personal bank account details and informed him that she could even transfer all of his amassed fortune into her own bank account.

"I can break you in a matter of seconds." She assured him.

She stared straight across the table at him.

She went on to inform him that she could do that right now, she could empty his entire bank account without even leaving the table.

"Why don't you sit there with that smug look on your face and ask me to prove it right now?" She dared him.

There was a silent electrified pause before Carmen spoke again.

"I know everything about you but here's your biggest problem." She continued.

She paused again as she casually picked up her wine glass and sipped before she once again returned it to the table.

"You will travel alone to Mamuju and pick up that girl." She informed him.

Her forefinger pointed to the photograph of Sasha on the table in front of him that he still hadn't even once glanced down at.

Throughout Carmen's entire outburst Miguel like his wife sat and stared in complete stunned silence.

So too did the just as startled Richard Willows.

"Your wife will remain at the hotel at Manisa." She added.

She then turned to Theresa.

"You could eat for two while he's away." She sarcastically suggested.

She returned her attention to Miguel.

"If you don't do as I say we go to the authorities with all of the evidence that we have and we have a lot of it." She continued.

"And you know Mr Sanchez that we can find you at any time." She added.

"We didn't *find* you at your hotel at Manisa at all because we already knew where you were."

"We watched you take our girl to that military base at Mamuju."

Carmen then knocked back the last of her white wine and then returned the empty glass to the table.

"Now I'm going to walk you pair of inbreeds back to your car and show you something before you fuck off out of my sight." She told them both.

She then climbed to her feet and glanced down to her right at Theresa.

"Do you need some help getting out of your chair princess?" She asked.

*'Now you know how to provoke somebody!'* She thought.

She still smiled down at Theresa.

Carmen again turned to Miguel.

"Take that photograph with you." She instructed as she pointed again.

For the very first time Sanchez glanced down at it.

Eventually the Spaniards both climbed to their feet.

Miguel Sanchez was smart and he wasn't prepared to react to Carmen's insults toward his wife until he knew exactly who and what he was up against.

However he vowed to himself that this big mouthed English bitch would pay for those insults.

Richard started to climb to his feet but Carmen gently pushed him back down.

"I have to do this alone." She quietly informed him.

"You stay here and stop talking." She whispered.

David Stringer chuckled in her ear.

A few minutes later Carmen stopped behind the Spanish couple outside next to their car that faced the bay of Foca.

"Before I give you specific instructions Mr Sanchez I want to show you something." She informed him.

"Place one hand behind your back."

Miguel stared at her in silence.

"Is that too difficult?" She sarcastically asked.

Eventually Miguel placed one hand behind his back with a sigh.

"Hold out as many fingers as you wish that I can't possibly see." Carmen continued.

Again he stared at her with confusion but eventually he hid three fingers from Carmen.

"Three." She immediately told him.

"Now you changed it to two." She added.

"Oh and now four."

Miguel Sanchez immediately spun around and stared out at the bay.

He knew that Richard who he only knew as Mr Handley was behind Carmen inside the hotel and he couldn't possibly have seen his hand.

"They never look up Carmen." David chuckled in her ear.

Eventually Miguel turned around to face her again.

"Oh he will now." Carmen very quietly uttered.

She slowly pointed a single finger toward the skies.

"We're watching you by satellite Mr Sanchez."

"When you drive back to your hotel at Manisa you now know that you're being constantly watched."

Theresa Sanchez suddenly glanced up toward the sky and Carmen chuckled.

"It's about eighty miles up and you can't eat it." She insulted her again.

She then returned her attention to Miguel.

"If you force me to go to the authorities I'll not only inform them exactly where you are in the world but I'll tell them what you're eating for breakfast." She assured him.

"You'll book a flight to the island of Sulawesi tomorrow and I will know if you have or you haven't." She continued.

"I would strongly suggest that you do it." She added.

"Your wife will remain at the hotel at Manisa and if you fail to do exactly as I tell you or you walk out of that army base without our girl." She continued.

Carmen paused.

"Your biggest problem that I told you about will become a reality."

"Theresa will be executed and you'll get a telephone call to listen to it happen live." She assured him.

Miguel stared into Carmen's eyes.

"This will not be easy to buy her back." He quietly uttered.

He raised the photograph in his hand.

Carmen shrugged.

"I really don't give a shit how easy or difficult it's going to be Mr Sanchez." She replied.

"I'm an incredibly wealthy woman and I will gladly spend every penny that I have to ensure your execution should you fail to carry this out and bring that girl to me." She assured him.

"When we see that you've arranged your flight to Indonesia tomorrow you'll receive a call and new instructions from me in person." She continued.

"You'll deal directly with me from now on." She informed him.

"Now fuck off out of my sight."

Carmen then turned on her high heels and headed back into the hotel restaurant and she didn't once look back.

*'That's how you do confident.'* She told herself with a smile.

A few minutes later back inside the restaurant she returned to her seat opposite Richard at the table.

"So do you think they'll do it?" He nervously asked.

Carmen raised her hand to get the attention of one of the waitresses before she glanced back at him.

"They don't have any bloody choice now." She replied.

"She was brilliant!" David giggled in both of their ears.

Richard nodded his head with a half-smile in full agreement with Stringer.

Carmen quietly laughed.

"Thanks for feeding me the information as I needed it David." She replied.

Richard stared across at her for a few moments.

"I wouldn't like to be on the wrong side of her Dave." He told David with a chuckle.

Carmen then stared back at him.

"No." She replied.

"You wouldn't."

## Level Seven
## Friday January 12<sup>th</sup> 2001

At just after eleven in the morning thirty five year old April Marsh sat behind Carmen's large oak desk at her office at Mount Street Mayfair west London.

She studied some properties on paper that were recently made available.

Her long dark brown hair was up and she was dressed in a thick black woollen pullover and a pair of old blue jeans with black flat heeled shoes on her feet.

Seated opposite her at the other side of the large desk was Carmen's new business partner forty eight year old property tycoon Arron Balcombe.

He supplied the paperwork that was placed in front of April and Balcombe was now fully aware of everything that was happening thanks to Carmen.

He actually took it upon himself to locate and obtain either the appropriate buildings that were required for Richard's somewhat elaborate plan or at least the use of them.

April now intently studied photographs.

"The maisonette at Tooting looks perfect." She quietly told him as she studied.

Balcombe flashed one of his smiles.

"It was just recently redecorated throughout." He replied.

"And in the middle of a housing estate it would be like looking for a needle in a haystack." He added.

April nodded in silent agreement without looking up at him.

Suddenly the new receptionist twenty one year old Polly Aldington who was hired by Carmen a month or so ago opened the door and stepped inside.

"April there's a policeman here to see Carmen." She announced with a look of concern.

Just as suddenly from behind her, Detective Inspector Sam Henning appeared with a smile.

"Hello April, it's been a while." He said.

Sam stepped past Polly and into the office.

April stared up at him for a brief moment before she turned her attention to Arron Balcombe.

*It hasn't been long enough.'* She thought to herself.

"Ok Mr Jones I have all of your details so as soon as we have tenants to rent your property somebody will give you a call." She told Balcombe.

With his back to Sam Henning, Arron Balcombe displayed another wry grin.

He winked at April before he officially thanked her.

He then turned to leave the office where he nodded to Sam Henning before he passed him in the doorway.

"Thank you Polly." April then said.

The twenty one year old receptionist also left the room and closed the door behind her.

Now April's attention finally turned to Sam Henning.

"What a lovely surprise it is to see you Detective Henning." She blatantly lied.

Sam knew it and he chuckled.

"Hello April actually it's Detective Inspector these days." He informed her.

April displayed another false wry smile.

"After a while you all start to look the same Mr Henning." She sniped.

Again Sam chuckled.

He pointed to the chair that Arron Balcombe had just vacated opposite her.

"Can I sit down?" He asked.

April stared up at him and shrugged her shoulders.

"Who knows what your arse is capable of Mr Henning?" She sarcastically asked in response.

Again Sam laughed as he sat down in the chair.

"So you're in the property business now."

April placed the details of the two properties that Arron Balcombe had personally brought over into Carmen's desk drawer.

Then she seemed to glance around the office before she stared into Sam's eyes.

"I can see why they made you a Detective Mr Henning." She sarcastically replied again.

Once again Sam chuckled.

He then also glanced around Carmen's lavish office for a few moments before he returned his attention to April.

"The receptionist tells me that Carmen is away on holiday." He began again.

This time April nodded her head in silence.

"Any idea when she'll be back?" He asked.

April shrugged her shoulders again.

"You know how these executive types are Mr Henning." She eventually replied.

Sam nodded his head with genuine full agreement.

"Oh I most certainly do." He replied with a quiet sigh.

There was a short pause as he watched April pretending to work before he resumed with his discrete line of questioning.

"Maybe you might be able to help me out April." He began again.

A wry grin appeared on April's lips.

"Oh I doubt that very much Mr Henning." She replied with another element of sarcasm in her tone.

Sam quietly chuckled again before he continued.

"Who was that young girl that used to work with you and Carmen back in the old days over at Alpha grove?" He casually asked.

April appeared to think on his question.

However Sam was no fool and he could see that she in fact wasn't thinking about it at all.

"A young girl that worked with us at Alpha grove..." She appeared to ponder.

For a few moments she continued to think out loud but then she glanced into Sam's eyes.

"No sorry I can't remember." She suddenly replied.

April's almost obstructive sarcasm brought yet another wry grin to Sam's lips.

Sam now also appeared to think hard.

"Oh what was her name?" He asked out loud.

"Was it Jane something?" He asked.

The plump thirty five year old brunette continued to stare back at him in silence.

"Like I said Mr Henning I can't remember." She eventually lied again.

"And I doubt I ever will." She added.

"Jade, that's it Jade Harris!" Sam suddenly miraculously recalled.

He noted that April's facial expression and body language slightly adjusted.

Suddenly April managed to recall absolutely everything.

"Oh Jade?" She asked with a look of surprise.

"She was lovely." She added.

Sam nodded his head with false agreement.

"Have you seen her lately?" He asked.

April provided yet another blank stare.

"Have I seen who?" She asked.

Again Sam chuckled.

He knew as soon as he learned that Carmen was away dealing with April was never going to be an easy task.

There was another pause before he continued.

"Have you seen Jade Harris recently?" He eventually started again.

April appeared to ponder for a few moments before she glanced back at him and eventually she shook her head.

"Not in years as a matter of fact." She lied again.

Eventually Sam slowly glanced around the office again as April still pretended to busy herself.

He slowly climbed back to his feet before he took from his inside jacket pocket a small white card that he placed down onto the desk.

"When Carmen comes back from her holiday could you get her to give me a call?" He asked.

April glanced up at him again and faked another smile.

"Oh you know me of course I will Mr Henning and she'll be so sorry that she missed you." She replied.

That response brought the biggest chuckle of all from Sam.

He headed back toward the closed door where he stopped and turned to face April again.

"You've done really well for yourselves." He said.

He nodded around Carmen's plush office.

April smiled again.

*'Don't let the door hit you on the way out.'* She thought to herself.

Sam opened the door and stepped outside it.

"It was good to catch up April." He said.

He slowly closed the door behind him and as it clicked shut April already displayed two fingers in the same general direction.

"It was lovely to see you too Mr Henning." She quietly uttered.

A few moments later Polly Aldington opened the door and walked back into the office and closed it behind her.

"I need you to get a hold of Carmen and tell her to call me." April told her.

Polly nodded her head.

"And pop upstairs to Carmen's flat and let Arron Balcombe know that he can come back down."

## Level Eight
### Wednesday January 17th 2001

It was just after ten in the morning and there was a temporary lull in the almost constant downpour of rain on the Greek island of Kefalonia.

Two days ago Richard Willows and Carmen Richardson returned from the hotel at Foca Turkey where they met with the Spanish husband and wife human traffickers Miguel and Theresa Sanchez.

In the lounge at Carmen's Mansion home Carmen and Richard sat with the native islander thirty year old Marinos Georgas and twenty nine year old half-sisters Jasmine Stiles and Jade Harris.

Richard's revised plan to get his twenty two year old sister Sasha out of Mamuju and back to London was somewhat elaborate and he assured both Jasmine and Jade that it would take considerable nerve particularly on their part.

In fact he particularly referred to Jasmine especially during the initial stages of it.

Richard's secondary plan was in his opinion preferable to the employment of a team of mercenaries to enter the base at Mamuju to remove Sasha during a clandestine military style operation.

From Carmen's financial viewpoint it was a far less expensive plan although that was furthest from her mind.

She would never consider backing out from any realistic option.

The revised plan especially since hearing news from his friend David Stringer at Bermondsey south east London this morning was now most decidedly preferable for all concerned.

Stringer reported via his wealth or resources that forty three year old Spaniard Miguel Sanchez had this morning booked flights just as he was instructed to by Carmen.

He would in fact depart and begin the journey to the Indonesian island of Sulawesi tomorrow.

Sanchez booked a short flight from the small airstrip not far from their hotel at Manisa where he would take an hour long flight north to the Turkish capital city of Ankara.

The next day he would board a flight from Ankara to New Delhi India where he would again have to wait to make another connection two days later.

On Saturday January 20th at 11am local time he would board a final flight from New Delhi to Makassar city on the south west coast of the Indonesian island of Sulawesi.

Those flights were all now booked and paid for.

Makassar city was north-west of the disused southern port at Bontosunggu where the Spanish super vessel the Indigo usually unloaded her highly illegal human cargo.

From Makassar city Miguel would have to travel around 112 miles north by road to the not so secret Indonesian military logistics base just south of Mamuju.

There he would hopefully buy back and collect Richard's twenty two year old sister Sasha.

The journey would take Miguel the better part of a week because of the connections.

The rest of the group listened as Richard relayed all of this new information and eventually Carmen reached across and took a hold of his hand and she gently squeezed it.

"Keep reminding yourself that he'll definitely do this." She told him.

"We left him with absolutely no choice." She added.

Richard now for the first time full of hope, half smiled in response.

"Trust me he doesn't have another option." Carmen assured him again.

The bold and brave Greek islander Marinos Georgas sat and listened in silence as everybody else in the room discussed Richard's new plan.

But now and even after his heroic deed at the port of Sami Marinos started to feel somewhat out of his depth.

Richard's plan was in his opinion insane and there was also another small matter.

Everybody in the room was aware of one vital piece of information with the exception of Jade's half-sister Jasmine Stiles.

Marinos was fully aware that it was a fact that Jasmine couldn't know of until the time was right and that time was definitely not now but somehow it still felt to him deceitful to hide it from her.

Eventually he glanced down at his wristwatch before he turned his attention to both Jasmine and Jade.

"Now that we know that this will happen we must leave for Argostoli." He told them.

Jasmine and Jade simultaneously nodded with acknowledgement.

"My cousin Veronica will soon be waiting for us." He added.

Jasmine stood up and so did her sister Jade.

Carmen and Richard watched them.

Marinos ushered them toward the door and out to the enclosed side entrance at the back of the house and they were eventually followed outside by Carmen and Richard.

"Remember to keep a low profile Jade." Richard reminded her.

"Interpol have put up flags at every European country for you and it only takes an off duty airport official to see and recognise you." He reminded her.

Marinos, Jasmine and Jade climbed into his silver Mercedes that slowly backed out of the driveway still watched by Carmen and Richard.

"I hate lying to her." Carmen uttered, referring to Jasmine.

They both watched the car drive away before Richard glanced at Carmen.

"You haven't lied to her." He replied.

"You just haven't and can't tell her that Jade killed that guy in her flat." He continued.

"Her reaction will be vital when she does hear it for the very first time." He added.

"Whatever happens, Jasmine can't know about it until she's back in the UK." He continued.

Carmen slowly nodded her head with a sigh.

"I know I just said that I don't like it." She quietly replied.

"Jade just wouldn't be able to pull that part off." Richard added.

Again Carmen nodded.

"I know."


The journey in the Mercedes west to the island's capital town of Argostoli took a little more than thirty minutes.

Eventually Marinos, Jasmine and Jade arrived outside one of the very few shops that had lights switched on inside and looked as though it was open for business.

Forty one year old Veronica Georgas was a very curvaceous five feet six inches tall with slightly greying but still very beautiful long straight black hair that was pulled back into a ponytail.

Her dark brown eyes widened with a warm smile when she met Jasmine Stiles and Jade Harris as both twenty nine year olds were ushered into her hairdresser shop by Marinos.

"Which of you is here for the appointment?" Veronica eventually asked.

It was Jasmine that raised her hand and at the exact same moment Jade pointed to her sister.

"I am." Jasmine said.

"She is." Jade added at the exact same moment.

Veronica smiled again even though her cousin Marinos had somehow managed to persuade her to open her shop for just this single appointment.

She reached forward and gently took Jasmine's long straight blonde hair in her left hand before she glanced into her blue eyes.

"Your hair is so beautiful." She said.

Jasmine broke into a smile.

"Thank you." She replied.

Again Veronica smiled back at her.

"What is it that you would like me to do with your beautiful hair?"

She then saw a slight frown appear but then just as quickly vanish from Jasmine's face.

She then pointed at her sister Jade standing beside her.

"I have to have it cut exactly the same as hers." She explained.

Veronica immediately placed a hand over her mouth to display a look of genuine shock.

She gasped.

She glanced at Jade's straight shoulder length reddish brown bobbed hair and then back to Jasmine's long straight blonde.

"All of your beautiful long hair must go?" She asked.

Jasmine nodded her head and displayed another frown.

After she recomposed herself Veronica ushered Jasmine to a row of four large black leather chairs that were situated in front of a long mirror.

Jasmine eventually sat down.

The middle aged Greek woman then tied a long purple vinyl cover around Jasmine's neck and stared into her blue eyes via the mirror in front of them.

She slowly brushed her long straight blonde hair.

"You are sure about this?" She quietly asked.

She hoped that Jasmine might change her mind and shake her head.

Jasmine nodded in silence as her blue eyes stared back.

Jade and Marinos suddenly turned and headed back toward the closed glass door.

Jasmine turned her head and watched them.

"Where do you two think you're going?" She enquired.

It was her sister Jade that turned and grinned.

"There's a shop just around the corner that sells nothing but chocolate." She replied.

"We're going to see if it's open." She added with a chuckle.

Jasmine's eyes widened and she shook her head.

"I'm going through hair amputation and you're off to buy chocolate?" She asked.

"If it is open you had better get me something really expensive for doing this!" She insisted.

The two sisters stared at each other for a few moments longer.

"If I find you with chocolate around your mouth later and you didn't get me some I swear I'll hit you with a house brick." Jasmine assured Jade.

Jade laughed before she glanced at Veronica.

"If she gives you any trouble just shave it all off." She joked.

Veronica giggled.

Eventually Marinos and Jade left the shop and closed the door behind them.

Veronica's gaze returned to Jasmine via the mirror in front of them.

"Now you're definitely sure of this?" She asked.

She again started to brush Jasmine's long straight blonde hair and Jasmine nodded again with a smile.

"Why do you do this to your beautiful long hair?" Veronica enquired.

"They're making me do it." Jasmine replied.

"They both kick me quite a lot too." She lied.

A telling smirk suddenly appeared on Veronica's red painted lips.

"Somehow I think that this does not happen." She replied with a chuckle.

"Maybe it does happen but the other way around."

"That's it take their side." Jasmine replied with a grin.


Back at Carmen's house at Lourdatta she stood up from the white dressing table inside her bedroom and dialled a number into her phone as David Stringer relayed it in her ear.

She walked across her spacious bedroom where she opened the door and stepped outside while the dialling number connected to the recipient of the call.

She then walked along the black railed balcony that completely surrounded the entire upper floor outside the house.

She suddenly broke into a smile.

"Mr Sanchez I see that you've booked the necessary flights to the island of Sulawesi." She informed him.

She then made a point thanks to David Stringer's continuous support in her ear to show Miguel that she knew all of the details of each flight.

She included flight numbers, expected departure and arrival times and even the seat numbers that he was booked onto.

She used the tip of her red painted fingernails to quietly drum onto another glass door before she opened it and stepped inside and then very quietly closed it behind her.

"When you leave tomorrow Mr Sanchez I want you to fully understand something." She began.

Miguel Sanchez was only in a position to listen for now.

"Nobody will approach your wife." Carmen continued to explain.

"Unless of course you decide to deviate from my instructions and we'll be watching the hotel at Manisa just like we'll be watching you during your entire journey." She added.

There was a pause as Carmen sat beside Richard's half-filled suitcase on the bed as he packed for their journey back to the UK tomorrow.

"If you fail to make it to Mamuju or you fail to pick up our girl you'll receive a call to listen to your wife's execution one hour after the time that you're scheduled to arrive." She vowed.

There was another pause before Miguel Sanchez eventually told Carmen that he understood.

"Bring that girl to me Mr Sanchez and you have my word that your wife will remain safe." She continued.

"I'll call you again tomorrow when I know that you have boarded the flight for New Delhi." She told him.

Richard Willows stood in his bedroom and listened to the one sided conversation before Carmen hung up the call.

"That was easy enough." She said as she reassuringly smiled up at him.

Even her heart however continued to pound heavily against her chest.

**Level Nine**
**Friday January 19th 2001**

It was just after ten in the morning when David Stringer sat inside his converted office bedroom and stared at all four of the monitors on the left side.

He was dressed in a black t shirt and a pair of knee length Tartan shorts with dark blue socks on his feet and he munched on dry toasted bread.

Yesterday he observed Miguel Sanchez board the flight from the small airstrip just outside Manisa for the short fifty minute flight to the Turkish capital city of Ankara.

Just twenty five minutes ago David watched Miguel board a Boeing 747 that departed for New Delhi India.

Several French and German spy satellites passed over Turkey allowing David to keep a close eye on the hotel that he knew Theresa Sanchez still hadn't left.

He concluded that the Spanish husband and wife knew that their only option was to go through this and get it done and that they really had no choice in the matter.

He also kept a close eye on the giant Spanish cargo vessel the Indigo.

She was anchored in the Mediterranean Sea fourteen miles south of the Turkish port at Antalya and just ninety six nautical miles north-west of Cyprus.

David expected very little or no activity from the 1,200 foot long ship for now.

Miguel Sanchez was no longer within the immediate vicinity and she was still reported as 'under repair' by her skipper Louise Fernandez and she would continue in this 'busted ship' condition until Sanchez returned.

Everything had suddenly stopped in its tracks since the incident involving the Romanians at Belmont road at Ilford Essex after the death of Dorin Christescu and the arrest and custody of Emil Hagi.

Vladimir and Inna Kolov had vanished into thin air and David could see that the highly professional human trafficking organisation had gone underground and it now appeared as if they never even existed.

But he knew of course that they did.

He kept a close eye on Unit 4F at the Stanley industrial estate beside north Woolwich pier where the bogus Indigo security services were based.

David knew that the auction room and holding pen were still located and were functional there.

There was no movement from there either.

In fact the entire already almost vacant estate appeared to be completely deserted.

There was no visible movement from the home of Jane Chapman at Glade road Watford or her bought and paid for sixteen year old Vietnamese message runner Kim Cuc Nguy.

She was also nowhere to be seen.

David however knew for a fact that she was still inside Chapman's luxurious five bedroom house.

There was no sign of Lisa Moore although again David knew that she was inside her own house at Uxbridge road Pinner just twelve miles south of Jane Chapman's Watford home.

David slowly nodded to himself with acknowledgement.

They had most decidedly gone into hiding even though the authorities were still quite clueless that any of them even existed.

To his surprise there was movement from the home of Debbie Davies at Rectory hill at Amersham.

As Stringer continued to eat dry toast he watched Davies climb into her gold Mercedes and head in a south easterly direction along the A413 toward Gerrards Cross just west of London.

"And where do you think you're going young lady?" He asked.

He stared at his computer monitor and waited to find out.


One hour and eighteen minutes later Debbie Davies pulled up outside a property that David wasn't aware of before today.

He guessed that she could be visiting a friend or a family member and because he took this into account and had other things going on elsewhere in the world David didn't check out the address at Larchwood drive Sidcup south east London.

He checked the overhead view of the hotel at Manisa and then hacked into the hotel files to ensure that Theresa Sanchez was still booked in.

She was still there.

He then glanced at the overhead view of the Indigo to ensure that everything there was as it should be.

The Indigo hadn't moved either.

Her skipper Louise Fernandez created the 'damaged ship' scenario that was under repair until his cousin Miguel Sanchez returned so David expected it to be right where it was supposed to be.

Debbie Davies remained inside the house at Larchwood drive for just under an hour before she climbed back into her car.

"You're the only one brave or stupid enough to move." David uttered to his PC monitor.

For a few brief moments his incredible mind pondered on the possibility that Miguel Sanchez or his wife had somehow managed to get word out.

Maybe they were now aware that every one of them was being watched from high in the sky.

"But then why would *you* venture outside?" He asked as he watched Davies.

He watched her climb back into her car and instead of returning home to Amersham she again headed in a south easterly direction.

"Where are you going now?" He asked.

It would be another hour and a half before he would discover her next point of destination.


Debbie Davies eventually reached the village of Whitfield just outside Dover on the south east coast where she pulled up behind a green eighteen wheeled truck at an out of the way very isolated layby.

"What the heck are you doing all the way down there?" David asked.

He then swigged red fizzy pop straight from the bottle as he watched.

"Ok whatever it is you just showed me that you don't know I'm here." He said.

He continued to watch as she climbed out from her gold convertible Mercedes and at the same time the driver of the truck that David identified as Polish climbed down from his cab.

"Ok what's going on here?" He wondered.

The driver and Davies shook hands before he unlocked and then opened the back doors of his huge truck as Stringer continued to watch from sixty miles above their heads.

Eventually he saw four figures climb out from the back of the truck and he could see that they were all women.

He could also see that these four women appeared to be young.

"Are you up to your old game Chapman?" David asked.

His question was aimed toward her although she couldn't hear him and he was right she had absolutely no idea that he was watching her.

He continued to watch as Davies shook hands with each of the four young women in turn before she ushered them toward her car.

He also noted that these four women all carried small holdall bags.

As they all climbed into her Mercedes Davies walked back along toward the cab of the truck with the driver where she appeared to hand over cash.

"Ok so you just bought those four girls and they don't even know it." David quietly uttered.

He guessed but couldn't actually see that it was cash that Davies had just handed to the truck driver.

He continued to watch as the green truck eventually departed and headed toward the city of London.

To David's surprise Debbie Davies climbed back into her car with the four young illegal arrivals and she headed in the opposite direction.

"You're not bringing them up to London?" He asked.

The Mercedes headed toward nearby Dover where the four girls had in fact just entered the country from.

They eventually pulled up outside a town house at York Street where they all including Davies entered a residential property.

While they were out of view David ran a check on the property and discovered that it was owned by forty seven year old Turkish Barak Yazici.

At the back of David's mind was the fact that Davies had just visited a house at Larchwood drive Sidcup a little more than two hours ago.

Considering that they were now at Dover her visit to Sidcup was more than likely not a social one at all.

He now ran a check on that property too.

The house at Larchwood drive was quite recently rented by the same man that owned the large town house at York Street Dover.

It was Barak Yazici.

David had somehow stumbled upon the hideaway of the Turkish group.

They were the very same Turkish group that took Jade Harris from her flat at Walworth.


Fifty two minutes later Debbie Davies left the house at York Street alone and made her way back to the house at Larchwood drive Sidcup.

She entered the house and remained there for around an hour before she eventually returned to her own home at Rectory hill at Amersham north-west of Watford.

"Well this crap just got interesting." David uttered.

He continued to stare at all four monitors as he picked up his telephone.

David didn't however call Richard Willows or Carmen Richardson.

**Level Ten**
**Tuesday January 23rd 2001**

It was just after ten on a pitch black evening at Carmen Richardson's huge home on the Greek island of Kefalonia.

Twenty nine year old Jade Harris stood outside her bedroom on the surrounding black railed balcony on the upper floor.

Carmen and Richard were now back in London and Jade knew that they were busy preparing even now at this late hour although back in London it was still only just after seven.

She was dressed in a thick chunky white pullover and a pair of tight fitting faded blue denim shorts with no shoes on her feet.

She rested her elbows onto the balcony rail and stared out at the silver grey swaying ocean in front of her with the lights on the neighbouring island of Zakynthos vaguely visible in the distance.

As she stared out to sea Jade sipped on a glass of brandy and contemplated everything that had happened over the past six months.

She also considered what would or could happen over the next three or four weeks.

She knew that she was Detective Inspector Nicola Garwood's very personal prime suspect.

Lights suddenly flickered into life inside the bedroom at the opposite end of the balcony and then the sliding glass door opened before Jade's half-sister Jasmine Stiles stepped outside too.

Jasmine was dressed in a long white towelling dressing gown with Carmen's white slippers on her feet.

She rigorously rubbed her now dark shoulder length hair as she glanced to her left to see Jade leaning on the balcony with a glass in her hand.

"Piss head." She quietly chuckled.

Jade still didn't see or hear her.

Jasmine slowly walked along the balcony toward her sister as she continued to dry her hair and Jade still didn't see or hear her until she eventually spoke.

"I'll give you a penny for your thoughts." Jasmine said with a smile.

Jade turned to see her there.

"Carmen's going to kill you." She chuckled.

She stood upright and sipped more brandy as she studied Jasmine.

Jasmine glanced down at the now blackened towel that she was using to dry her shorter and much darker hair.

"I'll bury it in the garden." She replied with a chuckle.

"Where's my drink then bitch features?" She asked.

She watched Jade sip more brandy and eventually the older of the two by just three months turned and slid open the glass door behind her that led into her own bedroom where she disappeared for a few moments.

Jade then re-emerged with a second glass and handed it to Jasmine.

The two girls now leaned onto the balcony and stared out at the Ionian Sea.

"Did you know that Loggerhead turtles swim to this island once a year to lay their eggs on the beach?" Jade asked as she still stared out at the dark swaying sea.

"What, right there?" Jasmine asked.

She pointed down toward the beach in front of them.

Jade shook her head and pointed to her left with her thumb.

"They swim in at Skala." She replied.

"Carmen and I sat down there for five hours one night and saw nothing after Marinos got his days mixed up." She chuckled.

Jasmine turned and stared at her sister.

"Are you ok?" She asked.

Without turning Jade nodded her head.

"It's been a strange old year." She eventually replied.

She sipped more brandy.

"No shit." Jasmine replied.

Jasmine placed Carmen's ruined towel onto the balcony rail and now Jade turned to study her.

"That colour suits you better than blonde." She said.

She continued to study Jasmine's ruffled and now darker hair and Jasmine turned and stared back at her.

"No, I'm starting to look alarmingly like you." She replied with a mock expression of horror.

Jade chuckled again.

"It could be worse." She replied.

"You could still look like you."

Eventually Jade leaned back onto the balcony rail and once again stared out at the shimmering silver grey swaying ocean.

"What did you tell your boss at work when you flew out here?" She asked.

Jasmine turned to face her again.

"I said I'm off to a Greek island so shove your job up your arse." She replied.

Jade spun around and stared at her.

"You did not!"

Jasmine rigorously nodded her head.

"What else was I supposed to say?" She asked.

"Would you mind if I fly out to a Greek island to help my sister because she was abducted?"

She chuckled at the mere thought.

"Shove your job up your arse was more plausible."

Jade shook her head.

"You're so Ashford." She uttered.

There was a momentary silent pause before Jade spoke again.

"Have you thought about what you're going to do when this is all over?" She asked.

Jasmine again rigorously nodded her head.

"I'm going to scrounge for a living in London." She replied.

Jade's eyes widened.

"Who exactly do you plan to scrounge from?" She asked.

Jasmine turned to face her again.

"From you of course." She casually replied.

"If you think I'm leaving you alone again you daft cow you're sadly mistaken." She informed Jade.

"And besides it's my name above your shop so I'm entitled to half the money for letting you use it." She added with another chuckle.

"You're so not living with me." Jade assured Jasmine.

"I so am." Jasmine assured Jade.

The two girls laughed for a few moments as Jade attempted to convince her half-sister that the name above her shop was actually after another Jasmine that she knew but this particular Jasmine was having none of it.

"Hey I know what we should do!" Jasmine said.

"I'll get my hair dried and we can dress identically and go and freak out the locals at a bar." She suggested.

Jade stepped into her room and then back out with the bottle of brandy and refilled Jasmine's glass.

"We have to stay here for tonight." She replied.

"It only takes one off duty policeman to see us together and we suddenly exist as sisters." She reminded Jasmine.

"Dad's name isn't on your birth certificate so right now we don't." She added.

"Carmen does however have a full wine cellar that we can completely abuse."

She refilled her own glass.

The two of them returned their elbows to the balcony and their eyes to the beautiful dark scenery in front of them.

"London's going to be different this time around." Jade quietly uttered.

Jasmine nodded with agreement.

"That's if we're not in bloody jail before we get there of course." She just as quietly replied.

At the exact same moment at 7:43pm with a three hour time difference at Tranton road Bermondsey David Stringer now watched two hotels from above.

Theresa Sanchez remained inside her hotel room at Manisa Turkey but David now also closely watched another hotel on the outskirts of Makassar city on the Indonesian island of Sulawesi.

Miguel Sanchez arrived there the day before yesterday.

He was a little less than one hundred and fifteen miles south of the military logistics base at Mamuju where Richard's twenty two year old sister Sasha Willows was being held.

David knew that Miguel was awaiting a hire car thanks to information from Carmen after her most recent call to the Spaniard.

David then confirmed it to be true via records from the hire car company.

**Level Eleven**
**Wednesday January 24th 2001**

It was just after nine the next morning when a slightly hung over Jasmine Stiles sat at the dressing table in her very quiet bedroom.

Her once long straight blonde hair was now almost identical to her half-sister's straight shoulder length reddish brown bob although Jasmine's was more of a light chestnut.

The completely silent atmosphere felt like the calm just before the storm as she stared into the large mirror in front of her.

She very carefully placed the first green coloured contact lens over her natural blue right eye and when it was finally fitted she stopped and stared at her reflection.

Eventually she reached down with her single left forefinger and took the second green lens onto the tip before she just as slowly and carefully applied it over her natural blue left eye.

After she blinked several times to lubricate it she stopped and stared again.

With her straight shoulder length reddish brown bobbed hair and now green eyes even Jasmine was quite startled at the transformation.

"Ok this is quite alarming." She quietly uttered to herself.

"I actually do look like her."

She sat and stared at herself again and it was almost like Jade was staring back at her.

She then glanced down again and gently took one of the two small dark brown moles from the top of her dressing table purposely using her right forefinger.

She grinned to herself as she recalled David Stringer from the occasion that he informed her that glue was not required as these moles actually reacted to body heat while he gently blew onto her neck.

"Chubby little Pervert." She uttered with another chuckle.

Before she placed it above her lip she once again stared at her reflection.

She reminded herself that she was staring into a mirror.

The mole had to be placed on the left side in the refection because Jade's real mole was on the right side just above her top lip.

She inadvertently waved her hand over it to ensure that the mole that needed no glue properly adhered to her skin.

Jasmine's new green eyes widened as she now stared into the mirror and her sister Jade stared straight back at her.

"Oh bloody Nora, no!" She suddenly said.

"My day just got worse than they've already planned it to be."

When Richard initially discussed part of his new plan to Carmen the day after Jade was bought and paid for by Marinos at the port of Sami Carmen told Richard of Jasmine's existence and her incredibly close bond with Jade.

"She has long blonde hair blue eyes and no mole but their facial features are like identical twins." She informed him.

"I often look at Jade and see Jasmine but with shoulder length hair." She added.

"But would she get involved in this?" Richard immediately questioned.

Jasmine and Jade never acknowledged or believed this pure natural fact that they were both the spitting image of their father.

Right now however in her bedroom at Carmen's Greek house Jasmine Stiles stared into a mirror, and her sister Jade Harris stared back at her.

"Why did I never see this before?" She asked herself in a whisper.

After a few more moments of staring into her sister's green eyes Jasmine eventually climbed to her feet.

"That's just too freaky."

She walked to a full length mirror at the other side of the room where she studied the outfit that Carmen had specifically prepared for her return to England.

"You shall pay for this Miss Richardson." She uttered with a look of utter disgust.

She stared at her own reflection dressed in a red and white short sleeved vertically striped Southampton football shirt and a pair of sprayed on bright red denim jeans with brand new bright white designer training shoes on her feet.

For a few moments, Jasmine considered what Carmen told her when she was initially introduced to her specific outfit for the day.

'We need you to stand out like a sore thumb.'

"No shit Carmen." She uttered as she stared at the mirror.

"I look like a complete twat."

Eventually she turned and walked back to the dressing table where she picked up Jade's flight ticket and passport.

She then turned again and picked up her dark blue canvas holdall bag and headed toward her closed bedroom door.

She suddenly stopped and then slowly turned to glance around the room.

She hoped that she would one day see this place again.

It was now that Jasmine's heart started to beat just that little bit faster than it normally did.

That time had finally arrived.

Down inside the lounge a just as hung over Jade Harris sat curled up in her usual cream coloured leather armchair with Marinos Georgas seated directly opposite her on a matching sofa.

Marinos silently watched Jade as she flicked through a Greek glossy fashion magazine.

Suddenly the door opened and Jasmine entered the room.

Even Jade's eyes widened as she watched herself walk into the room.

"Holy bloody crap!" She quietly uttered.

Jasmine smiled at her sister.

Jade slowly climbed to her feet and walked toward Jasmine without removing her gaze.

"I love your outfit." She chuckled.

Jasmine shook her head.

"They shall pay for this at some point in the not too distant future." She replied.

Marinos Georgas sat with his eyes widened and his mouth even wider.

"I cannot believe this, there are two Jades." He uttered with disbelief.

To this point only Carmen Richardson had ever seen this double vision.

Even April Marsh never understood what only Carmen saw.

"This is my ultimate fantasy." Marinos added.

Jade then turned and glanced at him.

"So what do you think?" She asked.

Marinos now slowly climbed to his feet and walked toward them both.

"This cannot be." He quietly uttered.

"When Carmen said this I did not believe." He added.

He still stared at Jasmine Stiles.

He saw only Jade Harris.

Two Jade Harris's in fact.

After a short while Marinos left the room to organise the car but mostly to give the girls a little time alone prior to Jasmine's departure.

"I'm not going to able to speak to you for a few days." Jasmine reminded Jade.

"Try not to get yourself abducted again won't you?" She asked with a giggle.

Jade smiled back at her.

"Are you going to be ok?" She asked.

Jasmine rigorously nodded her head.

"I'm a bit nervous but not as bad as I thought I was going to be." She replied.

She nervously fanned her own face with her hand.

There was a silent moment or two as the sister's stared into each other's green eyes before Jasmine spoke again.

"I'm not doing this whole emotional farewell thing." She told Jade.

"Keep yourself safe until this is over and we're drinking more brandy at Carmen's poolside." She added.

Jade chuckled.

"After last night I'm never drinking again." She replied.

Jasmine laughed.

"Of course you're not."

She then leaned forward and kissed Jade on her cheek.

"I'll see you in London bitch features."

Jade nodded her head.

"Try not to get arrested before I get there won't you?" She asked.

Jasmine walked away before she turned and smiled back at Jade.

"I'll give it a shot." She replied.

Before Jade knew it...

Jasmine was gone.


It was some forty minutes later when Jasmine sat in the passenger seat inside the silver Mercedes with Marinos in the driver seat.

The car now stood in the parking area away from the main doors of the airport terminal just outside the capital town Argostoli.

Jasmine's heart now pounded as she contemplated the first real task that lay ahead of her.

Eventually Marinos broke the intense silence.

"Are you ok?" He quietly asked.

Jasmine nodded.

"Yep and I'm going to do this right now." She replied.

Without uttering another word she opened the passenger door and climbed out of the car with her blue holdall bag in her left hand and Jade's passport and flight ticket in her right.

She turned and leaned back into the car where she kissed Marinos on his cheek.

"Keep an eye on my sister." She told him.

Marinos nodded.

"I will see you again when this is done." He replied.

Jasmine smiled.

"If I get arrested at the other side for being me and not Jade whatever anybody else says, keep her here." She told him.

Marinos nodded again but as he opened his mouth to speak Jasmine shook her head.

"I'm not doing that emotional thing especially before I walk into there." She said.

She nodded in the direction of the main terminal doors behind her.

Marinos sat and watched Jasmine as she quite casually strolled toward the front of the building and eventually disappeared inside.

"Very brave or very crazy, I'm not sure which one." He quietly uttered to himself.

Twenty five year old native islander Denis Christos was five feet seven inches tall and he had short jet black hair that was combed into a neat side parting.

He was dressed in a regulation long sleeved pale blue cotton shirt with a navy blue tie and dark blue cotton trousers with black leather shoes.

He stood behind the departure desk inside the terminal building and he was already aware thanks to the Interpol flag that she should arrive soon.

In an almost empty airport terminal building she wouldn't be difficult to spot.

When the glass sliding doors opened and he saw the woman with straight shoulder length reddish brown hair and large dark designer sunglasses he guessed that it must be her.

She *must* be Jade Harris.

The weather on the island in January was by no means warm and most definitely not for sunglasses and this immediately told him that this woman was attempting to avoid direct eye contact.

She was however dressed in a red and white striped top and the brightest red denim jeans possible and her new white designer training shoes were incredibly bright.

She completely failed Denis Christos's inconspicuous test.

Jasmine glanced at him behind the counter and thanks to David Stringer she knew that Denis was already aware that Jade Harris was due to arrive here and then depart around this time today.

She also knew that he wouldn't attempt to prevent her from boarding her scheduled flight.

All that Denis was required to do was positively identify Jade Harris upon her arrival.

Jasmine needed to make absolutely certain that he did just that.

She casually strolled toward him where she eventually tossed Jade's passport and flight ticket onto the desk in front of him before she studied the name badge on his shirt.

"Can you hurry this up please Denis?" She abruptly asked.

"Airport staff bore the hell out of me." She very quietly added.

Her statement was just loud enough for him to pick up.

She immediately irritated Denis with her remark regarding him and his chosen profession.

Denis Christos was having none of it and would stand his ground against this obnoxious woman and he purposely took time to check her flight ticket.

Then he just as slowly and meticulously checked Jade's passport before he turned to his computer to verify that this was the woman that was wanted by the Metropolitan police at London.

He glanced back up at her.

"Could you please remove your sunglasses Miss Harris?" He asked.

Jasmine stared back at him.

Eventually she sighed before she removed her large dark designer glasses and stared quite angrily back at him.

"Get a good look!" She snapped.

*'Airport staff bore the hell out of me.'* Denis recalled.

Everything that she said and did irritated Denis Christos but he smiled to himself.

She obviously didn't know that the moment that she arrived on British soil she would be arrested and detained.

If the truth be told Denis quite enjoyed that thought because this Jade Harris was completely obnoxious and very rude.

Now he opened an attached file to her destined flight and saw her British police issued photograph and he double checked just to make absolutely sure that it was her that they were looking for.

She had green eyes and a small dark brown mole just above her upper lip on the right side just like the woman with the exact same name that was *'wanted for questioning'* on his computer screen.

The highly trained Denis Christos knew that she was without a shadow of doubt the same Jade Harris.

Eventually he handed Jasmine, Jade's passport and her flight ticket and he smiled again.

"Have a pleasant flight Miss Harris." He said.

Jasmine shook her head without reply before she turned and headed toward the departure lounge.

*'I'm so sorry Denis!'* She thought to herself as she casually strolled away from him.

A few moments later, one of the local taxi drivers walked into the airport terminal and bought a takeaway cup of coffee.

Marinos Georgas stood and sipped his coffee as he watched Jasmine Stiles as Jade Harris stroll to the airport departure lounge where she sat down.

He then discretely turned his attention to the departure desk to see the clerk speaking on the telephone.

Marinos removed his own phone from the front pocket of his black denim jeans and dialled Carmen Richardson's number.

## Level Twelve
## Wednesday January 24th 2001

It was just after two in the afternoon UK time when thirty four year old Carmen Richardson sat behind her desk inside her office at Mount Street Mayfair west London.

She nodded her head before she glanced up in the direction of the forty eight year old property tycoon and her business partner among other relationships, Arron Balcombe.

Eventually Carmen broke into an inquisitive smile.

"How on earth did you manage to get a hold of that particular warehouse?" She asked.

Balcombe flashed one of his smiles and shrugged his shoulders.

"I've done occasional business with the guy that owns that patch of concrete and the buildings on it for about twenty years." He explained.

"I've actually stored furniture in that exact same warehouse." He continued.

"It wasn't that difficult and besides as you can see he'll do business with anybody that has the ready cash."

Carmen glanced back down at the completed paperwork on her desk.

She then slid the paperwork to her left side before she looked up at Richard Willows who sat beside Arron Balcombe.

"Have you also seen this Maisonette at Tooting?" She asked.

Richard nodded with a grin.

"It's perfect if only for that parking bay." He replied.

Again Carmen nodded with a beaming smile.

Her joy was however about to become short lived when realization arrived and it came in a familiar voice in her ear.

"Ok I can hear you all babbling so I know you can hear me." He began.

Carmen immediately raised her head again and stared directly at Richard.

"Jasmine Stiles departed from Kefalonia airport as Jade Harris seven minutes ago and she will arrive at Gatwick airport at around five thirty this evening our time." He informed them.

"Carmen obviously I know that Marinos called you when she walked through to the departures lounge and that the desk clerk was on the phone…" He continued.

David then took a swig of orange fizzy pop from the bottle before he continued.

"I can confirm that the clerk did call Gatwick airport to inform them that Jade Harris was inbound and that Gatwick have a security team preparing to take her into custody." He added.

"Detective Sergeant Saunders at task force headquarters has been informed by Gatwick."

Without even realising it Carmen nodded her head with acknowledgement before she glanced to her right at April Marsh standing in front of the bay window that overlooked Mount Street.

"I need you to drive over to Gatwick and see that they definitely take Jasmine into custody."

The plump brunette nodded.

"Do you want me to call you as soon as I've seen it?" She asked.

Carmen nodded with a smile.

"But don't hang around there waiting for Jasmine." She replied.

Again April nodded with acknowledgement.

"I hope I'm getting fuel allowance for this." She quietly uttered.

Both Richard Willows and Arron Balcombe chuckled as Carmen continued to stare April out.

After April left the office Carmen sat back in her brown leather office chair where she took in a long and deep breath.

"It's actually started." She quietly uttered.


Inside his office bedroom David Stringer glanced up at the clock on the wall because he had purposely adjusted it eight hours forward to display the current time at Makassar city on the Indonesian island of Sulawesi.

He knew that Miguel Sanchez had been waiting for a hire car that had just arrived outside the hotel.

He glanced up at the clock again to see that it was almost nine thirty in the evening at Makassar city and there was absolutely no way that Miguel could possibly make the mountainous journey at night.

He took in a deep breath and then sighed.

"Richard, I have some news about Indonesia." He began again.

"Miguel Sanchez will definitely leave for Mamuju in the morning as his hire car has finally arrived." He explained.

There was a pause before David continued.

"If everything goes according to plan Sasha should be out of that hell hole by this time tomorrow mate." He added.

There was no response from Richard.

He simply couldn't temp fate by responding.

Twenty nine year old Detective Inspector Nicola Garwood turned her car right at the junction when her personal phone suddenly started to ring.

She pressed the green button to answer it as she pulled into her parking space outside the task force headquarters building at Commercial Street Whitechapel.

The caller was Detective Sergeant Jacob Saunders.

"Guv I need to urgently meet with you at HQ." He informed her.

Nicola broke into a playful grin.

"Jacob, are you flirting with me you little tart?" She asked with a teasing giggle.

Nicola climbed out from her car and closed the driver side door before she headed toward the brown double doors that led into the task force headquarters building.

Jacob as usual completely misread her very dry sense of humour.

"No guv I'm not flirting." He assured her.

Nicola walked along the wide corridor past Chief Inspector Curtis's office on her left toward the wide staircase that led up to the first floor and she shook her head with disbelief.

There was a pause before Jacob eventually spoke again.

"Guv, I have something for you and I'm quite sure you're going to like it." He informed her.

Now Nicola chuckled.

"Stop being a phone pervert, Jacob." She replied.

With her phone tucked beneath her chin Nicola reached into her inside jacket pocket and removed her electronic swipe card to gain access into the operations room.

There was another pause before Jacob finally spoke again just as Nicola swiped her white card into the box and then pushed open the door.

"It's about Jade Harris guv." He informed her.

"She'll land at Gatwick airport in two hours."

Nicola started running toward the cubicle office that she shared with Sam Henning and when she pushed open the door she saw Jacob sitting on the edge of her desk and then pressed the red button on her phone.

"Where's she coming in from?" She asked.

Jacob stood up from the desk.

"She departed from the Greek island of Kefalonia a little more than an hour ago and the flight takes about three and a quarter hours." He replied.

Nicola walked around her desk where she sat down and opened a drawer.

"Jacob, how long does it take to get to Gatwick from here?" she asked.

He appeared to ponder.

"It depends on the traffic about an hour usually." He replied.

Nicola nodded as she searched through the drawer.

"Then don't you need to get us a car quite quickly?" She asked.

For the first time Saunders smiled.

"No guv because a security team at Gatwick are going to hold her for us." He explained.

"She won't be going anywhere."

Nicola suddenly stared up at him.

"I don't give a shit about the security team at Gatwick Jacob." She informed him.

"I'm interested in finally catching up with a certain little bitch by the name of Jade Harris!"

Jacob suddenly got the point and left the cubicle office to sign for a car.

Forty seven year old Detective Inspector Sam Henning sat at his desk in silence and until now he had only watched and listened.

"Nik, can we talk about this before you go off to Gatwick?" He asked in a calm and quiet tone.

Garwood briefly glanced across at him.

"There's no need Sam." She replied.

"I can't arrest Jade Harris unless she confesses all in a moment of insanity." She added.

"I get the picture."

Sam shook his head.

"I just want you to think this whole Harris situation through before you go." He replied.

"Something doesn't add up."

Nicola glanced up at him again before she closed her desk drawer.

"What part doesn't add up Sam?" She asked.

"Is it the blood samples that were found at her flat, the fragments of human skull or just the fact that she vanished off the face of the planet straight after it all happened?" She asked.

"What part doesn't add up for you?"

Sam took in a deep breath and exhaled it.

"It's not that I don't want you to question her Nik." He began again.

"I do want you to question her in fact she needs to be questioned without a doubt." He added.

"I just don't want you to automatically believe that she did all of this just from the evidence of a very conveniently timed anonymous call." He explained.

Again Nicola nodded.

"That little bitch has something to answer for Sam I just know it." She eventually replied.

She then stepped back out of the cubical office door and closed it behind her.

"Jacob, move your arse!" She yelled.

**Level Thirteen**
**Wednesday January 24th 2001**

Two hours and twenty three minutes later Jasmine Stiles followed the other seventeen passengers that had just arrived at Gatwick International Airport on flight XK774 from Kefalonia Greece.

Her heart now pounded very heavily against her chest.

*'Get a grip Jaz!'* She told herself.

She casually strolled into the arrivals lounge with her large dark designer sunglasses now placed on top of her straight shoulder length reddish brown bobbed hair.

Her green eyes discretely scanned the terminal building in search of something or somebody that she knew was waiting for her.

Wearing a red and white vertically striped football shirt and red skin tight jeans with brand new white designer training shoes Jasmine was actually more difficult to miss than she was to spot.

She made her way toward the luggage carousel where her heart started to pound even heavier when she suddenly realised that the people that needed to had now spotted her.

Across the vast open space on her left was a man that stood at around six feet tall and he had short slightly greying dark brown hair.

He wore a plain black suit and a white cotton shirt with a navy blue tie and she knew that he now stared straight at her.

"Oh crap here we go." She very nervously uttered beneath her breath.

"Hold it together." She just as quietly reminded herself.

Her heart pounded heavier and there was a shudder in Jasmine's very quiet tone.

On the man in the suit's left was a huge muscle bound security guard who was even taller and much, much broader.

The giant guard was dressed in a too tight pale blue cotton shirt that came with black epaulettes on his huge shoulders and a black clip-on tie and he wore plain black trousers with highly polished black leather shoes on his feet.

On the right of the man in the black suit was a pretty young woman that Jasmine guessed was in her early to mid-twenties and she had long blonde crimped hair that was pulled back into a ponytail.

The pretty young woman was around five feet six and she was dressed in the exact same uniform as the muscle bound body builder.

The man in the black suit suddenly smiled directly at Jasmine.

*'Shit here we go.'* She thought to herself.

He motioned with his hand but instead of approaching the trio Jasmine stopped walking and waited where she stood for them to approach her.

*'Keep calm you know what to do.'* She reminded herself.

Even her inner thoughts came with nervous apprehension.

As the three approached her the man in the black suit displayed another warm smile before he eventually spoke.

"Good day madam." He began.

Jasmine only smiled in response.

"My name is Mike Denning and I'm the head of security here at Gatwick." He continued.

Jasmine's false smile slightly broadened.

"Welcome home Jade." She very, very quietly uttered.

She said it just loudly enough for him to hear her mention her sister's name.

At the same time Jasmine reminded herself after specific detailed conversations with Richard that she was not making a statement of fact for Mike Denning or anybody else to hear.

After all her name was Jasmine Stiles and her quiet comment was only made to plant the seed into his head.

At no point would she tell him or anybody for that matter that her name was Jade Harris.


*'Because the mind often tells the eye what it chooses to see...'*


Richard already explained the psychology behind it.

She was identical to her sister and Mike Denning's subconscious had just heard Jade's name mentioned to link the two together.

He already knew without a shadow of doubt that this was the woman that they all waited for.

"Could I see your passport and flight ticket please madam?" He asked with the same warm smile.

Of course Jasmine readily handed to him Jade's passport and flight ticket.

The security chief studied Jade's passport as his highly trained mind systematically filtered all of the necessary information.

Kefalonia Airport yesterday informed Gatwick Airport that a person named Jade Harris who was wanted for questioning by London's

Metropolitan police had booked a ticket from the island and would be headed inbound from 2:15pm today.

A trained clerk at the departure lounge at Kefalonia Airport today positively identified her as the same Jade Harris.

He would never have done that unless he knew without doubt that she was Jade Harris.

That same clerk made a call to inform Gatwick to inform them that she was now on her way and even informed them of how she was unmistakeably dressed.

Even in a crowded Gatwick airport she wouldn't be difficult to spot.

Before flight XK774 landed Mike Denning studied Jade's passport photograph and he knew that without a shadow of doubt that this woman was the same person that was positively identified at Kefalonia earlier today.

He had also just heard her first name to clarify the fact.

He glanced up at Jasmine and smiled again.

"There seems to be some kind of issue." He began again.

Jasmine stared up at him and displayed a look of confusion.

"We've been asked to hold you for questioning." He continued.

"Officers from the Metropolitan police force are on their way to question you."

Jasmine looked somewhat bemused.

"Why would they want to speak to me?" She asked.

Mike Denning assured her that he had absolutely no idea and even suggested that this was more than likely some kind of mistake.

"If you would like to accompany us to an interview room Miss…" He began again.

Jasmine promptly stared up at the giant menacing male security officer before Mike Denning finished.

"And if I don't Conan here will rugby tackle me to the floor and beat me up?" She interjected with a nervous giggle in her tone.

Denning chuckled.

He knew that Jade Harris was no physical threat and he turned his attention to the giant security guard.

"We'll be fine from here thank you Jason." Denning assured him.

The muscle bound guard half smiled down at Jasmine before he left.

Denning returned his attention to Jasmine who he still one hundred percent *knew* was in fact her half-sister Jade.

He motioned toward the pretty young blonde security guard.

"This is Julia and she'll remain with you in the interview room until the police officers arrive." He informed her.

Jasmine turned to the pretty young Julia and beamed a grin after she discretely spied the engagement ring on her finger.

*'Good you're straight.'*

Now that she had convinced Denning, Jasmine went to work with fewer but still rapidly thumping heartbeats.

She hid it so well.

"Well you're much prettier than the other one." She commented.

She watched as the twenty four year old Julia Whitelaw started to blush.

Jasmine knew that she had to be accompanied by a female officer and she also knew exactly what to do with her.

It was absolutely essential from this point on that pretty Julia could not make or maintain any form of eye contact with Jasmine.

Fortunately Julia had been in the job for just two months by this time and this was her first serious assignment.

Jasmine beamed another grin at Julia's discomfort and offered her hand.

"Shall we hold hands or do you want to cuff me to stop mine from wandering?" She asked.

Of course Julia's face reddened more.

Mike Denning chuckled again as he ushered Jasmine toward a closed white door that he unlocked using his key bunch.

The pretty young and still profusely blushing Julia followed behind Jasmine.

Denning ushered Jasmine through the door where she immediately recognised the long quite dimly lit corridor in front of her from the blue prints that David Stringer sent over a few days ago.

She also recognised the staircase on her right that led up to the airport security operations room from the same drawings.

Denning closed the handle-less door behind them.

"Julia will escort you down to the interview room to wait for the police Miss Harris." He informed her.

Jasmine immediately turned to Julia again.

"We'll be alone at last!" She grinned.

Once again Julia's face burned.

Denning chuckled again as he climbed the staircase back up to the ops room where his own office was situated.

Jasmine, accompanied by the very uncomfortable Julia Whitelaw started to walk down the long dimly lit corridor toward the interview room at the far end.

Outside in the arrivals lounge thirty five year old April Marsh sat and watched who she knew was Jasmine Stiles as she was escorted behind the white door.

As April walked out from the terminal building she took her phone from the pocket of her black leather jacket and called Carmen to inform her.

At the same time Jasmine casually strolled down the corridor with Julia just slightly behind on her left side.

Julia was without a doubt avoiding any eye contact with the outlandish lesbian in front of her.

The Jade Harris lookalike knew that the closed door just ahead on the right was an unmarked unisex toilet.

She also knew that the toilet was windowless and because of that and because she had purposely flirted with the very uncomfortable naive pretty blonde Julia would not want to accompany her inside it.

Suddenly Jasmine stopped outside the door and pointed.

"Is this a loo Jules?" She asked.

The still very red faced Juliet sighed and purposely stared at the floor.

"Well I can't help it if I need to pee can I?" Jasmine asked.

"Want to come in with me?" She asked with a grin.

Finally Julia had listened to enough.

"Give me a fucking break will you?" She quietly asked with a snap in her tone.

"I've been here for a couple of months and I'm getting sick of this crap already!"

It was the one and only time that she very angrily stared into Jasmine's green eyes and it was in a very dimly lit corridor.

She would never do that again and that dimly lit corridor was the only place that she was ever going to be given the opportunity to.

Jasmine raised her eyebrows and giggled before she turned and pushed open the door but she stopped and turned to face Julia again.

"I'll try to be quick so don't run off." She said with another suggestive tease in her tone.

She then disappeared from Julia's view as the unisex toilet door slowly swung closed behind her.

Julia Whitelaw sighed and shook her head.

Inside Jasmine leaned her back against the door and took in a huge breath.

"Shit!" she silently mouthed to herself.

Her heart absolutely hammered against her chest.

'Do you even know what you're doing you dopey bitch?' She asked herself.

Eventually she composed herself and stepped into the centre of three cubicles where she closed and locked the door behind her.

Jasmine quickly but very carefully removed one of the green contact lenses and then the other to reveal her natural blue eyes.

She then held them both in her left hand as she just as carefully peeled away the small dark brown mole from above her lip.

She then folded all three items into tissue paper and dropped them down into the white porcelain toilet bowl where she left it to saturate.

She walked back out of the cubicle and checked in the mirror to make sure that there were no visible signs that the mole had ever been there.

She turned her head to the left and stared for a few moments at the closed white door knowing that the security officer still stood the other side of it.

Eventually she stepped back into the cubicle where she flushed and watched to ensure that everything disappeared.

When she stepped back out Jasmine stared for a few more moments at her reflection in the long mirror above the sinks and took in another long and deep breath before she exhaled.

"It's now time for the moment of truth." She very quietly whispered.

She also hoped that everything that Richard had assured her of was accurate.

Jasmine slowly walked toward the closed main door where she stopped and took in another long deep breath before she slowly exhaled again.

'Flirt some more with Julia.' She reminded herself.

She then opened the door and immediately broke into another beaming grin.

"Ok Jules let's go and sit in our comfy little room together." She grinned in the dimly lit corridor.

Julia's face reddened again as she shook her head.

"I'm engaged to be married!" She finally snapped.

Jasmine was finally ushered into a small white windowless room where she sat down at a table and glanced up at the CCTV camera and smiled again.

Mike Denning drummed his fingers onto the top of the monitor and stared back down at her.

The image that he viewed was in black and white which meant that he had no idea that her eyes had completely changed colour.

They were green when he stood in front of her and they were now blue but there was no way that he could see that.

The missing mole passed him by too because he wasn't looking for it and besides he knew something without a shadow of doubt.

Of course he already knew that he was staring down at Jade Harris.

Because Jasmine continuously flirted with Julia Whitelaw at no time did the pretty young blonde make any more eye contact with her but she only stared once into Jasmine's eyes in a dimly lit corridor.

Jasmine sat back in her chair where she secretly breathed a sigh of relief.

She now waited to fool Detective Inspector Nicola Garwood too.

Jasmine she had one important factor on her side.

It was a simple question.

Why would one person pretend to be another in order to be purposely questioned by the police?

Of course nobody would do that.

The mere notion would never enter anybody's head.

That's what Jasmine hoped anyway.

## Level Fourteen
**Wednesday January 24th 2001**

It was almost five that same evening on the Greek island of Kefalonia where Marinos Georgas sat and patiently waited at Carmen's spacious home.

He had one more task to carry out this evening.

Upstairs in her bedroom the real Jade Harris sat in front of her dressing table mirror and stared at her own reflection.

She was dressed in a crisp white cotton open necked blouse beneath a long thick black knitted cardigan and plain black slacks with black canvas low heeled shoes.

Her usually straight shoulder length reddish brown bobbed hair was tightly pinned back.

She continued to stare at her own reflection as she covered layer after layer, the small dark brown mole just above her lip with foundation.

It took around four minutes to make it appear insignificant unless the person staring at it already knew that it was there.

Her next task was the pale blue contact lenses.

She slowly and very carefully fitted them over her natural green eyes before she blinked several times to help them to settle and lubricate.

When she stared into the mirror again Jade half smiled because with no visible dark brown mole and blue eyes instead of her natural green she could already see Jasmine staring back at her.

"She's right this is quite alarming." Jade quietly chuckled to herself.

But just like her sister earlier Jade's heart was starting to beat just that little bit faster.

She glanced to her right at the long wavy blonde wig before she picked it up and carefully placed it over her tightly pinned straight reddish brown hair and adjusted it to fit and look natural.

She then brushed it out and now Jasmine really was suddenly staring back at her.

After a short while she took from the top of the dressing table Jasmine's passport and flight ticket and then she climbed to her feet and did exactly as her sister did earlier.

She casually strolled across the room and studied Jasmine's appearance in the full length mirror for around a minute.

"It's no wonder you're single." She quietly uttered.

It didn't matter that Jade quietly joked about her sister.

She was truthfully starting to feel very nervous indeed.

She picked up her small black canvas holdall bag and headed out of the room.

Before she closed the door behind her she stopped and turned and as her new blue eyes studied the room.

Jade also hoped one day to see this place again.

Then she closed the door and made her way downstairs.


Thirty year old Marinos Georgas sat in the lounge where he read the same glossy magazine that Jade read just a few hours ago.

The door slowly opened and he glanced up.

It looked just like Jasmine had entered the room and his eyes widened yet again.

Just like earlier today when he stared at Jade but knew that she was actually Jasmine he now stared at Jasmine but knew that it was in fact Jade standing in front of him.

Marinos slowly climbed to his feet and walked toward her and as Jade often did she half smiled as he approached her.

"This is insanity." He quietly uttered.

He still stared at Jade but only saw Jasmine.

"We have to leave now." She calmly informed him.

"My flight leaves in an hour."

Marinos nodded without taking his eyes off her.

"Are you ok to do this?" He eventually asked.

Jade shrugged her shoulders before she nodded her blonde head in response.

"I wouldn't be standing here if it wasn't for Richard." She eventually replied.

"I owe him at least this."


It was around twenty eight minutes later when they reached Kefalonia airport where this time Marinos parked in the vacant taxi rank right outside the main doors and where he and Jade sat inside his car in silence.

Marinos like everybody else had concerns when it came to Jade because she had been through so much over recent months and yet she seemed fine.

To Marinos that itself wasn't quite right.

He knew that Jasmine was bold and brash and that she could pull this off.

Jade had never discussed the things that happened to her on that night at her flat, inside the warehouse and auction room at the Stanley Industrial estate or on board the Indigo before Marinos himself collected her from the small fishing boat at the port at Sami.

She never once spoke to him of anything that happened to her.

He knew that the three Turkish men fractured her jaw and cheekbone and smashed most of her back teeth with her own heavy baseball bat.

Jade still remained silent about everything.

The only person that she ever told anything was Carmen.

It was the reason that Marinos feared her walking through the airport terminal just like her sister had earlier because nobody knew what was going on inside Jade's head.

Jasmine was a completely different matter.

Jade was now so calm too calm in fact.

She sat in the car and stared to her right at the glass doors that led into the airport terminal and Marinos watched her in silence.

Her sister was purposely dressed in bright red and white with obvious signs to trained officials like twenty five year old Denis Christos who contacted Gatwick when the blatantly obvious Jasmine stood in front of him.

Jade was dressed in black so that unlike Jasmine she *didn't* stand out.

Unlike the incredibly busy holiday season there were just two flights in and out of Kefalonia airport every two days in January and Jasmine successfully boarded the first flight out.

Jade was about to board the second.

It had to be right now or never.

Eventually she turned to Marinos and smiled again.

"I can't put this off." She nervously told him.

Marinos smiled back at her.

"I will follow you in five minutes to make sure that you're booked in." He replied.

Jade then leaned across and they hugged.

"Just get to the other side." He told her during their embrace.

Jade nodded her blonde head in silence.

Eventually they broke off and she climbed out of the car with Jasmine's passport and flight ticket in one hand and her small black canvas holdall bag in the other.

Marinos sat and watched her walk into the airport terminal where she eventually disappeared out of sight.

"Please be safe." He quietly whispered.

Twenty six year old departures clerk Ruth Venizelos sat behind the desk when a woman with long wavy blonde hair approached her and handed over a flight ticket and passport.

She smiled up at the woman as she briefly studied her passport before she glanced up to ensure that the woman in front of her was the same and then she moved onto the flight ticket before she handed them both back to Jade.

"Please have a pleasant flight Miss Stiles." Ruth said with a smile.

Jade Harris smiled back at her.

"I hope that one day you visit again." Ruth commented.

Jade's smile broadened.

"I plan to." She replied.

She turned and headed toward the small departure lounge.

Standing in the small airport shop Marinos Georgas watched Jade Harris walk into the glass departures lounge with Jasmine Stiles passport and flight ticket in her hand.

He then turned his attention to the check-in clerk Ruth Venizelos.

The Greek clerk did absolutely nothing because nobody was looking for the girl from Ashford Kent and Interpol's alert had already located the one that they were waiting for.

Jade Harris was after all being held at Gatwick airport in the United Kingdom.

Nobody was waiting for a blonde by the name of Jasmine Stiles.

**Level Fifteen**
**Wednesday January 24th 2001**

The moment that everybody feared particularly Carmen Richardson had just passed.

David Stringer informed Carmen via the tiny brown electronic device inside her ear that the real Jade Harris had just boarded her flight at Kefalonia airport bound for Gatwick in the United Kingdom.

In approximately three hours and ten minutes from now flight GS777 would land on runway twenty eight at Gatwick international airport.

Jade would hopefully walk straight out and onto British soil as the completely unwanted and unknown Jasmine Stiles.

"I can't believe that we're actually going through with this." Carmen quietly uttered.

It was all now beginning to sink in.

She sat at her desk and stared out of the window with only Richard Willows remaining inside her office.

"This is bloody insane!" Carmen uttered.

Richard sat directly opposite her and after hearing her quiet statement he reminded her of the reasons that it had to be done this way.

At around two in the morning on Sunday November 5th three Turkish abductors entered Jade's flat and their efforts resulted in one of their deaths courtesy of a solid wooden baseball bat in the hands of Jade Harris.

Detective Inspector Nicola Garwood's forensic team identified a blood group stained onto the brand new carpet inside Jade's half decorated living room and they also discovered three tiny fragments of human skull that matched the blood sample.

It meant that the skull fragments and unknown blood source came from the same victim and that victim was most likely now deceased.

Jade was aware that she killed a man during the struggle that night before she was shot in the back with a Taser and the fact that she knew about it could be used by Detective Inspector Nicola Garwood to hold her in custody on suspicion of murder.

Richard knew that the police would see during an interview that Jade was aware of the death by reading her body language and facial expressions along with intricate strategic trick questioning even though they had no physical evidence to link her to the crime scene.

Without some kind of confession or suspicion Richard also knew that they would have to release her.

This information was purposely kept from Jasmine.

Of course it was she that sat in the interview room at Gatwick airport in Jade's place and awaited the arrival of DI Nicola Garwood and DS Jacob Saunders.

Her body language and facial expressions would convince them that she knew nothing of the death that occurred on the night in question night.

Jasmine Stiles genuinely knew absolutely nothing about it.

It was the information that had been purposely kept from her for this very reason.

Jasmine could not give away those obvious signs of body language and facial expressions because she genuinely didn't know.

Richard went on to explain to Carmen that changing a person's identity was easy but having them pull it off was something completely different.

They all knew that Jasmine could do it and it was why her sister Jade played the minor role in his plan because nobody knew what could possibly be going on inside her mind after her ordeal.

Carmen understood everything that he explained but she assured him that it didn't make this moment in time any easier.

It was the reason that she added another small safeguard of her own just to be sure.

Carmen had a very valuable little black book.

Jasmine and Jade were the ones taking the risks today but Carmen wasn't about to play their luck with just chance and hope.

"When they're both where they're supposed to be I'll calm down." She informed Richard.

David Stringer suddenly interjected in both of their ears.

"Ok here we go boys and girls." He began.

"Detective Inspector Garwood and Detective Sergeant Saunders have just pulled up in the visitor's car park at Gatwick to interview Jade who isn't jade but Jasmine." He began.

"The actual Jade is heading to the exact same place as Jasmine and the cops." He informed them in his own way.

There was then a short pause before he spoke again.

David considered the information that he had just relayed to Richard and Carmen.

"You're an idiot Richard." He quietly added.

David returned his attention to watching the hotel at Manisa where Theresa Sanchez remained in her room.

He also watched the hotel at Makassar city on the Indonesian island of Sulawesi where Theresa's husband remained until the morning when he would drive north to the military installation just south of Mamuju.

He checked on the Indigo that remained on southern Turkish waters in the Mediterranean Sea.

He also kept a close eye on the homes of Jane Chapman at Watford, Lisa Moore at Pinner and Debbie Davies at Amersham.

David was in for a busy few hours.

He continued to monitor unit 4F at the Stanley Industrial Estate and the recently discovered house at Larchwood drive at Sidcup.

Then he checked the town house at York Street at Dover that was owned by forty seven year old Turkish Barak Yazici where he knew four Polish illegal immigrants were now temporarily housed.

As David ate chocolate he continuously rotated his observations.

"Garwood and Saunders have just entered the operations building at Gatwick." He announced.

## Level Sixteen
**Wednesday January 24ᵗʰ 2001**

The forty seven year old Gatwick security chief, Mike Denning stood in his office and stared at the live black and white CCTV image of who he wholeheartedly believed to be twenty nine year old Jade Harris.

From his viewpoint she was the exact same woman Jade Harris that he identified down in the arrivals lounge and he was absolutely right, she was the same woman but she still wasn't who he believed her to be.

Mike Denning was an expert in his field and he had been completely fooled.

In the same moving images he could see the pretty young security guard Julia Whitelaw as she stood beside the closed door and he had no reason to believe that something, anything as insignificant as a tiny mole had changed.

Bold Jasmine Stiles suddenly glanced up to the corner where the CCTV camera pointed directly down at her and she smiled back at him and again Mike Denning quietly chuckled to himself.

Suddenly he was aware that somebody was behind him at the opened door that led into his office.

When he turned he saw a man with short dark curly hair and a woman with long straight blonde hair that was pulled back into a ponytail.

He smiled at them both before he pointed toward his CCTV monitor.

"There's your girl." He told them.

Detective Inspector Nicola Garwood courteously smiled back at him before she stepped into his office where she shook his hand.

"Hi I'm DI Garwood and this is DS Saunders from Whitechapel." She announced.

She glanced at the monitor herself before she stepped a little closer to take a more detailed look.

"I found you at last you little bitch." She very quietly uttered beneath her breath.

"So what did she do to warrant a visit from the Met to rural old Gatwick?" Denning asked.

Jacob Saunders now shook his hand too.

"Nothing at all in fact she's as clean as a whistle." He replied.

"Jade is helping us with enquiries as a key witness but because she travels around a lot she's very difficult to pin down." Saunders lied again.

Denning nodded his head with a smile.

*'I wish I'd purposely missed her now you lying pair of bastards.'* He thought to himself as he continued to smile.

Garwood finally took her eyes from the monitor and returned her attention to Denning.

"Can we borrow your interview room for half an hour?" She asked.

Denning still smiled.

"Of course you can." He replied.

Downstairs in the almost clinical white interview room Jasmine Stiles took in a long deep breath before she sighed and then turned to the pretty young security guard and smiled at her again.

"Jules, I've been kept here for over an hour now." She pointed out.

Julia obviously knew this due to the fact that she had been subjected to constant flirting from Jasmine for the entire time and the red faced naïve security guard still refused to be drawn in or make eye contact with her.

"I do love your crimped hair." Jasmine continued with a grin.

She watched Julia's face turn just a little redder than before.

Suddenly the door beside Julia opened before Nicola Garwood and Jacob Saunders entered the room.

Nicola immediately turned to the pretty young blonde.

"You can go." She told her with a smile.

Julia didn't need a second opportunity and she thanked Garwood before she hurried out of the room.

"Bye Jules." Jasmine giggled.

Jacob Saunders smiled at Julia too before he closed the door behind her.

Jasmine sat and watched in silence as Nicola strolled to the corner of the room right in front of her where she reached up and unplugged the CCTV camera.

She knew that Mike Denning would be observing from upstairs in his office with far too much interest.

Saunders sat down on a chair that was a few moments ago against the wall beside the security guard Julia Whitelaw.

Jacob's main role was to watch the facial expressions and body language of Jade Harris when Nicola eventually asked that all-important question.

Nicola turned and for now she remained standing where she stared down at Jasmine Stiles.

"So where have you been for the past two months Jade?" She finally asked.

*'The mind tells the eye what it chooses to see...'*

Jasmine glanced up at her and smiled.

"I would hazard a guess that because I just flew in from a Greek island that I've been there." She replied.

Garwood very briefly glanced across at Saunders before she quietly mocked a chuckle and shook her head.

Now she pulled out a seat directly opposite Jasmine.

Everything that Garwood did was methodical and designed to make Jade Harris wait and become increasingly anxious.

That was how she would slip up and make a mistake.

She slowly sat down where she stared into her eyes for a brief moment and Jasmine grinned back at her despite the fact that her heart was just about ready to explode.

*'There's something about you that I can't quite put my finger on.'* Nicola thought as she stared into Jasmine's blue eyes.

"It's nice to see that they make pretty police women these days." Jasmine said with the same smile.

Garwood continued to stare at her.

*'Is the little bitch flirting with me?'* She wondered.

Jasmine's remark caused her to briefly stare down at the table before she glanced back up but the distraction was just enough to halt the close examination

"Have you been on that Greek island for the past two months?" Garwood enquired.

Jasmine nodded her head and continued to smile.

"The next time I go you really should come with me or meet me there it's quite beautiful." She replied.

A broad flirtatious grin suddenly appeared on Jasmine's lips but Nicola completely ignored the remark.

Jacob Saunders watched the initial stage of the interview with complete surprise.

*'Is she seriously hitting on the guv?'* He wondered.

"Could you tell us how you got to this Greek island, Jade?" Nicola then asked.

There was a momentary pause before Jasmine responded.

"You haven't told me your name yet." She reminded Nicola.

The attractive blonde high ranking police officer seated opposite her sighed.

"My name is Detective Inspector Nicola Garwood and that is Detective Sergeant Jacob Saunders." She began again.

"We're from the task force investigating the case of the missing homeless." She added.

Jasmine then displayed a look of confusion.

"But I'm not homeless or missing, Nicola." She replied.

Jasmine could see that Garwood was already becoming frustrated.

"How did you get to Kefalonia?" She enquired.

This time there was a snap in her tone and it was followed by another pause.

"I went on a boat." Jasmine finally replied.

Nicola glanced across at Saunders again before she returned her attention to who she still believed was Jade Harris, the suspect that she had become somewhat obsessed with for the past two months.

"There are absolutely no records of you ever leaving the country by any route so tell me about this boat." She insisted.

Jasmine smiled again.

"It was a blue boat Nicola." She replied.

"And it belongs to a man called Dave." She then recalled.

It transpired during the next few minutes of the interview that the boat was owned by a man that she could only remember as 'Dave' and he lived somewhere near the sea in Ramsgate, Margate or Dover in the county of Kent.

She couldn't remember which but she did recall that 'Dave' dealt with all of the necessary paperwork involved.

Of course there was really none.

Jasmine hadn't necessarily lied because Nicola Garwood believed that she was talking to Jade Harris and Jade did arrive at the island of Kefalonia on a boat and she had very little knowledge about anybody else on it.

The boat that delivered her was also in fact blue.

As Richard pointed out to her one of the men on it could have been called 'Dave'.

Jasmine's body language displayed all of the right signs for Saunders to observe.

Nicola however chuckled.

"So you went all the way to a Greek island by boat instead of by plane and you were taken there by a man that you don't know?" Nicola enquired.

Jasmine nodded with another smile.

"At least I think his name was Dave." She eventually replied.

Garwood took in another deep breath and exhaled before she sat back in her seat.

"Ok let's talk about your flat at New Kent road." She began again.

"In fact let's talk about your flat at New Kent road sometime prior to Wednesday November the eighth of last year when we visited it."

Jasmine nodded with another beaming smile.

"Don't you just love the shop name *Jasmine Fashions*?" She asked in response to Nicola's next line of enquiry.

"I love that name." Jasmine again truthfully added.

Nicola stared into Jasmine's blue eyes and not Jade's green but her relentless obsession continued to blind her from the completely obvious fact that was staring straight back at her.

"What I'd like to talk about is the huge pool of dried blood that we discovered on your brand new carpet." Nicola suddenly revealed.

"We know that your own blood group is O negative and the blood on the floor was O positive so it wasn't yours." She continued.

"Neither were the tiny fragments of human skull that we know were from the same person so my next question would be *who died in your flat, Jade?*"

"And then my next few questions just from the top of my head would be who was it, how did they die and where is the body?"

This was the information that was purposely kept from Jasmine by Richard, Carmen, Marinos Georgas and the real Jade Harris.

The expression of shock on Jasmine's face and the reaction of her body language as she immediately sat bolt upright showed Jacob Saunders that she had absolutely no idea of what Garwood was talking about.

*'She doesn't know.'* Jacob immediately concluded.

"What the hell are you talking about?" Jasmine eventually asked.

It was finally Garwood's turn to smile.

"You didn't know that somebody died in your flat Jade?" She asked.

"Did some little deal go wrong?"

Even Nicola could see that Jade Harris in front of her had absolutely no idea of what she was talking about.

"Did you kill whoever bled out in your flat?" She continued to push.

Jasmine could only stare wide eyed back at her.

Saunders attempted to silently get Nicola's attention because she was now treading on very thin ice.

He could clearly see that this woman had absolutely no clue.

"What do you mean somebody died?" Jasmine enquired.

Richard's plan had worked.

Jasmine now only had to keep her nerve as soon as everything filtered through.

Garwood and Jasmine stared at each other for what seemed an eternity before the white door suddenly opened again.

Jacob Saunders jumped to his feet with surprise.

"Good afternoon ladies and gentlemen my name is Oliver Alcott QC." The unexpected visitor announced.

As he approached the desk he dropped a white business card down onto it for Nicola Garwood to examine.

Alcott was a portly man and stood at five feet eight inches and he had balding grey swept back hair and his grey eyes widened as he smiled down at Nicola.

He was dressed in a dark brown pinstriped suit and carried an old brown leather briefcase.

"Are you going to charge my client?" He enquired.

Alcott was Carmen's safeguard, the surety and the call that she made earlier.

Nicola glanced down at the table where she picked up the business card and studied it.

*'How the hell did he even know she was here?'* She wondered with stunned surprise.

Alcott smiled down at the now grinning Jasmine.

"Do you need a lift somewhere Jade?" He asked.

Jasmine climbed to her feet and nodded.

"Do you know the King's road in Chelsea?" She asked.

Alcott smiled again.

"Carmen's old flat?" He asked.

Again Jasmine nodded her head while she displayed the same beaming grin mostly from utter relief as her heart was just about ready to explode.

Oliver Alcott redirected his attention down toward Nicola Garwood.

"If you have any further questions for my client please feel free to contact my office." He informed her.

He then ushered Jasmine out from the interview room and courteously closed the door behind him.

Nicola Garwood and Jacob Saunders sat in complete silence for a few moments.

She eventually glanced up at him and then held up Alcott's business card for Jacob to see.

"How the hell could he even possibly know that she was here?" She asked with anger in her tone.

Jacob could only sit and shrug his shoulders with nothing but wonder.

"I don't know guv." He quietly replied.

"But I do know that girl definitely didn't have a clue about the blood inside her flat." He added.

Garwood climbed to her feet and kicked back the chair so hard that it fell to the floor.

"This isn't right Jacob!" She snapped.

"Something here stinks." She added.

"That bastard had no way of possibly knowing that she was here!" She snapped again.

Nicola headed toward the door.

"But we do know that she's going to Carmen Richardson's old flat on the King's road." Saunders reminded her.

He followed her out through the opened door.

**Level Seventeen**
**Wednesday January 24<sup>th</sup> 2001**

Carmen Richardson's heart still pounded even after she heard the news that the highly regarded lawyer Oliver Alcott had just departed from Gatwick Airport with Jasmine Stiles.

Even Alcott believed that Jasmine was in fact Jade Harris and he had very briefly met her once before today.

From the moment that Jasmine was apprehended at the arrivals lounge at Gatwick until this moment had taken almost three hours and Carmen could finally breathe a sigh of very temporary relief.

David just informed Carmen and Richard that Detective Inspector Nicola Garwood and Detective Sergeant Jacob Saunders had not yet left Gatwick.

This was a valid reason for Carmen's next anxiety attack.

He also informed them that flight GS777 from Kefalonia had just landed on runway twenty eight and taxied to the arrivals area.

Jade Harris was about to walk through the arrivals area while Nicola Garwood was in the exact same building.

Although Jade looked just like her sister Jasmine this could easily turn into a brand new problem because Jade also had a specific task to perform.

"I'm having a very large scotch if we get through this unscathed." Carmen quietly uttered.

Twenty nine year old Jade Harris strolled through the customs area at Gatwick international airport and approached one of several operating check-in desks.

She handed over her sister Jasmine's boarding ticket and passport and immediately placed her small black canvas holdall bag in front of the woman to check.

The clerk glanced up to see the same woman from the passport photograph standing in front of her with long blonde hair and blue eyes and she smiled up at her.

"Welcome to Gatwick international airport Miss Stiles." She said.

She then ushered Jade through without checking the black bag that contained only a pair of white denim jeans, a lilac coloured t shirt, a short white matching denim jacket, a small black hair brush and a packet of baby wipes.

Jade walked through the check-in and into the arrivals lounge itself.

Of course she had never met Detective Inspector Nicola Garwood before.

Nicola Garwood suddenly stepped out from the same white door with Jacob Saunders and Mike Denning that Jasmine was escorted through when Jade was in the process of boarding her flight at Kefalonia three and a half hours ago.

In a brief moment of surreal madness the real Jade Harris walked straight past Nicola Garwood.

She was close enough to reach out and touch her as the two police officers obliviously thanked Mike Denning for his assistance.

Jade walked through another door and into the ladies toilet while Nicola Garwood and Jacob Saunders walked past her from behind as they left the airport building and headed back toward their car.

Nicola had no idea that she was the real Jade Harris and Jade had no idea that Nicola was the police woman that was hell-bent on charging her with murder and human trafficking offences.

In a second moment of insanity Nicola Garwood walked past, and then Jacob Saunders stood aside to allow thirty five year old April Marsh pass them as she entered the building to pick up the real Jade.

That same Jade stood inside the locked toilet cubicle where she removed the clothes from her black canvas bag and placed them onto the lowered white seat.

She then removed the natural looking long blonde wig from her head and then bundled it into the now empty black canvas bag.

She carefully removed the blue coloured contact lenses from her eyes to reveal her own natural green and then she did as Jasmine did earlier.

She wrapped the lenses in tissue paper before she slightly raised the lid and dropped them inside.

Jade quickly unpinned her reddish brown hair and brushed it out and back to its original straight shoulder length bobbed style.

She opened the pack of wipes and removed all of the layers of foundation to reveal the dark brown mole just above her upper lip on the right side.

Jade Harris was back just eighteen minutes after she walked straight past Nicola Garwood and Jacob Saunders outside at the arrivals lounge.

After another minute or so she stood inside the locked cubicle where she took a moment to compose herself before she bundled all of the items of black clothing into the black bag along with her sister's passport and flight ticket.

*'At least I'm in England now I just have to get out of this place.'* She told herself.

She took in a huge deep breath.

Jade flushed the now saturated tissue and blue contact lenses and watched them vanish before she stepped out of the cubicle.

She was now dressed in a short white denim jacket over a lilac coloured t shirt and white denim jeans with the same black flat heeled shoes on her feet.

She briefly checked in the mirror above one of three porcelain sinks to ensure that there were no signs of that she had ever been Jasmine Stiles and more importantly that she looked like Jade Harris.

She stared at her reflection for a few more moments.

"Welcome home." She quietly uttered.

She walked to the door, opened it and left the toilet with only one resemblance of the twenty nine year old woman that had just entered Gatwick Airport twenty four minutes ago.

It was a black canvas holdall bag that was slung over her right shoulder.

For the next five or six minutes Jade purposely stood not far from the exit doors at Gatwick airport and directly in front of a CCTV camera before she eventually headed out.

April Marsh followed her outside and continued to walk behind until they finally left the vicinity and CCTV coverage.

In the short stay parking area the already tearful Jade finally turned to the just as tearful April and the two women hugged each other tightly.

They had not seen each other for more than two months since just before Jade was taken.

The tears flowed from both of them.

"Where have you been you stupid bitch?" April sobbed.

"I went on holiday." Jade blurted her sobbing reply.

Eventually Jade started to pull away but April held her tightly for longer than an additional minute until finally she did release her.

As both women wiped their tear filled eyes April glanced up at her.

"I have to take you to Tooting." She croaked as the tears still rolled down her cheeks.

Jade continued to wipe her own.

"What's at Tooting?" She asked.

April started to walk toward her small blue Ford car.

"That's where the maisonette is that we're sharing." She replied.

Now Jade suddenly stopped sobbing.

"We're what?" She asked.

April turned and showed a still tearful smile.

"We're going to be roomies."

Jade stood and stared at April as she walked away.

"You have got to be kidding me!" She quietly uttered.

**Level Eighteen**
**Wednesday January 23rd 2001**

Carmen Richardson sat back in her office chair and sighed with relief that both Jasmine and Jade had now left Gatwick international airport.

She stared across her desk at Richard with almost disbelief at what she had just audibly witnessed.

"How the hell did we get away with it?" She quietly asked.

Richard smiled before he glanced back up at her.

"It helps that Dave can see everything from above and everybody else's CCTV footage." He replied.

"And the girls both held their nerve."

David Stringer now interjected.

"Jasmine is just being dropped off at your old flat at the Kings road Carmen." He informed her.

"April and Jade are heading toward Tooting." He added.

There was a pause before he chuckled.

"I just read Detective Inspector Garwood's personal log and she's not a very happy woman at all." He said.

David went on to remind them both that at Carmen's old residence at the Kings road Chelsea were the same small mole communication devices for Jasmine to coordinate her next moves with him.

At the maisonette at Tooting Jade would find hers too.

Carmen subconsciously nodded despite that as far as she was aware David couldn't actually see her.

Eventually she glanced toward the window and Richard could see that she was again deep in thought.

"Jasmine must have played one hell of a game." She quietly uttered.

She glanced down to stare at her own still trembling hands.

Richard nodded in agreement with her observation but he was now listening to what David was informing him in a private conversation that Carmen could no longer hear.

"I had a conversation with Major Green today." David informed him.

"Something has or is about to happen." He continued to explain to Richard.

"In order for me to continue helping here, you have to do something off the record for Major Green."

Carmen continued to stare out at Mount Street completely oblivious of the fact that this one sided conversation between David and Richard was taking place.

Because Richard knew that this was an isolated conversation he didn't react at all and he just listened to what David was now telling him.

"It's connected to what we're doing so you can just think of it as tying up loose ends." David continued.

"Come and see me tomorrow once we have these two girls settled in." David finished.

Then he switched back the frequency so that Carmen was again included and he knew that she had absolutely no idea that she had been temporarily isolated.

David then beamed a grin as he heard a brand new voice on the frequency.

"Hello Jaz it's so nice of you to join us." He chuckled.

## Level Nineteen
## Wednesday January 23rd 2001

It was around seven that evening when Jade Harris sat on the passenger seat inside April's dark blue Ford car and stared at a short block of five maisonettes at the end of Pitcairn road just south of Tooting railway station.

"It's a shit hole." She quietly uttered.

April Marsh was however a little more enthusiastic.

"That's because you're looking at it from the main road but just wait until you see inside and what's at the back inside the cul-de-sac." She replied.

Jade turned to her.

"April, it's a shit hole surrounded by thousands of other shit holes." She uttered with a sigh.

Her comment brought a grin to April's lips.

"Everything around here looks the same as the place next door." Jade complained.

She stared at all of the surrounding identical buildings.

"And who could possibly find you here?" April asked in response.

April went on to explain that this property came with a very large rear garden and an enclosed drive-in garage.

She then restarted the engine and drove the car into the cul-de-sac on her left where she eventually parked in front of the large wooden drive-in parking bay.

"Just wait until you see inside." She told Jade with more enthusiasm.

Jade still wasn't impressed.

*'My sister gets that lovely flat in Chelsea and I end up in a crap hole in Tooting and I'm sharing it with the walking ashtray.'* She thought to herself.

Eventually Jade followed April through the unlocked back gate and with the huge wooden drive-in structure on their left they headed for the front door that was opened by April before they both stepped inside.

"How many bedrooms does this place have?" Jade asked as April closed the door behind her.

"Three." She replied.

"There's one for you, one for me and one for whatshisname." She added.

"Thank god for that." Jade whispered.

She then glanced to her left to see a fully equipped and spacious pale yellow kitchen and directly on the right was a narrow dark brown carpeted staircase.

"So how can you walk into the garage from the house without being seen by nosey neighbours?" She asked.

Jade asked this particular question because there was a tall block of flats that faced the garden.

April pointed directly ahead.

"That's the living room and when you go through the door you turn left and then double back on yourself and walk straight through another door and into the garage." She explained.

"The living room like all of the others is quite lovely." She added.

"I stayed here for the past couple of days and it's surprisingly a really quiet area."

Jade nodded her head and continued to glance around at her new surroundings.

"And it's just for a few weeks." She quietly reminded herself.

April nodded with agreement.

"Let's have a nice cup of tea and then I'll show you around the place." She said.

Jade watched her light her first of many cigarettes.

## Level Twenty
**Thursday January 24th 2001**

It was a little after nine in the morning when Chief Inspector Keith Curtis called a meeting to discuss the events that unfolded yesterday at Gatwick airport.

He sat with his elbows rested on his desk and stared one at a time at the three senior officers in front of him.

On the left was Detective Sergeant Jacob Saunders, in the centre Detective Inspector Nicola Garwood and on the right was the broad figure of Detective Inspector Sam Henning who Curtis knew personally and had worked with in the past.

The chief slowly shook his head after a continued silence.

"Come on people speak up exactly what happened?" He asked them all.

Eventually Nicola Garwood began.

"Sir, we arrived at Gatwick Airport at..." She began.

Curtis shook his head again.

"Nik, I'm not the local magistrate and I don't need a perfectly worded incident report just tell me what bloody went on over there."

Jacob Saunders interjected.

"Sir a barrister by the name of Oliver Alcott somehow showed up at Gatwick and he was representing Jade Harris." He said.

The chief raised his eyebrows.

"Alcott was there?" He asked with surprise.

Jacob nodded.

"Oliver Alcott works on high profile trials at the bloody Bailey." Curtis informed them all.

"How can Jade Harris afford his services?"

Sam Henning shook his head because he had already worked out the answer to that particular question.

"Carmen Richardson." He uttered.

Curtis now turned his attention to Sam.

"Go on."

Sam filled Curtis in regarding the association between Jade Harris and Carmen Richardson at Alpha grove on the Isle of Dogs and then explained that Oliver Alcott represented Carmen on a solicitation charge a few years ago.

"Carmen knows Jade, Carmen knows Alcott and Alcott then meets Jade." Sam explained.

Curtis nodded.

"Ok but we still don't know how he knew that he needed to be there." He said.

"Harris had no idea that we'd be waiting at Gatwick for her."

Then he turned his attention to Nicola.

"So what did you get from Jade Harris?" He asked.

Nicola shrugged her shoulders.

"Not that much really." She replied.

"She lied about how she left this country to travel to Greece." She explained.

"And she played the lesbian flirting card with me which I think is quite ironic considering she slept with men for a living before she moved into the flat above the shop at New Kent road." She added.

Curtis chuckled.

Jacob Saunders interjected.

"But she had no idea about the blood samples and bone fragments at her flat." He pointed out.

Nicola sighed as she was forced to nod her head with resentful agreement.

The chief sat back in his chair and placed his hands behind his head.

"So where do you want to go with this now Nik?" He asked.

Nicola stared back at him for a few moments.

"Guv she may or may not have killed whoever bled out in her flat, but that doesn't rule her out from the human trafficking case." She pointed out.

Curtis nodded with agreement.

"Her body language and reaction suggests that she was shocked but that doesn't mean she isn't a good actress." She continued.

"Don't forget that it was her name that was given to us as a tip off." She reminded him.

Now Sam Henning interjected again.

"It was also an anonymous tip off don't forget." He reminded her.

Nicola nodded.

"But she has just lied to me about how she left the country to go to Greece." She retorted.

"And she made a silly joke about the missing homeless during the interview." She lied.

Saunders stared at her.

Keith Curtis considered all of the facts for a few moments before he returned his attention toward Nicola.

"I'm going to be completely up front here." He began again.

"Let's assume that we're going to discover no more of these connected abductions within the next four to six weeks." He continued.

"They'll begin to pull our non-essential resources in or around that time." He added.

"With that in mind Nik tell me what you want to do now."

Nicola already knew the answer to his question.

"Guv, Vladimir Kolov has already fled the country and you have Martin Roberts banged up somewhere." She replied.

"No Indigo security vans have been sighted anywhere and as you know the abductions have abruptly stopped." She correctly pointed out.

"I'd like to pull some of the manpower from the safe houses and have Jade Harris placed on around the clock surveillance." She said.

Her request stunned Jacob on her right side while Sam Henning slowly shook his head on her left.

Curtis stared at Garwood for a few moments.

"I swear Garwood if this goes south and one of those houses gets done that should've been supervised I'll personally hang you up by your tits." He quietly uttered.

Garwood beamed a grin.

"Thanks guv." She replied.

She promptly climbed to her feet.

"Jacob, start organising a car to the Kings road as soon as possible." She instructed.

Saunders stood up too and followed her toward the office door.

Curtis now turned his attention to the only officer still seated in front of him.

"Well?" He asked.

Sam Henning seemed to ponder.

"I'll pay another visit to Carmen Richardson just to verify that she sent Alcott to Gatwick airport." He replied.

Curtis nodded.

"How well do you actually know her?" He asked.

Sam smiled.

"Carmen and I go way back." He replied.

"Like I said before she's one of the good ones if I'm honest guv." He added.

"She wouldn't be involved in the human trafficking ring of that I'd stake my pension."

Curtis nodded again.

"But would her friend Jade Harris?" He asked.

Sam now climbed to his feet and raised his eyebrows with a shrug of his broad shoulders.

"That's what I want to find out guv." He replied.

**Level Twenty One**
**Thursday January 24th 2001**

When she arrived at the flat at the Kings road Chelsea early yesterday evening Jasmine Stiles found on the smoked glass coffee table a note that was handwritten by Carmen Richardson.

It explained to her how the two small dark brown communication moles worked.

The smaller was a receiver that rested inside her ear and the slightly larger was a transmitter that worked perfectly using the vibrations from her throat whenever she spoke.

She inserted the smaller mole inside her left ear and placed the larger onto her neck and then reintroduced herself to a somewhat delighted David Stringer.

The note also explained that beneath the mattress in Carmen's bedroom was a large beige envelope that contained two thousand pounds in cash.

Inside the attached garage was Carmen's second car a black Saab convertible that she only ever used whenever her pale green Aston Martin was being serviced.

Those moles would prove to be an invaluable resource because David informed her that he just had read Detective Inspector Nicola Garwood's personal log.

The log showed that around the clock surveillance was to be placed on Jade Harris at the Kings road Chelsea.

Of course the Jade Harris at the King's road at Chelsea was in fact her, Jasmine Stiles.

He then informed her that a silver Ford car was parked just fifty feet away and the two male occupants were watching the flat until they would be relieved by a second team.

Jasmine also now knew that her sister had passed through Gatwick airport less than an hour after her own release thanks to the intervention of Oliver Alcott QC.

She also learned that Jade was with April at the maisonette at Tooting.

"Jade did everything that she was supposed to do." David informed Jasmine.

The invaluable moles also meant that everybody could now communicate with everybody else wherever they were although Jade had still not activated hers.

It was around eight last night when David heard from Jasmine for the second time.

"Is that unmarked police car still sitting down the road from here David?" She asked.

David confirmed that it was and that it wouldn't be leaving until the morning or if she left the flat and even then she would still be able to see it.

"Because they believe that you're Jade they're watching you around the clock." He assured her.

Jasmine broke into a wry grin.

"I've always wanted to do this." She chuckled.

David listened in with a bigger grin as he heard what followed.

"Hi, can I order two pizza's please?" She asked on Carmen's landline telephone.

"Can I have one ham and pineapple and one pepperoni?"." She asked.

She grinned again.

She then gave the address on the Kings road for the delivery driver to pick up the cash but then she made a very strange request.

"I'll pay in cash when the delivery gets here but do you think that he could actually deliver it to some friends of mine that are parked in a car just down the road?"

A short while later David watched as Jasmine paid the driver for the pizza delivery before he went on to deliver it to two stunned undercover surveillance officers in a silver Ford Mondeo car on the King's road.

This morning Jasmine climbed from Carmen's huge bed and walked from the bedroom to the kitchen where she made herself coffee and then she sat down to watch the news on TV.

"Are you there David?" She eventually asked.

After a few moments Stringer confirmed that he was listening in for all transmissions.

"So am I still being watched?" She asked.

Again David confirmed that she was and would continue to be.

"But something quite strange happened." He then informed her.

David went on to explain that the two startled police officers that enjoyed pizza last night were actually relieved around an hour ago by none other than Detective Inspector Nicola Garwood herself and Detective Sergeant Jacob Saunders.

"She must really like me." Jasmine chuckled.

"Or really hate you." David replied with a chuckle of his own.

"But you're about to find out which one." He added.

Jasmine raised her eyebrows.

"What do you mean?" She asked.

"She's crossing the Kings road and heading for your front door as we speak." David informed her.

Jasmine immediately leaned forward and placed her coffee cup onto the glass table and her wry grin suddenly vanished.

"She's coming here, now?" She asked.

Then she heard the chimes from the doorbell.

"I think that means yes." She quietly uttered.

She headed toward the door and again her heart started to beat just that little bit faster.

"Here we go again." She nervously uttered in a quiet tone.

"Considering she recently met Oliver Alcott she has some balls I'll give her that." David said.

He watched Garwood standing outside the front door of Carmen Richardson's old flat and there was a pause before he spoke again.

"Well obviously she's a girl so I don't mean she actually has balls, what I mean is..." He began to explain.

Jasmine interjected.

"Yes I got that bit David." She assured him.

She stopped halfway down the staircase and checked her appearance in the mirror before she continued down seven more steps where she opened the front door and beamed a fake smile of surprise.

"Nicola, I just made coffee do you want one?" She asked.

Detective Inspector Nicola Garwood was dressed in a white cotton open necked blouse beneath a smart black suit jacket and a pair of blue designer jeans with white training shoes.

Her long straight blonde hair was as usual pulled back into a ponytail and her blue eyes looked Jasmine Stiles up and down.

"Good morning Jade I thought I'd come and thank you in person for feeding my surveillance team last night." She quipped.

Jasmine beamed another false grin.

"They looked bored and hungry sitting there watching nothing happen all night." She replied.

The two women stood and stared into each other's blue eyes for a few moments before Jasmine's wry grin reappeared.

"So are you coming in for coffee or shall I go make it and bring it down for you?" She asked.

Without uttering another word she turned and started to walk back up the stairs before she heard the door close again and she knew that Garwood followed behind her.

"So what do you have planned for today Jade?" Nicola enquired.

Without turning to face her Jasmine grinned.

"The usual, rob a few banks and commit a few murders." She replied.

Garwood almost grinned as she shook her head.

Jasmine couldn't see her reaction.

"I'm going to do a stock check today." Jasmine eventually told her.

As she stepped into the small kitchenette Garwood stood and stared at her.

"You can't go into the shop or the flat above it at New Kent road." She pointed out.

"It's still a crime scene."

Jasmine glanced across at her and smiled.

"I know that's why I'm going over to my warehouse at north Woolwich." She replied.

As Garwood continued to stare at her with surprise she sat down on one of the two facing cream coloured leather sofas.

"What warehouse?" She asked.

Jasmine glanced away from her and grinned again.

*'You wouldn't have found it before because I haven't bloody been there myself yet.'* She thought to herself.

She turned to Detective Inspector Garwood again.

"Gosh Nicola it's no wonder you haven't caught anybody yet." She replied.

"But as you're probably going to follow me there I might as well give you the address." She chuckled.

"It's at unit 2A on the Stanley industrial estate near north Woolwich pier." She added.

Garwood studied Jasmine as she finished making the coffee.

Jasmine was dressed in a pale green t-shirt over a pair of peach coloured cotton shorts.

"For somebody that's been on a Greek island for so long you don't look very brown." She observed.

Yet another secret grin appeared on Jasmine's lips.

"Detective Inspector Nicola Garwood, are you staring at me legs?" She asked.

Jasmine then turned and walked toward Garwood where she placed two coffees in front of her and then sat down on the opposite sofa and faced her.

Jasmine then picked up and sipped her coffee before she spoke again.

"If you must know I was working in an office for most of the time there." She lied.

Garwood nodded her head.

"Ah yes for Carmen Richardson?" She asked.

Jasmine nodded.

"You don't go very brown in an office Nicola." She pointed out.

"And besides it's the raining season over there and you have a better chance of drowning walking to the shops than getting a tan."

Garwood pondered on how one would sell houses during this so called *season of rain*.

She sipped her coffee without taking her eyes off Jasmine.

"So tell me the truth how did you actually get over there Jade?" She enquired.

Jasmine sipped hers again.

"I went on Dave's boat." She lied again.

Her reply brought an immediate sarcastic chuckle from Nicola.

Eventually she climbed back to her feet and headed toward the door.

"I'll see you at the Stanley industrial estate later today Jade." She uttered as she left.

Jasmine smiled as she sipped again.

"I'll have the coffee ready Nicola."

## Level Twenty Two
**Thursday January 24th 2001**

It was a cold and grey morning when David Stringer sat on the right side of his office bedroom at Tranton road Bermondsey and watched several computer monitors at once.

Earlier he watched Jasmine Stiles drive out from the garage at Blacklands terrace just off the Kings road Chelsea in Carmen's black Saab convertible.

He then watched Detective Inspector Garwood and Detective Sergeant Jacob Saunders pull away in a silver Ford to follow her to north Woolwich.

He also watched thirty eight year old Theresa Sanchez step onto the balcony at the hotel at Manisa Turkey to purposely show herself.

The Indigo was still anchored north-west of Cyprus in the Mediterranean Sea.

So far today everything was running as expected.

He kept an eye on the progress of Theresa's husband Miguel Sanchez.

He left the hotel at Makassar city south west of the Indonesian island of Sulawesi in a rented car and was currently headed north toward the secret military logistics base just south of a small town called Mamuju.

David then switched to the Stanley industrial estate at north Woolwich pier east London where he knew that Jasmine Stiles was headed Carmen's the black Saab.

She was indiscreetly followed by Detective Inspector Nicola Garwood and Detective Sergeant Jacob Saunders in a silver Ford.

He knew where they were headed but they were not the reason that he switched to and from the industrial estate.

The reason was that nine units south from the warehouse that Arron Balcombe secured for Jasmine was Unit 4F.

It was the bogus office of Indigo security services and the still operational warehouse and auction room that was managed by Jane Chapman's brother in law Mark Downing.

David then switched to the house at Larchwood drive Sidcup south east London that he now knew that Turkish Barak Yazici rented.

Everything was quiet there too.

He briefly switched to Mount Street Mayfair to keep an eye on Carmen Richardson and his friend Richard Willows and from above David saw the roof of Carmen's pale green Aston Martin parked outside with Richard's own black Saab parked behind it.

In the blink of an eye David just missed something.

He checked on Jade and April at Pitcairn road at Tooting to ensure that they were also safe.

He then switched to the house that was owned by Jane Chapman at Glade road Watford and then the home of Lisa Moore at Pinner south of Watford and finally the home of Debbie Davies at Amersham north-west of Watford.

David checked on the progress of Miguel Sanchez one more time as he headed north toward Mamuju before he sat back in his black leather office chair and swigged from a bottle of red fizzy pop.

"Well you lot are all boring." He quietly uttered.

He screwed the white plastic cap back onto the bottle.

Suddenly David saw an incoming typed message on his fourth monitor from his employer.

He immediately typed a response.

*'Yes I'm going to talk to him about it today.'* He typed before he pressed the 'enter' key.

He sighed and saw his own response displayed to the recipient.

Then something caught his eye on monitor one.

"Oh you're back there are you?" He asked Debbie Davies.

Her Mercedes pulled up outside the rented house of forty seven year old Barak Yazici at Larchwood drive Sidcup.

Carmen Richardson sat behind her desk inside her office at Mount Street Mayfair and Richard Willows sat opposite when they both heard the situation report from David that things were very quiet.

But David didn't yet know that he had only just missed something.

A third car had pulled up directly behind Richard's.

Suddenly there was a knock at the door and when it opened Carmen glanced up to see her most recent employee Polly Aldington.

Polly quietly entered and closed the door behind her.

"Carmen, that policeman that came and spoke to April is here again." She whispered.

Carmen nodded her head with acknowledgement as Richard climbed to his feet.

Polly opened the door again as Carmen climbed to her feet before she reached across and shook hands with Richard.

"I'm sure that we'll have no problem finding you a professional tenant Mr Handley." She told him.

Richard turned and headed toward the opened door where he passed Detective Inspector Sam Henning in the doorway and the two men gave each other glancing nods as Richard left.

The broad frame of Sam Henning entered the office and he smiled at Carmen.

"I'm sorry to intrude Carmen." He said with a smile.

She smiled back at him before she nodded to Polly and the pretty young black haired receptionist left the room and closed the door behind her.

"Mr Henning I thought you'd have retired by now." She told him in jest.

They shook hands and Sam chuckled.

"I'm not that bloody old!" He replied.

Carmen ushered him to the same seat that Richard had just vacated.

"I'm guessing that you're here about Jade." Carmen said.

She sat back down and Henning smiled again.

He sat right back in his seat and took in a deep breath.

"Straight to the point as always, that's one of the things I like about you." He replied.

"Can I confirm that it was you that sent Oliver Alcott to Gatwick?" He asked.

Carmen glanced out of the window to her right.

"Yes I did." She replied.

Sam's next obvious question was how she knew that Jade was being held at Gatwick.

Carmen now chuckled.

"It's not a great big mystery Mr Henning." She replied.

"If you check the CCTV footage at Gatwick you'll see April." She added.

Sam nodded his head as he listened.

"April was there to pick up Jade and watched her being taken away so she called me and then I called Oliver."

Sam patted his thighs.

"That's the mystery solved!" He said.

"Nobody could work out how the bloody hell Alcott knew to go there in the first place." He said with relief.

Carmen half smiled.

There was a silent pause for a few moments before Sam continued.

"Carmen, you and I have always managed to see eye to eye." He began again.

"I know that you're by no means stupid and you've never lied to me in the past." He continued.

"I'm going to ask you one simple question because I trust you and I'm already more than sure of the answer." He added.

There was another pause before he continued.

"Is Jade Harris or has Jade Harris ever been involved in this human trafficking ring?" He asked outright.

Carmen appreciated that Henning was always up front and direct with her in the past and although she knew more than she could possibly divulge she believed that he deserved at least something.

She wanted to give him *something* but without giving anything of vital importance away of course.

After all they had known each other for well over a decade albeit from opposite sides of the fence.

"Sam, you know that Jade worked for me at Alpha grove for more than ten years." She finally replied.

Henning nodded in silence as she continued to respond.

"Do you really think that I would tolerate her doing such a thing?" She asked him just as outright.

Eventually Sam replied to her question.

"You're actually one of the good ones Carmen and I genuinely believe that." He said.

"I know that you wouldn't but I just wanted to hear it come from your own lips." He added.

The conversation eventually turned to *'the good old days'* for a few more minutes before Sam climbed back to his feet and then he turned and slowly glanced around the office and then back to Carmen.

"This suits you." He told her.

Then he smiled with a wink of his eye and walked toward the door.

As Sam opened the door he turned again.

"There is one other little thing that still seems to be something of a mystery." He said.

Carmen raised her eyebrows.

"Is there any chance of giving me the heads up about how Jade really travelled from here to Kefalonia?" He asked.

Carmen smiled back at him and there was a pause.

"She went on Dave's blue boat Mr Henning." She eventually lied with another smile.

Sam chuckled again.

"It was worth a shot." He said with a grin.

Sam winked at Carmen again and when he left he closed the door behind him.

"Is everything ok Carmen?" David asked in her ear.

Again she unwittingly nodded although David couldn't see her, to the best of her knowledge anyway.

"Yes David I was expecting that at some point." She replied.

She strolled to the window with her arms folded in front of her and watched Sam Henning climb into his silver pool car.

"It does feel like they're closing in on us though." She quietly uttered.

David stared at his computer monitors and watched the gold Mercedes that was owned by Debbie Davies as it now headed south east on the M20 motorway toward Dover.

He then glanced at the earlier message on another monitor that came from Major Green and then David suddenly typed to him again.

*'We need to do it soon because they're just about to get picked up.'* He typed.

He stared at the screen for a few moments and saw that no response from Major Green was incoming as yet.


An hour or so later David watched the same gold Mercedes as it pulled up outside the town house at York Street Dover in Kent that was owned by Barak Yazici.

It was also where he knew that four young Polish illegal immigrants were temporarily staying inside.

After a few more moments Debbie Davies climbed out from the driver seat of the car and entered the house and her arrival caused David's heart to pound.

'This isn't good at all.' He anxiously thought to himself.

The situation that was unfolding at Dover wasn't the only thing that was causing him considerable emotional discomfort.

Another situation somewhere else was beginning to unfold at the exact same time and his busy over magnified eyes continued to switch between the two monitors.

An hour ago nothing was happening at all.

After a short while he watched Debbie Davies leave the house and he waited to see what would unfold.

To his utter dismay behind her he watched the four Polish girls that he saw almost a week ago when they climbed from the back of a Polish truck and now all four climbed into the gold Mercedes.

"Don't go with her." David quietly uttered to the girls.

He glanced back at the other monitor and stared at the unanswered response that he earlier typed to Major Green.

Now when he stared back he saw that the gold Mercedes was heading toward the end of York Street as it made its way back toward the M20 motorway that would take it and the four young women to London.

David knew exactly where in London the car was headed.

He once again stared at the unanswered communication to Major Green.

Suddenly his attention was drawn toward the other unfolding incident and he leaned forward to scrutinise the screen.

"Is it?" He quietly asked himself.

At her office at Mount Street Mayfair Carmen and Richard were again discussing the plan in general terms when David Stringer suddenly interjected.

"Richard there's something that I have to tell you but I don't want to tell you but I think I have to tell you." He announced in his own unique way.

Carmen glanced across at Richard and she broke into a silent grin.

Richard quietly chuckled as he stared back at her.

"Let me get this straight." He replied.

"You have something to tell me that you don't want to tell me but you're going to tell me anyway?" He asked.

Carmen covered her mouth with her hand in an attempt to stifle her giggles.

At Bermondsey, David stared at his microphone.

"That's exactly what I just said!" He replied.

He then returned his attention to the same monitor.

"What is it Dave?" Richard eventually asked.

He continued to quietly chuckle.

His question was followed by a lengthy pause from David but eventually he responded.

"I think I can see Sasha."

The grins suddenly disappeared from both Richard and Carmen at Mount Street and there was a very long silent pause.

"W…What do you mean?" Richard eventually asked.

David Stringer could watch half a dozen computer monitors at the same time and could even switch from satellite to satellite while eating dry toasted bread or swigging from a bottle of fizzy pop.

He also had the uncanny ability to solely focus on whatever his attention faced and that's what happened next.

Right now his over magnified eyes stared solely at the image in front of him and he didn't even hear Richard's question.

"Dave?" Richard asked.

There was another lengthy pause.

"Dave what's going on?"

Still Stringer didn't respond and by now Carmen could see the pure anguish displayed on Richard's face.

"Dave can you please answer me?" Richard pleaded.

Eventually David did.

"Well…" He began and then he swigged from his favoured bottle of red fizzy pop."

Richard's head fell into his own hands on Carmen's desk.

"I'm looking down at Mamuju." David continued in his own time.

There was yet another lengthy pause as David leaned forward once again.

"I can't get close enough to be absolutely sure." He uttered to himself.

Of course everybody could hear him including Jasmine Stiles.

"You see…" He began again.

"I know your sister I've met her." He continued.

"And from my chair it does look like Sasha." He added.

Richard glanced up at Carmen with tear filled eyes.

"David just tell me what you can see right now." Carmen interjected.

She climbed to her feet and walked around the desk where she held Richard in her arms.

Stringer took another swig of red fizzy pop from the bottle.

"Well…" He started again.

"This girl looks like Sasha and she's being helped into the car that Miguel Sanchez hired and drove to the military base." He continued.

There was another silent pause.

"Do you know Richard I think we might just have your sister?"

He continued to intently stare at the monitor and at Mayfair Carmen reached up and covered her mouth with her hand again but this time it was for a different reason.

This time she wasn't stifling a giggle.

Tears started to roll down Carmen's face as she listened to David assuring himself more than anybody else.

At Unit 2B at the Stanley industrial estate north Woolwich silent tears also rolled down the cheeks of Jasmine Stiles.

David took yet another swig of fizzy pop from the bottle.

"Well it's not like they're going to bring us somebody else is it?" He asked.

For some unknown reason to David he received no reply whatsoever.

"Well I'll just talk to myself then shall I?" He asked in an uttered tone of discontent.

**Level Twenty Three**
**Thursday January 24th 2001**

In the front passenger seat inside Debbie Davies gold Mercedes sat nineteen year old Polish illegal immigrant Gita Budz.

The excited teenager was a slender five feet five inches tall and she had long straight light brown hair and incredibly beautiful pale blue eyes.

Gita was dressed in a short faded blue denim jacket over a pale peach coloured t shirt and tight fitting faded blue denim jeans with white training shoes.

She glanced behind her toward the long back seat of the car and displayed an excited grin.

Directly behind the driver seat was sixteen year old Kassia Zoldak.

Kassia was five feet four inches tall with long straight dyed jet black hair and she had dark brown eyes.

She wore a white cotton open necked blouse beneath a short black leather jacket and skin tight white denim jeans with beige leather strappy sandals.

In the centre of the beige leather bench seat sat eighteen year old Magda Gronek.

She was five feet six inches tall and had long wavy blonde hair and stunningly beautiful blue eyes.

She wore a thin beige canvas jacket over a turquoise t- shirt and tight fitting blue denim jeans with white training shoes.

Seated directly behind Gita was another sixteen year old and her name was Dominika Laski.

Dominika was a slender girl that stood at five feet six and she had long straight blonde hair and blue eyes.

She was dressed in a black canvas bomber jacket over a pale yellow cotton open necked blouse and beige cotton slacks with black canvas flat heeled shoes.

All three of the pretty young women in the back seat of the car grinned excitedly back at the oldest of the group nineteen year old Gita Budz.

"I bet you're all excited aren't you?" Debbie Davies asked.

Gita turned to face Debbie with a beaming grin and she nodded her head.

"In our home town Slonsk in Poland there are no jobs." She replied in English but her Polish accent was evident.

Debbie Davies returned her attention to the road in front of her.

"And here you all have a job and you can all share the same house." She lied with a smile.

She was truthful about one fact.

They would all reside at the same house for the time being.

Gita beamed another excited smile.

"It is so exciting." She replied.

Davies glanced back at her and smiled again.

After a few more miles on the M20 motorway Davies turned to Gita again.

"I need all of your passports by the way." She said.

Gita now looked confused.

"We create work permits so that if you ever get questioned the permit matches your passport numbers." Davies lied.

To Gita and the three girls in the back of the car this seemed absolutely plausible.

All four girls reached into their bags or pockets and handed their passports to Davies as she continued to drive.

"When will we begin work at the factory?" Eighteen year old Magda Gronek enquired from the back seat.

Davies made eye contact with her via the rear view mirror and she smiled.

"You have the weekend to settle into the lovely house and then you all begin work on Monday." She lied again.

The initial stage of their future employment would in fact begin today and very soon.

It was around two hours later when the gold Mercedes turned into leafy Larchwood drive at Sidcup south east London.

Halfway up the tree line street it turned right and drove straight into a pre-opened brown garage door.

Davies climbed out from the driver seat and pressed a white switch on the brick wall and then she stood and watched the garage door slowly electronically close as internal bright lights flickered into life.

She then opened a white door and ushered all four pretty young Polish girls into the house before she stepped inside herself and closed it.

She then locked the door behind her.

They were all now inside a fully locked house with no means of an exit.

The first to walk into the cannabis smoke filled living room was the black haired sixteen year old Kassia Zoldak and as soon as she entered she saw three middle aged men.

Thirty nine year old Atif Rahman stood on her left side and stared at her.

Forty two year old black cab driver Firat Alican stood on her right and he also stared in silence.

Barak Yazici stood directly in front of her and he smiled at Kassia as her three young friends joined her in the opened doorway with Debbie Davies behind them.

The girls all turned to Davies with confusion in their eyes.

They were previously of the belief that they alone would share a beautiful house.

This cannabis smoke filled room was far from beautiful.

The three middle aged men were never mentioned either.

The naïve teenagers still hadn't figured it out.

Barak Yazici with a smile approached the group of confused girls before he reached out his hand for sixteen year old Kassia Zoldak to shake.

Kassia instinctively moved her trembling hand toward his but as she did Yazici reached back with his right hand.

Without warning and with a tightly clenched closed fist he swung and punched the sixteen year old directly onto her left cheek.

She squealed as she was sent sprawling across the living room floor.

The three other girls started to scream with terror as Atif Rahim and Firat Alican also walked toward them.

On the threadbare carpeted floor Kassia Zoldak received a very hard kick in her stomach from Barak Yazici.

"Get down onto the fucking floor!" Atif Rahman yelled at the remaining three girls.

He then screamed his instruction again.

Over the next ten minutes all four of the pretty young women were stripped completely naked before the first, sixteen year old blonde Dominika Laski was dragged out of the room and up the narrow threadbare carpet by Atif Rahman and Firat Alican.

She was like those before her taken into the back room where she was relentlessly beaten with metal belt buckles.

Twenty minutes or so later down inside the living room her terrified friends could hear her being dragged whimpering across the landing to the front bedroom.

Debbie Davies smiled down at the three remaining naked girls that knelt trembling on the living room floor and when Rahman and Alican returned she pointed down at eighteen year old Magda Gronek.

"Take this one next." She told them.

As Magda screamed pleas while she was dragged toward the door Davies walked into the kitchen to prepare four new syringes with Heroin.

**Level Twenty Four**
**Friday January 26th 2001**

It was around eleven in the morning when Richard Willows stood beside David Stringer inside his converted spare bedroom.

The two men stared at one of David's computer monitors and together they watched the play back of what David saw at Mamuju on the Indonesian island of Sulawesi.

A young blonde woman was helped into the hire car by Miguel Sanchez outside the military base.

It occurred thirty six hours ago by this time.

The still image that was now displayed on the monitor was an overhead projection of the large hotel at Makassar city south west of the island.

David knew that the young blonde woman was inside with Miguel Sanchez.

"I gave this situation some thought." David said.

"I doubt that Sasha has ever seen Miguel Sanchez before so he'll have convinced her that he's a friendly face."

Richard silently nodded his head with acknowledgement.

"After all he did just get her out of that hell hole so she'll think he saved her." David added.

Again Richard nodded.

"So when and where do they go next?" He asked.

David typed onto one of three keyboards in front of him and brought up a new file that was displayed on a different monitor while Richard continued to stare at the hotel rooftop at Makassar city.

"They fly out from the airport at Makassar city tomorrow morning our time to Johannesburg South Africa." David began to explain.

"On Monday afternoon they fly from Johannesburg to Lisbon in Portugal." He added.

David then glanced up at Richard.

"This is where I think Sanchez probably decided to play a little trick on us." He continued.

"He's trying to test us." He added.

"They haven't booked any form of transport from Lisbon to London."

David went on to explain that Carmen called Sanchez earlier today just to show the Spaniard that she knew exactly where he was at that precise moment in time and what flights he had booked.

She also informed him that she knew that he was taking *her girl* to Lisbon Portugal.

"So he definitely knows that we can see him wherever he is." David assured Richard.

"I'm guessing that because Sasha doesn't have a passport he has to bring her into the UK using the same secret methods that they used for taking people out."

"The same way that they took Sasha out you mean." Richard quietly corrected him.

David then pointed out that Lisbon was a Portuguese coastal town and it caused him to think that Sasha would be brought into the UK via the river Thames.

Richard knew to trust David's instincts and he slowly nodded his head again.

"We almost have her mate." David quietly told him.

There was a lengthy moment of silence before David approached another topic that he knew Richard was completely unaware of.

"I want to show you something else." He eventually began again.

"I did something that you're not going to be happy about." He added with a visible cringe.

David then showed Richard a play back recording of the four Polish girls when they climbed out from the back of the truck at Dover a week ago on Friday.

He then skipped forward to the second sighting of the four girls just twenty four hours ago when they were driven to Larchwood drive at Sidcup by Debbie Davies.

He then glanced up at Richard.

"I haven't seen them since." He quietly uttered.

Richard stared back at him.

"What does this have to do with us?" He asked.

"And what did you do that I won't like?"

David glanced back at the screen but mostly to avoid making eye contact with Richard.

"I asked Major Green for some help to get those girls out from that house." He very quietly replied.

Richard's eyes widened.

"You did what?"

David continued to focus his full attention on nothing in particular in front of him while Richard continued to stare at the back of his head.

"I told you before that Major Green knew what we were doing." David reminded him.

Again Richard nodded but he also knew that there was more to this because David was now shuffling papers on his desk.

*'What the hell have you done?'* Richard wondered.

"Ok so why am I not going to be happy about this Dave?" He eventually asked again.

He watched as Stringer continued to busy himself.

"Because Major Green says that you have to deal with this situation on Sunday." He finally replied.

Again Richard's eyes widened.

"If you don't do it I'm not allowed to help you anymore." David lied.

Richard and David had been friends for long enough for him to know when Stringer was being liberal with the truth.

Eventually Richard sat down beside him.

"So this has been fully authorised by Green?" He asked.

David nodded but still without making eye contact with Richard.

"They left the things here that you'll need to do the job." He replied.

There was another silent pause.

"And this has to be done on Sunday?" Richard asked.

Again David nodded his head.

"It's going to pour down with rain on Sunday night so there will be plenty of noise reduction." He replied.

Richard sat back in his chair where he took in a deep breath and then blew it out.

"Your timing is impeccable Dave do you know that?"  He asked as he stared at Stringer.

"Thank you."  David nervously replied.

He genuinely thought that Richard was paying him a compliment regarding his knowledge about the rain on the forthcoming Sunday night.

**Level Twenty Five**
**Saturday January 27th 2001**

It was around midday when Detective Inspector Nicola Garwood sat in the passenger seat inside a silver Ford pool car with Detective Sergeant Jacob Saunders in the driver seat.

"Guv taking into account that we met Oliver Alcott at Gatwick when she came back, can I just say that I don't think that it's a good idea for you to walk in there alone?" Saunders said.

Nicola glanced across at him and smiled.

"She isn't going to make a complaint Jacob." She replied.

"She would've done that when I went to her flat the other morning." She added.

Garwood and Saunders both stared at the closed dark green door that led into unit 2B at the Stanley industrial estate at north Woolwich.

"I still think you're leaving yourself wide open guv." Jacob replied.

Again Nicola nodded with acknowledgement.

"It's as if she wants me to pester her." She uttered.

"If she was completely innocent and knew nothing Jacob she'd be filing complaints to Alcott left right and centre." She added.

Then she turned to stare at him again.

"Why isn't she doing that if she has nothing to hide?" She asked.

Jacob shrugged his shoulders.

"All I know is that we have to find something soon." He replied.

The new chief thinks they'll start to pull our resources in three weeks." He added.

Nicola once again nodded her head with acknowledgement.

"Jade Harris is so close to slipping up Jacob I can feel it."

There was another silent pause before Nicola eventually opened the passenger side door and placed her left foot onto the grey concrete floor outside.

"She definitely lied to us about how she got to Kefalonia." She reminded Jacob.

"And she's playing little games with us like feeding pizza to the night teams that watch her." She added.

Once again Jacob nodded.

"She's by no means innocent or ignorant about any of this." Nicola continued.

Then she stepped out of the car and closed the door behind her.

Saunders sat in the driver seat and watched Nicola casually stroll toward the green closed door at Jade Harris's warehouse building.

"You're still bloody insane going in there by yourself." He quietly uttered to himself.

Three days before the almost identical sisters returned to the UK, Carmen Richardson bought stock for Jade's business venture.

It was delivered to the warehouse and signed for by April Marsh in preparation and today twenty nine year old Jasmine Stiles sat behind an old wooden desk and checked through the paperwork.

She was dressed in a thin white knitted pullover and a pair of tight fitting faded blue denim jeans with dark blue designer training shoes on her feet.

As she sat and stared down at the detailed receipt she heard the green door in the narrow corridor slam shut.

She secretly smiled to herself although her heart rate immediately started to climb because her visitor would only be one person.

She then glanced up to see Detective Inspector Garwood as she appeared in the opened doorway.

Jasmine smiled.

"You took your time Nicola."

Garwood's long straight blonde hair was pulled back into a ponytail and she was dressed in a navy blue suit jacket over a white cotton open necked blouse and a pair of dark blue designer jeans with black flat heeled shoes.

"Hello Jade." She said with a fake smile as she strolled toward the desk.

Jasmine faked one back at her.

"Well if it isn't my new girlfriend!" She chuckled.

"Have you come to play dress up with me Nicola?" She asked.

"I have all of these new outfits that you could try on!"

She nodded toward several large boxes of delivered teenage fashion clothing.

Nicola took in a deep breath and sighed as she shook her head.

"Actually I'm here because I promised that every time you look up or turn around you're going to see me watching you." She reminded Jade Harris.

Jasmine Stiles beamed another grin back at her.

"I know and as we're going to be seeing so much of each other I bought you your own coffee cup!" She replied.

Jasmine then climbed to her feet and walked to her right where she switched on the brand new white electric kettle.

"You just have to christen your new cup!" She added.

Nicola sat down at the opposite side of the desk.

*'Was this bloody chair placed here for me to sit on?'* She suddenly wondered.

"Wasn't it three sugars Nicola?" Jasmine asked.

When she turned to face her she saw that Garwood simply sat and stared back at her.

"Were you staring at my arse Nicola?" She asked with another grin.

"Do you know Jade that there are people within the task force that actually believe that you're innocent and just got caught up in this thing?" Nicola asked.

Jasmine turned to face her again and smiled.

"But you're not one of them are you?" She asked.

"Convince me by telling me how you left the country and ended up on the Greek island." Nicola retorted.

Jasmine then carried two white coffee mugs over to the table and placed one in front of Garwood.

Nicola immediately glanced down at it.

"You see?" Jasmine said.

"I bought you your own cup." She added.

Nicola slowly picked up the once plain white cup that was now modified with indelible bold black marker.

**Nicola's cup**

"You're not funny Jade." She uttered.

Jasmine then sat down opposite her.

The two women sat and stared at each other for a few moments before Garwood broke the silence again.

"You see Jade those that believe that you're innocent don't see what I see every day." She started to explain.

Jasmine sipped coffee and still stared back at her.

"I see a woman that lied to me about how she left the country." She continued.

Jasmine's only response was a smirk.

"I see a woman that I still believe killed somebody inside her flat at New Kent road." She continued.

"And I see a contradictive Lesbian sitting right in front of me that used to shag men for a living." She added.

"I often wonder how that works Jade."

Nicola was pushing buttons to find out which one worked.

Instead of the reaction that she hoped that her last statement would incur Nicola now watched Jasmine chuckle in response.

"I should imagine in the same way that a woman could climb so quickly up the ranks of the police force Nicola." She sarcastically retorted.

"We do what's necessary, don't we?"

Garwood shook her head.

*'You're not turning the tables on me you little bitch.'* She thought to herself.

Garwood slowly climbed to her feet and walked back toward the corridor while Jasmine watched her.

"See you again soon Jade!" She called back without turning around.

Jasmine beamed another grin while inside she breathed a deep sigh of relief.

"I look forward to it Nicola!" She called back.


Across London inside her office at Mount Street Mayfair Carmen Richardson sat behind her desk opposite Richard Willows where she carefully peeled away the small dark brown mole from her neck and placed it down onto the table.

"And now you do the same." She quietly insisted.

"I want a private conversation with you."

Richard showed her a look of confusion but Carmen continued to stare back at him.

Eventually he did the same and removed his mole so that David could not hear the conversation between them.

"On the day that you and I first met we promised each other as part of this agreement complete and total honesty at all times." Carmen reminded him.

Still Richard showed her a look of confusion.

"I remembered that David informed me that he could isolate the frequencies on these things." She continued.

She pointed down at the small mole that was removed from her neck.

Richard nodded his head.

"Yes if he needs to talk to you in private he can do that." He replied.

Carmen nodded with acknowledgement.

"And lately he keeps doing that with you." She replied.

"I noticed it the other day when you were sitting in that very same chair Richard." She told him.

"And yesterday when I tried to talk to David when you drove over to him it happened again." She added.

"Call me paranoid if you like but not stupid."

She watched him as he sat back in his chair and eventually she did the same and continued to stare across her desk.

"We keep no secrets Richard." She reminded him.

"Those were your words." She added.

Richard took in a long and deep breath before he exhaled with a sigh.

Eventually he explained the reasons that David asked him to visit Tranton road yesterday regarding the situation with the four Polish girls inside the house at Larchwood drive at Sidcup.

"He spoke with my old boss of the company." He continued to explain.

"But this is all Dave's doing not Major Greens."

Carmen now looked confused.

"But why would he do that?" She asked.

Richard slowly shook his head.

"He sometimes comes across as very nonchalant about things but for him to react in this way means he's hurting because of something he saw or knows." He replied.

"And then his mind convinces him to fix the situation."

Carmen now held her head in her hands and sighed.

"So how do you have to fix this new situation for him?" She enquired.

Eventually she glanced back at Richard to see that he now stared out of the window.

"Can this affect us Richard?" She asked.

Again there was a lengthy silent pause before he replied.

"Not if I get it dead right tomorrow night."

**Level Twenty Six**
**Sunday January 28th 2001**

It was twenty three minutes to midnight and just as David Stringer predicted yesterday it was absolutely pouring with rain.

Richard Willows sat in the driver seat of his old dark blue Bedford van at Maylands drive Sidcup and was parked thanks to David Stringer's guidance directly in line with the house one street away at Larchwood drive.

Richard sat and stared out of the rain soaked windscreen and waited for the street lights to go out which he knew would soon again thanks to David's intelligence report.

"You see the house right next to you?" David asked in his ear.

"I'm talking about the one right beside you."

Richard turned his head to stare at the property in question on his right side.

"It's empty so you can go through that little side gate and then over the garden wall at the far end and into the next garden." David explained.

"I've been watching the area since Friday." He continued.

"The reason we're going this route is because there's a speed camera on the corner of Larchwood drive and you and your crappy old van were never here."

Eventually Richard replied.

"Ok mate I'm ready when you are." He quietly replied.

"Remember don't use your overshoes until you're actually inside the house." David reminded him.

Inside the house at Larchwood drive thirty nine year old Turkish Atif Rahman walked into the dingy narrow kitchen where he switched on the electric kettle.

He glanced up at the ceiling and shook his head at the obvious heavy rhythmic thumping sounds that came from one of the bedrooms.

He knew exactly what his two friends Barak Yazici and Firat Alican were doing.

He placed his smoking marijuana cigarette into the ashtray before he prepared instant coffee in a cup with the same heavy rhythmic thumping sounds continuing above his head.

Former Captain of the elite British Army SAS regiment Richard Willows stood completely motionless in the pouring rain just in front of the closed dark brown garage door.

He was almost invisible to the naked eye.

He was dressed in a black vinyl boiler suit that had elasticated wrists and ankles with flat black training shoes on his feet and he had a small black vinyl holdall bag draped over his right shoulder.

Richard didn't move a single muscle.

He simply wasn't there.

"Ok let's do this strictly by the numbers." David eventually said into his ear.

"We need your gloves and mask on before you approach the front door."

Richard pulled on ultra-tight fitting black latex gloves and tucked them inside the elasticated wrists of his boiler suit.

David watched from sixty miles in the night sky via a passing American spy satellite that officially didn't exist.

He then reminded Richard that the gloves needed to be tucked inside the sleeves of his boiler suit so that not even a single skin cell could be discovered later.

Richard had of course already done it and didn't respond.

Eventually he also pulled a black vinyl mask over his head that had just a single rectangular mesh covered gap for his eyes.

"Don't forget your goggles as soon as you're inside." David reminded him.

Again he received no reply from Richard because he would now only speak when it was absolutely necessary and when he did he would use very few words.

Richard approached the white UPVC front door of the house where he stood on the red brick door step.

"I'm really sorry about this Richard." David quietly uttered.

Richard stared down at the ground for a few moments.

"Let's just get it done." He replied.

Then there was a momentary pause.

"No more little surprises though Dave."

"Now stop talking." David chuckled in response.

Richard then removed two thin slithers of silver metal and pushed them both into the lock of the door one above the other and twisted them just twice before he heard the lock quietly 'click!' in the pouring rain.

"I'm in." He very quietly uttered.

Because the mole on the left side of his neck operated using the vibrations of his throat his voice came across loud and clear at Bermondsey.

With his latex encased left hand on the handle of the slightly ajar front door Richard used his right hand to pull one vinyl elasticated overshoe over his right training shoe.

He then silently pushed the door forward and placed his now dry covered right foot onto the dark brown carpet inside before he slipped the second overshoe over his left trainer and then stepped inside with completely dry vinyl encased feet.

Richard then just as silently pushed the door closed behind him.

He was inside.

As he opened his small black vinyl bag Richard glanced up the narrow staircase as he heard the same rhythmic thumping sounds that Atif Rahman heard from the kitchen.

"At least one of them is upstairs." He very quietly informed David.

He stood motionless and listened more intently.

"Make that two."

Richard then pulled clear plastic goggles from the bag and placed them over his eyes and tightened the elastic at the back of his head.

Then he removed a small black pistol from the same bag.

He very slowly glanced around the door frame and into the living room without making a single sound.

David scrutinised the blue print layout of the house.

"You have a living room to your right." He informed Richard.

'Keep up Dave.' Richard thought to himself.

"At the far end of the living room is a step down into the kitchen directly ahead." David continued.

"But be aware that about two thirds of the way down on your left there's another doorway that leads out to the attached garage."

Unbeknown to Turkish Atif Rahman in the kitchen he was no longer alone.

Richard silently entered the living room to approximately half way down just before the slightly obscured doorway that led out to the garage on his left side.

He then stopped and stood completely motionless.

Thirty nine year old Atif Rahman was suddenly aware that somebody stood in the living room to his right and he naturally assumed it to be Firat Alican or Barak Yazici.

The pouring rain outside had completely stifled the sounds of Richard's entry into the house.

Rahman glanced across with a half-smile.

Instead of Yazici or Alican he now stared into a completely focussed gaze that was behind sealed plastic goggles.

His smile suddenly disappeared as he stared down the short barrel of a black pistol.

No words would be spoken.

Richard Willows wasn't here to talk to him.

Without any hesitation he squeezed back the trigger twice in rapid succession causing two loud echoing gunshots.

The first 9mm round hit Rahman on the right side of his temple and killed him immediately while the second passed lower straight through his nose and exited out from the back of his head.

They both caused loud crimson blood splatters to hit and spray up the hard ceramic white tiled wall behind him.

For Richard everything occurred as an instantaneous formality.

As soon as he saw and heard the blood splatter behind Rahman and before the Turkish immigrant had even slumped to the floor Richard began to approach him.

He knew that although he still stood and stared, Rahman was in fact already dead.

He just didn't know it yet.

"One." Richard quietly announced.

Rahman finally slumped onto the linoleum covered concrete floor in front of him.

Richard stepped over him before he removed a secondary pistol from the bag.

"Received that." David replied.

He then swigged from a bottle of orange fizzy pop as he continued to study the blueprints of the entire house.

Using his own latex encased hand Richard placed the second clean unused pistol into the right hand of the now dead Atif Rahman and he waited and listened to heavy footsteps that rushed down the stairs in the hallway.

The forty seven year old leader of the Turkish group Barak Yazici obviously heard the gunshots from upstairs and as he still refastened his trouser belt he rushed into the living room.

Yazici now stared down the barrel of a gun that was in the dead right hand of his friend Atif Rahman.

He stood and stared as he defensively very slowly raised both of his hands to plead for his life.

Richard immediately used Atif Rahman's forefinger to squeeze back the trigger of the second pistol three times in just as rapid succession as before.

All three rounds thudded into Yazici in a dead straight line.

The first hit him in his throat and went straight through and exited at the back of his neck.

The second thudded deep into his chest.

The third thudded into his stomach.

He was in fact also dead long before he slumped to the floor.

"Two." Richard uttered.

Again he climbed to his feet but he left the second pistol in the dead hand of Atif Rahman so that it appeared that it was in fact he that shot Barak Yazici.

"Received that." David replied.

As he approached the now dead Barak Yazici Richard removed a third clean unfired pistol from his black vinyl bag and placed it into Yazici's lifeless right hand.

"Waiting on a third." Richard announced as he waited in otherwise silence.

"There are definitely three inside the house, nobody has left there today." David replied.

Richard sat beside the dead body of Barak Yazici clutching the pistol in Yazici's right hand.

He listened and waited motionless to the very quiet footsteps that crept down the carpeted staircase toward him.

Suddenly out of the darkness the terrified face of forty two year old London taxi driver Firat Alican appeared.

His hands were raised in the air as Richard silently motioned with the pistol to ensure that he entered the room.

Alican wasn't about to do anything stupid.

In front of him was his dead friend Barak Yazici and as he very slowly entered the room he saw his other now dead friend Atif Rahman slumped in the kitchen and also covered in his own blood.

"W...We can come to an arrangement." He quietly proposed to Richard.

Richard silently motioned him into the room and directly to where he stood earlier when he shot Atif Rahman in the kitchen so that the future calculated distance of the rounds in Rahman would match forensics.

Richard then placed a single forefinger to where his mouth was covered by the black mask and he motioned for Alican to kneel.

With the gun aimed directly at him Alican did exactly as Richard instructed.

With the trembling Firat Alican now knelt directly in front of him Richard fired just one shot.

It cracked into Alican's forehead and the blood splatter sprayed over the wall directly behind him.

Firat Alican immediately slumped to the floor with his eyes still wide open.

"Three." Richard calmly announced.

There was a pause before David responded.

"Is there any more movement?" He asked.

Richard's eyes slowly scanned but his heightened senses were actually listening, not watching.

"No." He replied.

"Ok mate clear up and get out." David told him.

Richard left the third pistol in the hand of Barak Yazici.

He stepped forward the removed the first pistol that was used for the initial shots at Atif Rahman from his black bag and placed it into Firat Alican's hand and used his forefinger to leave the only imprint on the trigger.

"Now it should look as if they all shot each other in an argument when you're finished." David clinically announced.

Richard stood and although he thought it all thoroughly through the sequence of events was instantaneous in his mind.

Pistol number one was used to shoot Atif Rahman in the kitchen by Firat Alican.

Pistol number two was used by Rahman's hand to shoot Barak Yazici in the cannabis smoke filled living room from the kitchen.

Richard then used the third hand gun to shoot Firat Alican directly between his still terrified wide eyes but it now appeared that Yazici pulled the trigger.

"Ok I'm clearing out." Richard announced before he left the house.

This time he made his way back to his van via the back door of the house and into the back garden.

He headed in the exact same straight line toward his blue Bedford van that was parked at Maylands drive.

David then made a masked call from his converted office bedroom.

"Hello can I speak to the police please?" He asked.

"I just heard what I think were gunshots from a house across the street." He informed the emergency operator.

Richard climbed back into the driver seat of his van where he finally removed the vinyl overshoes from his black training shoes and tossed them onto the passenger seat before he heard the sound of police sirens.

After a short while he watched the first two police cars speed past on the main road ahead of him.

He started the engine of his van and slowly pulled away.

After a few moments David spoke again.

"Thank you Richard." He quietly uttered.

Richard turned his van right onto Faraday road.

"No more little surprises Dave, or you might just find me standing behind you one day." He replied.

There was however a chuckle in his tone.

There was another pause before Stringer replied.

"I received that too." He quietly answered.

Richard again quietly chuckled and shook his head.

**Level Twenty Seven**
**Monday January 29th 2001**

At just after eight the next morning Jasmine Stiles left Carmen's flat and casually walked down the King's road at Chelsea.

She was of course watched by Detective Inspector Nicola Garwood and Detective Sergeant Jacob Saunders from across the street inside a silver Ford police pool car.

As she passed them Jasmine glanced across and smiled before she gave a little wave to Jacob Saunders.

She then continued to walk and from inside the car Garwood stared at Saunders with a look of utter disbelief.

"Jacob, don't wave back to her!" She angrily snapped.

Saunders turned to glance back at Nicola.

"I was just being polite guv." He replied.

Eventually they watched as Jasmine walked into a greasy spoon café around two hundred feet away on the King's road.

Garwood quickly checked her make up in the vanity mirror above her head.

"It's time for some breakfast I think." She uttered.

Saunders beamed a smile.

"Great I'm starving."

Nicola suddenly stopped and stared at him.

"No you wait here." She insisted.

"Whenever it's just her and me she drops little snippets and little insinuations." She informed him.

Nicola then broke into a smile and reached across and ruffled Jacob's curly hair.

"I'll bring you something back." She promised.

She then climbed out of the car and slammed the door shut behind her.

Jacob sat in the driver seat of the car and watched Nicola cross the street via his left wing mirror as she made her way down toward the same greasy spoon café.

"I think I might definitely travel Europe when you get us both fired." He quietly uttered to himself.

Inside the café Jasmine sat facing the door and she glanced up from the menu and beamed a smile when Garwood entered and then closed the door behind her.

"One of these days I'll make you breakfast in bed." She chuckled.

Nicola sat down at the same table.

Before any more words were spoken a young waitress approached the table and smiled down at Nicola.

"Can I just have a coffee to drink here and a bacon sandwich to take away please?" She asked.

She watched as the young woman scribbled down her order.

"Put it on my bill." Jasmine said.

Garwood continued to stare up at the waitress and she shook her head.

"I'll be paying for my own." She insisted.

When the waitress eventually departed Nicola turned her attention to Jasmine.

"Do you know what I find intriguing Jade?" She asked.

Jasmine glanced up from the menu again.

"Is it that I maintain such a fantastic figure considering that I just ordered a full English breakfast?" She asked in response.

"You had Oliver Alcott come to get you out at Gatwick airport on the day that you arrived back here." Nicola reminded her.

"And I'm sure that you think that I'm harassing you right now and yet you've never threatened me with him since."

Jasmine displayed a wry grin as she glanced back down at the menu in her hand.

"First and foremost Nicola I didn't arrange Oliver Alcott's arrival at Gatwick." She reminded Garwood.

"And maybe you're giving out the wrong signals." She continued in a quiet tone.

"And maybe, just maybe I'm enjoying the attention from you." She added.

The waitress suddenly returned with coffee for Garwood and placed it onto the table in front of her before she promptly left again after Nicola smiled up at her.

Her attention soon returned to Jasmine.

*'There's still something about you that I can't quite put my finger on.'* She thought to herself as he studied Jasmine Stiles.

She couldn't see Jasmine's blue eyes because Jasmine purposely stared down at the menu.

Jaz then watched Nicola scoop three heaped teaspoons of sugar into her coffee before she stirred it.

She then she glanced up into Nicola's eyes and grinned again.

"I'm going to so enjoy looking after you when you're diabetic." She chuckled.

"I'm sure I have a nurse's uniform somewhere."

Garwood nodded.

"Why wouldn't that surprise me?" She asked before she sipped her hot coffee.

Nicola placed her coffee cup down onto the table and stared straight into Jasmine's blue eyes.

"So what have you got planned today Jade?" She enquired.

Jasmine now sipped her own coffee before she responded.

"I have another day over at my warehouse." She eventually replied.

"Let me know what time you're coming in so that I can hide all of the dead bodies and I'll have your new cup ready." She added.

Garwood sat back in her chair and again stared across at Jasmine.

"The moment that you call Oliver Alcott is the moment I know that I hit a raw nerve." She informed Jasmine.

The twenty nine year old half-sister of Garwood's personal obsession stared back at her.

"I'm not going to let you out of my sight." Nicola assured her.

Jasmine slowly broke into another grin.

"I'm banking on that Nicola." She replied.

*'We can't have you accidentally stumbling across my sister now, can we?'* She thought to herself.

She continued to stare back at Garwood with a smile.

David Stringer sat and stared at a monitor that showed him that Miguel Sanchez had already boarded a flight with who he still believed to be twenty two year old Sasha Willows.

The flight that they boarded today from Johannesburg South Africa was headed toward Lisbon Portugal.

"Flight ST444 is scheduled to land at Lisbon airport at around four tomorrow morning." David explained to Richard and Carmen via their earpiece moles.

"As I told you earlier Theresa Sanchez left the hotel at Manisa Turkey and she is also headed toward Lisbon to meet with Miguel." He added.

"I'm still guessing that they're coming to the UK by boat from somewhere around the Lisbon area." He finished.

On a different monitor David occasionally glanced and read updated incident reports from the Metropolitan police database regarding an incident that occurred last night at Larchwood drive Sidcup.

The initial reports read that at around midnight last night an unknown caller contacted the emergency services and informed them that he heard what he believed to be gunshots from inside the property.

An armed police response unit was dispatched to the address where they gained entry after around an hour and discovered three dead men on the living room and kitchen floors.

The three men were later identified as forty seven year old Barak Yazici, thirty nine year old Atif Rahman and forty two year old Firat Alican, all originally from Turkey.

A forensic team was immediately called to the scene as the initial investigating officers began a search of the entire house.

In the master bedroom at the front of the house they discovered four young women.

Nineteen year old Gita Budz, eighteen year old Magda Gronek, sixteen year old Kassia Zoldak and sixteen year old Dominika Laski all from the small town of Slonsk western Poland were chained to individual beds.

All four had been injected with heavy doses of Heroin.

All four had been very recently repeatedly raped and beaten.

Samples of semen taken from the girls revealed that their attackers were two of the three dead Turkish immigrants in the living room and kitchen.

Forensic evidence of Barak Yazici's indented fingerprint on the trigger of the pistol that was discovered in his right hand showed that he shot and killed Firat Alican at point blank range.

The pistol in Alican's hand fired the two shots that killed Atif Rahman in the kitchen.

The pistol that killed Barak Yazici had been fired three times from Rahman's hand.

The initial reports showed that the three men killed each other in a three-way fight probably over drugs or another illegal deal.

One other prominent unidentified DNA sample was found.

It belonged to a woman.

Debbie Davies however had never been arrested.

The discovered DNA sample found no matches on the Metropolitan police database.

**Level Twenty Eight**
**Monday January 28th 2001**

It was just after six on the same evening when Jade Harris sat in front of the dressing table mirror in her bedroom inside the maisonette at the end of Pitcairn road Tooting south London.

Her straight shoulder length reddish brown bobbed hair was brushed and she had just finished applying her make-up.

For the very first time she removed two small dark brown moles from a small clear sealable plastic bag.

Jade was dressed in a shimmering gold sleeveless top and an incredibly tight fitting black leather thigh length skirt with glossy black patent leather knee high boots that had a four inch heel.

She stared at her reflection in the mirror as she recalled what Carmen had told her regarding the two small moles.

*'The smallest one rests inside my ear.'*  She told herself.

She took a hold of the tiny mole with her short tweezers and watched in the mirror as she very, very carefully placed it inside her ear and then she returned the tweezers to the dressing table.

"Ok, well I can't hear anything."  She said out loud.

The larger of the two moles was placed on the tip of her right forefinger.

Jade shrugged her shoulders.

She pressed the second mole onto the side of her neck as she recalled more of what Carmen explained to her.

"The smallest mole rests just inside your ear and the larger of the two is a transmitter and it actually transmits by the vibrations of your throat."

Jade shrugged her shoulders again.

She removed her finger from the mole that was now placed on the right side of her neck.

"Right I've done that so what now?" She asked herself again out loud.

Suddenly and without warning a clear voice spoke in her ear.

"Hello Jade it's nice of you to finally join us." David Stringer said.

Jade suddenly leapt up from her seat and fell backward over her bed and landed on the floor beside it.

"Holy bloody shit!" She squealed.

She stared around the room to ensure that whoever just spoke her wasn't actually there with her because that's exactly what it sounded like.

"W…Where are you?" She asked him in a state on utter confusion.

I'm in Bermondsey did I make you jump?" David asked.

Jade slowly climbed from the floor and straightened her clothing.

"Not at all, I was sitting down." She eventually lied.

There was a short pause before Stringer spoke to her again.

"Are you as hot as your sister?" He enquired.

Jade sat back down on the same chair that she had just fallen from and sighed as she shook her head.

"Oh please she's as rough as they come." She insisted.

She suddenly heard Jasmine's voice.

"I heard that bitch features!" Jasmine retorted from Carmen's old flat at Chelsea.

"Great they're going to have a fight." David interjected.

It was now Richard Willows that interrupted the conversation.

"Jade, I'm about five minutes away from Pitcairn road." He informed her.

"Are you ready?"

Jade nodded her head.

"Yes I look like a Charing Cross whore." She informed him.

"Good." Richard replied.

"Perfect actually." David promptly added.

Jade shook her head with another deep sigh.

"Shut up pervert." She uttered.

She heard Stringer chuckle.

Jade then climbed back to her feet and headed toward her bedroom door.

"Are you here yet Richard?" She asked.

"I'm just pulling up outside now in a dark blue van." He replied.

Carmen Richardson sat in her darkened office and listened with a smile because Jade's last remark that was directed toward David Stringer sounded just like the old Jade.

Jade cautiously climbed down the narrow staircase in her high heeled boots and informed April that Richard was now parked outside and that she was leaving.

She stepped outside the door and into the small cul-de-sac where she saw the parked dark blue Bedford van.

She took her usual long strides out of the back gate beside the huge wooden roofed parking bay where she was immediately seen by David Stringer from above.

"Ok yes you're hot." He quietly uttered.

Jade heard his remark but she wasn't the only one.

"David, do you think she's hotter than me?" Jasmine suddenly asked him.

As he stared at the screen in front of him David's huge magnified eyes widened.

"No comment on the grounds that one of you will beat me up." He replied.

David complex brain suddenly switched into the more serious professional mode.

"Richard, Huy Nguy has been in the Hare and Hounds pub for an hour now." He informed Willows.

David went on to explain to the entire group that the older brother of the sixteen year old Vietnamese girl that was kept at Jane Chapman's residence visited the same pub almost every evening.

"He'll be absolutely plastered within the next hour." He added.

David had been watching Huy Nguy for the past week in preparation for tonight.

Jade climbed into the passenger seat of Richard's old dark blue van and closed the door behind her before she glanced across at him and he stared back at her.

"Let's get this done as quickly as possible." He told her.

Jade nodded her head.

Richard then started the engine and pulled away from the cul-de-sac at the end of Pitcairn road.

Together he and Jade headed north for around forty minutes toward Holborn in the city of London itself.

Nineteen year old Huy Nguy sat inside the Hare and Hounds public house and already in a drunken condition at around eight in the evening as he did every single night.

He was a thin young man that stood at just five feet six inches and he had short dark brown hair and dark brown now very blurred eyes after his third pint of weak lager.

Because most of the pubs in the city centre closed at around eight every night the Hare and Hounds was tonight as usual very busy because it kept regular trading times and would remain open until eleven.

The nineteen year old Vietnamese student never ever once made it to that time.

He studied medicine at the nearby college and would later attend university courtesy of his sponsor.

His sponsor was a Russian by the name of Vladimir Kolov.

Huy Nguy also had an allowance that allowed him to drink every night but this was obviously still a new concept to him.

He sat at the bar dressed in a plain black t shirt and a pair of blue denim jeans with black training shoes on his feet and he ordered his fourth pint of Lager.

He would as usual at around nine o'clock be thrown out from the pub and somehow manage to stagger back to his rented flat just around the corner.

He glanced to his right at a young woman that stood at the bar beside him and he grinned.

She was around five feet six inches tall and she had long straight blonde hair that was pulled back into a ponytail and she was dressed in a smart black business suit over a white open necked cotton blouse.

"Hello pretty lady." Huy Nguy slurred.

The woman completely ignored him.

He then glanced straight ahead before he glanced to his left where another woman stood.

This woman was considerably taller and she had straight shoulder length reddish brown hair.

"Hello pretty lady." Huy Nguy slurred with another grin.

Jade Harris smiled back at him.

"Hello handsome what's your name?"

Huy Nguy suddenly sat upright and with the forefinger of his right hand he pointed toward his own narrow chest.

"I am Huy Nguy from Vietnam." He announced in good English.

Jade watched as he swayed on his bar stool and she smiled at him again.

After a few moments she turned her head to her left and appeared to glance around the bar.

"I found him Richard." She very, very quietly uttered.

Because the tiny mole that was attached to her neck worked on the vibrations of her throat Richard heard her message loud and clear.

"How drunk is he?" Richard asked.

Jade now ordered a Brandy for herself and another pink of weak Lager for Huy Nguy.

She glanced across at him and smiled yet again.

"Oh he's absolutely plastered." She very quietly replied.

When the barmaid returned in front of Jade with their drinks she informed her that this would be the last drink for Huy Nguy and Jade smiled back at her.

"I know him and I'll take him home after that one." She assured her.

For the next ten to twelve minutes Jade Harris sipped her Brandy with his hand rested upon her bottom and she listened as he talked about his home country.

"Tonight's your lucky night because I'm going to take you home now." She eventually informed him.

A huge grin appeared on his lips.

After a few moments Jade helped Huy Nguy toward the door and outside to the car park.

She continued to help him walk while his right hand remained firmly placed on her right bottom cheek.

As they walked past a dark blue van the sliding side door suddenly opened on their right side.

Jade suddenly stopped and held Huy Nguy upright before he glanced inside the van.

"I am Huy Nguy from Viet..." He began.

Richard used the index finger from his right hand to tap the temple on the right side of Huy Nguy's head just once.

He suddenly slumped into Jade's arms.

She raised her eyebrows with surprise as she stared at Richard.

"What the bloody hell was that?"

Richard dragged the Vietnamese teenager into the van and climbed out before he slid the door closed behind him.

"Just a little trick I know." He replied.

He then walked around to the driver side of the van and Jade watched him.

"Can you teach me to do that?" She asked.

Richard glanced across at her and smiled.

"No."

Jade could hear David Stringer chuckling in her ear.

She climbed into the passenger seat of the van before she closed the door behind her.

Richard started the engine and pulled away while Jade continued to stare at him.

"If you teach me to do that I promise never to use it on people." She assured him.

The van began to head south and back toward Tooting.

Richard glanced across at her.

"No." He replied again.

David continued to chuckle into Jade and Richard's earpieces.

"Ok what if I promise only to ever use it on David?" She asked.

When Richard glanced back at her he saw a wry grin before Jade winked her left eye.

"I'll think about it."  He replied with a grin of his own.

In the converted office bedroom inside the house at Tranton road Bermondsey David Stringer's eyes widened again.

"You bastard Willows!"

"And I always knew that Jasmine was the nicer one."  He added.

**Level Twenty Nine**
**Tuesday January 30th 2001**

At around ten the next morning nineteen year old Huy Nguy slowly opened his blurred eyes and eventually focussed on a man with blonde swept back hair that stared down at him.

His head pounded from the combined effects of too much alcohol and a prolonged enforced sleep that was induced by the same man that continued to stare at him.

Richard however wasn't alone.

"Are you the so called medical examiner that works for Vladimir Kolov's little organisation?" Carmen Richardson bluntly enquired from Huy Nguy's right side.

He now glanced across at her.

Beside Carmen was the woman that he vaguely recalled meeting at the pub last night and standing beside Jade Harris and also staring down at him was the slightly plump figure of April Marsh.

Huy Nguy slowly sat upright and very gently shook his head in order to test the throbbing pain.

"W...Where is this place?" He croaked.

"I just asked you a question." Carmen replied.

"Are you working for Vladimir Kolov as a medical examiner?" She asked again.

Eventually Huy Nguy glanced back up at her before he buried his head back into his hands.

"I am medical student not examiner." He replied.

Carmen then handed him a glass of water.

"Drink this." She told him.

When he looked up and saw the glass he reached up and took it in his trembling right hand.

"Why am I here?" He asked.

He then slowly turned his head to his left again as Richard held an overhead satellite image.

"This picture was taken over as bus stop at Watford." He began.

"Do you know who the girl in the red coat is?" He asked.

Huy Nguy stared at it and tried to focus.

Eventually he shook his head and then stared back up into Richard's blue eyes.

"I do not know this person." He replied.

Richard then looked across at Carmen before he returned his gaze down to Huy Nguy.

"Her name is Kim Cuc Nguy." He informed the Vietnamese teenager.

Huy Nguy immediately stared back at the image that showed a bus stop and a busy main road and most decidedly not anywhere near South Vietnam.

He stared back up at Richard.

"Th…This cannot be." He quietly croaked.

"She is at home in my village at Vietnam."

Richard half smiled back at him.

"You're going to need our help to get your sister back." He began again.

"And we need your help to do it." Carmen Richardson added.

In a very clever twist dreamt up by Vladimir Kolov, Kim Cuc Nguy was currently forced to work for Jane Chapman purely to ensure the safety of her older brother.

However when the nineteen year old medical student was fully qualified he would be informed that should he fail to comply, his sister would be at risk.

The tables would be completely turned.

Huy Nguy was not yet the medical examiner currently working for Indigo.

His sixteen year old sister would be twenty years of age by the time he was fully qualified.

**Level Thirty**
**Thursday February 1st 2001**

It was two days ago when Spaniard Miguel Sanchez arrived at the hotel at Lisbon Portugal along with the young blonde woman that was picked up and taken from the Indonesian military base at Mamuju.

David Stringer was now almost certain that she was Richard's sister twenty two year old Sasha Willows.

Miguel's wife Theresa Sanchez arrived at Lisbon a day earlier than her husband and now it was time for David to break other important news to his friend and Sasha's older brother Richard.

Richard sat right beside him in his converted office bedroom at his home at Tranton road Bermondsey.

"Jane Chapman, Lisa Moore and Debbie Davies have pretty much gone underground since the unfortunate Turkish incident at Larchwood drive." David began.

"I read the initial forensic reports yesterday and all evidence regarding it is pointing to the simple fact that all three of the Turks were stoned and killed each other in a fight." He added.

"You left no trace of DNA anywhere."

"Jasmine is doing a great job keeping DI Garwood busy and away from her sister." David continued.

He then typed onto one of his keyboards.

"At the warehouse at the Stanley industrial estate I estimate that there are still around twenty captives remaining inside unit 4F." He continued.

Then he stared into Richard's eyes.

"That estimate is from what you told me from when you went there to buy Jade back from them." He added.

A few moments after David typed onto the keyboard an image flickered into life on one of the monitors and Richard leaned forward to study it.

"Where is this?" He asked.

David pointed his finger to a large black rooftop on the live overhead satellite image.

"That's the hotel at Lisbon Portugal where Sasha is at." He explained.

He glanced back at Richard.

"And before you even think about going there to get her I have something to tell you." David promptly continued.

"By the time you manage to book a flight and get there she'll already be on her way to the UK." He added.

"You'd go straight past her."

David's forefinger then slowly moved west on the PC monitor from the hotel at Lisbon to the nearby sea port at Cascais and in particular at a large feeder ship that was moored there.

"That big old Betty is a British ship called *the Candlelit Queen* and it also arrived there yesterday." He explained.

"Miguel Sanchez climbed on board it as soon as he arrived in Lisbon." David added.

"The ship departs from Cascais tomorrow and arrives at North Woolwich pier on the river Thames in four days." He said.

"And try to remember that Miguel Sanchez knows that we can see him when he's taking a dump so they will expect us to try to take Sasha back." He continued.

"They're not stupid Richard and they'll have some kind of safeguard in place."

Richard stared at the screen while his brain operated almost as quickly as David's.

"Ok so when do we get the girl at the bus stop?" He asked.

David turned to stare at him.

"It has to be tomorrow." He replied.

"She'll be at the bus stop near Glade road Watford at eleven o'clock." He added.

Without removing his stare from the monitor and the image of the black rooftop where he knew that his sister Sasha was agonisingly close Richard eventually nodded his head.

David then opened a desk drawer where he removed a black mobile phone and handed it to Richard.

"It's fully charged." He explained.

"So do me a favour and don't make a call on it." He added with a chuckle.

Richard broke into a chuckle of his own.

"I'll try to remember that."

**Level Thirty One**
**Saturday February 3rd 2001**

It was just after eleven on a cold dark night when one silver Ford car pulled up beside another at the Stanley industrial estate at north Woolwich east London.

The window at the driver side of the second car lowered at the same time as the passenger side window of the first.

"She's still inside?" Detective Inspector Nicola Garwood asked.

Both surveillance officers inside the first car nodded.

Nicola glanced toward the closed green door that led into unit 2B.

She arrived here just under an hour ago." One of them informed her.

"What the hell can she be doing in there at this time of night?" Nicola quietly uttered to herself.

"She knows she's being watched so she's probably playing one of her silly little games." She added.

She then turned again to the two officers in the first car.

"Is she in there alone?" She asked.

Again they both nodded.

Nicola glanced toward the green door again.

"Ok I'm going to take a walk over there and find out what she's up to." She said.

Jasmine Stiles sat at the small brown wooden table inside unit 2B and sipped coffee while she waited.

She knew of course thanks to David Stringer that Detective Inspector Nicola Garwood was also parked right outside and that she was about to enter the warehouse.

"Here she comes now, Jaz." David had just informed her.

It was a cold night and Jasmine was dressed in a long black coat with black woollen gloves on her hands.

Suddenly she heard the unlocked entrance door open and then eventually it swung closed again.

"Here we go." She very quietly uttered to David Stringer.

"Remember to really let her have it tonight." David replied.

Carmen Richardson, Richard Willows and Jade Harris all listened in silence from Mayfair and Tooting.

"Well if it isn't the lovely Detective Inspector Nicola Garwood." Jasmine uttered with a wry grin.

Nicola Garwood stepped into view.

"You're up late Nicola." Jaz continued.

Garwood's eyes scanned around the warehouse as she slowly approached Jasmine at the desk.

"I was informed that you drove out to here at ten o'clock at night so I thought I'd come and see what you're up to Jade." She replied.

"What exactly are you doing here at this time of night?"

Jasmine's wry grin broadened.

"You really are obsessed with me aren't you?" She asked.

Her question received no response from Nicola.

She had heard that statement made too many times of late.

"Why *are* you out here at this time of night?" Nicola asked again.

"Did you rush out to see me so quickly that you didn't have time for coffee?" Jasmine asked.

"You seem a little cranky tonight." She added.

David Stringer continued to quietly chuckle in Jasmine's ear.

Jasmine placed her cup down onto the desk before she climbed to her feet and walked to her new white electric kettle and switched it on.

"Actually Jade I don't want to sit and socialise with you." Nicola told her.

Jasmine turned and mocked a frown.

There was a silent pause of a few moments.

"Actually you do." She eventually replied.

Nicola adamantly shook her head.

"What I want is for you to slip up just once so that I can throw you into a cell." She replied.

Again Jasmine broke into a wry grin.

"But I never slip up Nicola." She replied.

She continued to make Garwood coffee.

Nicola stared at her for a few moments before she responded.

"That was almost an admission of guilt Jade." She said.

This time Jasmine chuckled before she turned to face her again.

"Ok let's pretend that I do know something that would be of use to you." She began.

"And let's presume that I actually wanted to give it to you too." She continued.

"This is obviously all theoretical of course and *not* an admission of guilt so you can't throw me into that cell." She promptly added.

Now Garwood slowly stepped closer to listen more intently.

"Go on." She said.

"But before I do that if I do that, you have to drink coffee with me." Jasmine added.

Garwood now chuckled.

"And if I agree to drink coffee with you, you're going to give me something regarding the case?" She asked.

Jasmine then turned and handed her the same coffee mug that she had already personalised for Nicola.

"Oh you're really good." David Stringer said in Jasmine's ear.

Jasmine smiled again before she picked up her own coffee cup from the desk and then sipped while they maintained continuous eye contact for a few moments longer.

"It's a lovely evening Nicola." Jasmine said.

It was absolutely freezing cold as a matter of fact.

"Why don't we drink our coffee outside?" She suggested.

"Is being outside relevant?" Nicola enquired.

Again Jasmine smiled.

"I don't know yet." She replied.

"That actually depends on what it is that you want Nicola."

Eventually Garwood followed Jasmine out into the narrow hallway and through the main green door where they then stood outside.

Jasmine then turned and locked the door behind them.

"Ok maybe it's not such a lovely evening." She chuckled.

Garwood purposely sipped her coffee and then stared into Jasmine's blue eyes.

"Ok I'm drinking coffee with you Jade." She began again.

"Let's see your side of this little deal." She added.

Jasmine chuckled again.

"It's no wonder you're still bloody single Nicola."

She then slowly turned and faced south and pointed in the general direction of the river Thames.

"Ok, tell me what you see down there." She said.

Garwood glanced down toward the end of the estate and the river Thames as a small river boat passed by.

"I see the lights from the other side of the river." She began.

"I see a river boat passing." She added with a sigh.

Jasmine turned and smiled at her.

"What else do you see?" She asked.

Nicola sighed again.

Her trained eye now thoroughly scanned the area directly in front of her because she suddenly felt that this wasn't one of Jade Harris's cryptic little games.

*'What do I see?'* She asked herself.

"It's right in front of you Nicola." Jasmine informed her with a clue.

Garwood now meticulously scanned the industrial estate itself.

*'A Street light that isn't working, a silver van, four waste bins, one yellow Skip, a river boat, buildings...'* She told herself as she continued to scrutinise.

Then it suddenly dawned on her.

Her busy eyes darted back to the silver van.

She stared at it for a few moments more not quite believing what she was looking at.

"What the fuck..." She quietly uttered.

She immediately handed Jasmine her coffee cup without removing her stare and slowly edged forward.

"It can't be..." She quietly told herself.

"They've been bringing them out one at a time all day and taking them away." Jasmine informed her.

She now sipped coffee from Nicola's personalised cup.

Garwood turned and stared at Jasmine.

"And tell me how would you know that Jade?" She asked.

"You didn't get here until ten o'clock tonight."

Nicola's attention promptly returned to the silver van that was just twenty feet or so away from her.

As she neared it the imprints that were left from the original signage on the side of the van were becoming more and more visible.

Garwood reached into her inside jacket pocket and removed her police two-way radio and immediately pressed the black button before she spoke into it.

"You two make some calls and get everybody down here now!" She instructed the two watching officers in the first silver car.

"Are you ok guv?" One of them asked.

Nicola stopped and turned to stare at them both through the windscreen of their car.

"Make the calls and get everybody out from their beds like I just told you to!" She snapped.

*'Really give it to her tonight.'* David Stringer earlier instructed.

"Well I gave it to her David." Jasmine quietly uttered.

"Can I leg it now?"

Nicola then coincidentally turned to Jasmine and pointed her right forefinger.

"You, don't you dare bloody well move!"

Jasmine broke into yet another grin.

"Of course Nicola I'll stay right here like a good girl." She quietly uttered with a chuckle.

The two surveillance officers from the car now ran past Jasmine toward Garwood.

Jasmine watched for a few more moments.

"Go get them Detective Inspector Nicola Garwood." She whispered to herself with an almost tearful smile.

She then placed the two cups onto the floor in front of the green door and then casually made her way toward her car.

Around six minutes later Jasmine drove west on Factory road where she passed six police cars coming from the opposite direction with flashing blue lights and Sirens.

"Ok guys they're going to be very busy tomorrow." She chuckled to everybody that listened in.

"Good job Jaz." David told her.

"Great job Jasmine." Richard Willows added.

## Level Thirty Two
## Sunday February 4th 2001

The next morning David Stringer sat and stared at one of his computer monitors and at Miguel Sanchez, his wife Theresa and the young blonde girl that David believed was Richard's younger sister Sasha Willows.

Together they walked up the gang plank and on board the British cargo vessel *the Candlelit Queen*.

"I now have absolutely no doubt that this girl is Sasha." He said into his microphone.

The Candlelit Queen was still moored at the sea port at Cascais just west of Lisbon Portugal and she was due to disembark within the next two hours.

"This big old boat will arrive at north Woolwich pier at around midday in three days from now." He continued to explain.

"That's how long we have to get the rest of this done." He added.

Richard confirmed that he had received and fully understood David's statement.

"We've nearly got her mate." David quietly uttered on a personal note.

Richard Willows still didn't dare to even dream that it was even possible.

David turned his attention to the second operational monitor.

"How far are you from the bus stop?" He asked.

There was a pause before Richard responded.

"About ten minutes away." He finally replied.

"Is she there yet?"

He glanced across to the passenger seat inside his old dark blue van at nineteen year old Vietnamese medical student Huy Nguy.

"Yes and her bus will arrive in about eleven minutes to take her to Pinner." David replied.

"So you had better move your arse Willows." He added with a chuckle.

Richard again glanced across at his passenger Huy Nguy.

"Your sister is at the bust stop." He said.

The blue van climbed the hill just around the corner from Glade road at Watford and as it continued to climb a lone figure eventually appeared beside the bust stop and she wore the same unmistakable red duffle coat.

Huy Nguy stared with disbelief.

"How can this be?" He quietly uttered to himself.

Richard glanced across at him again.

"Are you certain that she'll help us?" He asked.

Huy Nguy briefly glanced back at him.

"If we help you do this we can go back home together?" He asked in response.

Richard nodded with a genuine smile.

"Then she will help." Huy Nguy assured him.

Timid sixteen year old Kim Cuc Nguy stood at the bus stop and watched an old dark blue van as it indicated to pull into the layby.

Her eyes immediately stared down at the floor to avoid making eye contact with the occupants or to attract any unwanted attention.

She suddenly heard a very familiar voice that spoke to her in her native Vietnamese tongue.

When she glanced up her eyes widened with just as much disbelief as her older brother.

Huy Nguy immediately climbed out from the passenger side of the van and they hugged each other tightly.

"How and when did you arrive here?" He asked her in their native tongue.

Richard Willows watched on from the driver seat of the van in silence.

It was mostly Kim Cuc Nguy that talked as she explained and confirmed what her brother was told by Richard and Carmen regarding Vladimir Kolov and Jane Chapman.

It was true that she was threatened with his life should she ever choose to disobey Jane Chapman's instructions.

Eventually with his sister's hand in his own Huy Nguy walked toward the closed door of the blue van and stared across at Richard through the lowered window.

"My sister will help." He informed Richard.

"What do we do now?"

Richard broke into a grin.

Huy Nguy ushered his sister into the centre of the dark brown leather bench seat where she immediately stared at Richard.

She had seen him somewhere before.

She still however had no idea that he had stolen ten strands of her long straight jet black hair.

Huy Nguy climbed in beside her and slammed the door before Richard's van indicated to pull out from the bus lane.

"Outstanding." David uttered in Richard's ear.

"Do the first one today." He advised.

"Detective Inspector Garwood still appears to be quite busy at the moment."

**Level Thirty Three**
**Sunday February 4th 2001**

Inside Chief Inspector Keith Curtis's manically busy full office at task force headquarters Nicola Garwood stood beside Sam Henning with her arms as usual folded in front of her.

The entire ground floor office was a buzzing hive of activity and full of TV photographers and small film crews.

Garwood and Henning watched in silence as Keith Curtis revealed to the world that last night task force detective's discovered an undisclosed human trafficking warehoused holding facility in London.

Nicola and Sam continued to watch as Curtis revealed that at the same undisclosed warehouse facility several also currently undisclosed arrests were made.

A total of twenty six people were discovered inside unit 4F although at this time specific details regarding their identities, welfare and the location itself were not disclosed.

Nicola leaned to her left as Chief Inspector Curtis stared into a rolling camera in front of his desk and revealed non specifics regarding last night's incident.

"And you thought I was being paranoid and obsessed with Jade Harris." She very quietly whispered.

Sam glanced back at her and he nodded with acknowledgement.

"We need to discuss the Harris situation when we get back upstairs." He replied.

"You never know what microphones this lot have hidden." He reminded her.

He referred to the room full of Journalists.

It was Nicola's turn to silently nod with acknowledgement.

Sam and Nicola discretely left the full office on the ground floor and headed up the wide staircase toward the operations room where Nicola swiped her electronic card into the box and pushed open the door.

Sam followed her inside and the door swung closed and relocked.

There was an instant very strange electrified atmosphere inside the operations room.

PC Chris Breslin slowly climbed to his feet and stared directly at Nicola.

For a very brief moment as she stared back at him she thought that one of the unmanned safe houses had been hit.

He slowly started to clap his hands together.

Garwood stood and still stared back at him as her heart pounded against her chest.

Eventually one or two more surveillance officers climbed to their feet and joined Breslin in a genuine round of applause.

After a few moments more the entire team of two hundred plus camera operators were on their feet clapping their hands together.

It was because Garwood uncovered the holding facility warehouse late last night.

Sam Henning leaned forward.

"News travels fast doesn't it?" He quietly uttered into her ear.

Nicola turned and stared into his eyes.

"We haven't cracked anything yet Sam." She replied.

"That little bitch knew that they were at the end of that industrial estate the entire time." She added.

Sam shrugged his broad shoulders and shook his head.

"You don't know that for certain and even if she did she gave us the warehouse and that shows me that she's not a part of the trafficking ring." He replied.

"And besides, we have all of these new suspects and victims to interview before you start pointing your finger at Jade Harris again." He added.

Sam continued to stare back at Nicola before he also started to clap his hands together.

"However you got the warehouse Nik, it was you that got it." He said.

Last night when task force officers gained entry into the warehouse unit 4F at the Stanley industrial estate Nikki Fright from the abduction at Love Lane Micham near Croydon on August 4th last year and Veronica Willard from the abduction at St Andrew's Road Enfield on August 11th were discovered amongst the captives.

**Level Thirty Four**
**Sunday February 4th 2001**

It was some four hours after Kim Cuc Nguy was picked up at the Watford bus stop by Richard Willows and her nineteen year old brother Huy Nguy in the old dark blue Bedford van.

She was taken to the Maisonette at Pitcairn road at Tooting mainly to allow enough time to pass.

Jane Chapman sent her on her routine trip to the house owned by Lisa Moore at Pinner and then onto the house owned by Debbie Davies at Amersham and those trips would take considerable time.

She was also introduced to the latest technology that was created by David Stringer and because Kim Cuc Nguy spoke limited English her brother translated.

Richard only hoped that Huy Nguy instructed his sister well.

To be on the safe side he would only hand her the new mobile phone just before she was due to return to Chapman's house.

At the maisonette at Pitcairn road she met Carmen Richardson, Jade Harris, April Marsh and the now missing from Nicola Garwood's radar Jasmine Stiles.

It was also now that she was shown proof that she and her brother Huy Nguy would begin their journey back home to their village in South Vietnam in one week via pre-booked flight tickets.


A few hours later David Stringer watched from above as sixteen year old Kim Cuc Nguy walked along Glade road at Watford with her hands inside the pockets of her red duffle coat.

After a short while she turned left and walked across the gravelled driveway toward the front door at Jane Chapman's house.

"Ok get ready she's knocking on the door now." David informed Richard.

Richard was parked just around the corner inside his dark blue van and in the passenger seat was Jade Harris.

Suddenly the front door opened and thirty six year old Chapman stood and glared down at Kim Cuc Nguy.

"Where have you been?" She asked.

"You're more than half an hour late!"

Chapman's blonde shoulder length hair was pulled back into a short ponytail and she was dressed in a black cotton sleeveless top and a pair of light beige cotton shorts with expensive new beige leather sandals.

To Jane Chapman Kim Cuc Nguy seemed unlike her usual self.

She couldn't pinpoint why but what she hadn't realised was that under normal circumstances the Vietnamese teenager appeared very fearful.

That was the difference.

Kim Cuc Nguy knew that one way or another her slavery would end today.

It brought hope of a normal life and a nonchalant acceptance should everything go wrong.

Chapman took a hold of her wrist and roughly pulled her inside before she closed the door behind her.

"Why are you late?" She angrily asked.

She then followed Kim Cuc Nguy into her spacious kitchen.

David Stringer waited for another few moments before he picked up a small black electronic home-made device and on it he pressed one of three small black buttons.

Jane Chapman stared at Kim Cuc Nguy and waited for an answer.

She then heard a quiet electronic 'bleep' that came from somewhere on the Vietnamese teenager's person.

David had just purposely pressed the button.

"What the hell was that?" Chapman demanded to know.

Kim Cuc Nguy's heart pounded against her chest because she knew that whatever was going to happen this afternoon had just begun.

She slowly shook her head and remained completely silent.

All that she could think of was going back home to the village in South Vietnam with her brother.

"It sounded like a mobile phone to me!" Chapman snapped.

"Where did you get a phone from?" She angrily asked.

Again Kim Cuc Nguy only shook her head in silence.

Chapman then stepped closer and stared down at her.

"What did I tell you?" She asked.

"What did I tell you about what would happen to your brother if you do anything other than what you're told you little bitch?"

She then held out her hand.

"Give me the phone!" She snapped.

Reluctantly Kim Cuc Nguy removed her trembling right hand from her coat pocket.

Chapman stared down to see that she held a black mobile phone and she immediately snatched it before her angry gaze returned to Kim Cuc Nguy's terrified dark brown eyes that immediately returned to the floor.

"Where the fuck did you get this from?" Chapman asked.

What Jane Chapman didn't and couldn't possibly see or know of was one of David's tiny dark brown moles.

It was a receiver, a listening device that was stuck behind the top red button of Kim Cuc Nguy's fully fastened coat and he along with Richard, Jade, Jasmine and Carmen could hear the entire one sided conversation.

"Richard I don't know if Kim Cuc is freezing up but she hasn't spoken once." He pointed out.

"But Chapman has the phone in her hand so get to the house now."

Richard Willows glanced across at Jade Harris.

"Here we go." He told her.

He then started the engine of his van.

From his converted office bedroom at Tranton road David pressed his finger onto the second of the three black buttons and then he patiently waited.

At Glade road Watford Jane Chapman glanced down at the black phone in her hand as it vibrated.

Displayed on the green screen were just two initials.

VK.

*The things that we see in front of us are not always as they first appear to be….*

*The mind often tells the eye what it chooses to see….*

She slowly returned her angry stare at Kim Cuc Nguy.

"Did Vladimir Kolov give this to you?" She asked with more venom.

"Are you in touch with him you little bitch?"

Kim Cuc Nguy once again silently shook her head as her heart pounded with sheer terror before Chapman pressed the green button on the phone and then held it to her ear.

"Hello who's this?" She asked with a snap in her tone.

David Stringer grinned.

"Oh it's only me." He quietly uttered to himself.

As David watched Richard's dark blue van pull up outside Chapman's detached house his forefinger pressed the third button on the small black device.

David's third button sent a signal to the home made Taser device that was now pressed against Jane Chapman's ear.

There was a 'snap!' from the phone and the signal immediately sent 20,000 volts through her skull and then down through the rest of her body.

Kim Cuc Nguy leapt back when she heard the same electronic 'snap' that came from the device.

Chapman's entire body turned completely rigid.

She let out a quiet squeal before she slumped down to the floor.

The terrified Vietnamese teenager stared down at Chapman's still trembling body until she heard a loud knock at the front door and then she stared out toward the hallway.

Her own body trembled as much as Chapman's and she was at first too shocked to move.

Eventually she managed to make her way out of the kitchen and into the hall where she slowly opened the front door.

Richard immediately entered and passed her with Jade Harris behind him.

"You had better keep an eye on her." Richard told Jade.

He nodded in the direction of a completely stunned Kim Cuc Nguy.

Jade took a hold of Kim Cuc Nguy's slender wrist and pulled her back into the kitchen.

Richard moved toward the back of the house and then to his right before he stepped inside a darkened closed attached garage.

He crossed the empty space and opened the white garage door from inside before he stepped back outside to his van.

After a few minutes he reversed the van right up to the opening and partially into the fully opened garage.

He then turned off the engine and made his way back into the house.

Kim Cuc Nguy stood in a daze and watched Jade Harris roll Jane Chapman's still trembling frame over before she roughly pulled her lifeless arms behind her back.

Jade then tightly bound Chapman's wrists together using a roll of sticky grey duct tape before she did the same at Chapman's ankles.

She rolled Chapman back over onto her back before she used her teeth to bite off another much shorter strip of sticky grey tape.

"I'm really hoping that you're conscious enough to know what's happing to you bitch." Jade told her.

She firmly pressed the shorter strip of duct tape vertically from just beneath Chapman's nostrils to just beneath her chin.

Only Chapman's eyes showed signs of life as they flickered.

Jade suddenly slapped Chapman's face hard.

"Can you fucking hear me?" She yelled.

Only Chapman's eyes continued to flicker.

Jade bit away yet another strip that she just as firmly pressed horizontally across the first covering Chapman's mouth to ensure that there was no way that she could possibly open it.

"I want you to know who I am." She informed the now bound and gagged Jane Chapman.

"I want you to know that you sold me." She continued.

"So just remember that every good kicking that I give you from now on is repayment." She added.

She then she slapped Chapman's face very, very hard again.

Richard stood in the doorway and stared down at Jade before he eventually spoke.

"Jade, let's just get her into the van." He quietly and calmly said.

She glanced back up at him and as she stared Richard could see that Jade Harris was finally venting her anger.

"We can't negotiate for my sister if you beat her to death." He reminded her.

Jade slowly calmed before she glanced back down at Chapman's trembling torso.

"You're getting the first of those kicking's tonight I promise." She quietly assured the convulsing stunned blonde.

Richard and Jade eventually carried Chapman's bound limp frame into the garage where she was unceremoniously dumped into the back of the van.

After he moved the van forward Richard closed the garage door again.

His main concern was now Jade Harris not Jane Chapman.

Something had definitely snapped.

His original intention was to leave Jade in the back of the van to keep an eye on Chapman but he knew that now wasn't such a good idea.

"Keep your eye on the young girl." Richard told her.

"She's suffering from shock."

"Don't forget my phone." David reminded Richard in his ear.


Ten minutes later Jane Chapman's house at Watford was locked and the dark blue Bedford van began to make its way back to Pitcairn road at Tooting.

Beside Richard in the front of his van was a completely shell-shocked sixteen year old Kim Cuc Nguy, and beside the passenger door was a completely different kind of Jade Harris than he had seen before.

On the steel floor in the back of the van was a bound, gagged and semi-conscious Jane Chapman.

## Level Thirty Five
**Monday February 5th 2001**

The next morning David Stringer sat in his office room and stared down at the British feeder ship the Candlelit Queen from sixty two miles in the sky.

The vast cargo vessel headed toward her destination point that was deep into the river Thames and into the heart of the city of London.

She left the Portuguese sea port of Cascais yesterday morning and she was now in the Atlantic ocean just thirty seven miles north west from the port at Ferrol north west Spain.

Yesterday David watched as Miguel Sanchez, his wife Theresa and the young blonde that he was convinced was Richard's twenty two year old sister Sasha Willows boarded the Candlelit Queen just an hour before she left Cascais.

*'They wouldn't bring us the wrong girl I'm sure.'* David pondered and convinced himself.

This thought had been at the back of his mind since she was picked up from Mamuju on the Indonesian island of Sulawesi.

He just couldn't positively identify her as Sasha.

Eventually he relayed the information to Richard via the tiny mole inside his ear.

"They'll dock near north Woolwich pier the day after tomorrow." David explained.

"But that's going to be a reasonably hairy moment." He added.

"How so?" Richard asked.

David stared down at the exact point where the Candlelit Queen would arrive in two days from now.

Less than two hundred metres from the docking port stood guarding task force police officers that manned the entrance gate that led into the Stanley industrial estate.

The industrial estate was still closed to the public while forensic teams continued to work since the discovery of the human trafficking warehouse at unit 4F.

David continued to stare at the reserved docking point for the inbound Candlelit Queen and then at the long row of terraced buildings on the left side of it.

His eyes then moved to the left of the buildings he stared down at five probably armed police officers.

David slowly shook his head with a sigh.

"This is cutting it really close." He quietly uttered to himself.

If the row of terraced warehouse buildings were not exactly where they were everybody involved would quite clearly be able to see everybody else.


At the maisonette at Pitcairn road Richard also shook his head at David's remarks but he chuckled because David was personally more than simply protected by certain powers in authority.

He slowly glanced around the living room to see Jade seated on the sofa next to her almost identical sister Jasmine and they casually chatted as if none of this was happening.

Sixteen year old Kim Cuc Nguy sat on one of the armchairs and her nineteen year old brother sat on the arm of the same chair and they quietly conversed in their native Vietnamese tongue.

He wondered what they were talking about.

Richard knew that April Marsh was in the kitchen either cleaning or making more tea.

It suddenly dawned on him that they were all managing quite well while in the middle of his elaborate plan.

Everybody was holding up.

Upstairs in the otherwise empty spare bedroom thirty six year old Jane Chapman laid helplessly still bound and gagged on the light brown carpeted floor.

She watched as Carmen Richardson left the room and closed the door behind her.

She then heard the key once again turn inside the lock from the other side.

As soon as she was alone Chapman started once again to try free her hands.

She eventually exhausted herself again and lay there motionlessly staring up at the window to see that today was a reasonably warm and sunny day.

*'I've got to get out of here.'* She calmly told herself.

Down in the living room Richard heard from David again.

"We have two days before the Candlelit Queen docks at north Woolwich pier mate." David reminded him.

Both Jasmine and Jade turned to stare at Richard after they heard the same transmission.

"You really need to take the next one today." David added.

Richard then glanced across at Jade before he responded.

"And we need to do this one calmly." He replied to David.

He continued however to stare at Jade.

**Level Thirty Six**
**Monday February 5th 2001**

Thirty year old professional photographer Lisa Moore walked from the studio at the back of her home at Pinner into the kitchen.

She was dressed in a tight fitting pale grey pinstriped suit over a white cotton open necked blouse with new beige leather designer shoes on her feet.

Her straightened shoulder length reddish brown hair was brushed and her make-up was applied because she prepared for what was under normal circumstances something completely out of the question.

She had not seen her friend and business partner Jane Chapman's sixteen year old message carrier Kim Cuc Nguy and the Vietnamese teenager should have routinely appeared two days ago.

It was never a simple case of calling Chapman on the telephone because when they originally started this venture Chapman, Moore and Debbie Davies purposely changed all of their contact details.

It was currently impossible to contact each other by any traceable means such as landline, mobile phones and emails.

Because there was no traceable electronic means of communication between them whatsoever and no sign of the sixteen year old message carrier it left Lisa Moore with just one option.

She was about to drive thirteen miles north to Chapman's house at Watford.

She was aware of what had happened to the three Turkish immigrants at Larchwood drive Sidcup and she knew that something wasn't right.

By chance from her kitchen window she saw the familiar red duffle coat that was worn by sixteen year old Kim Cuc Nguy as she walked across the gravelled drive toward the front door.

"Where the hell have you been?" Moore quietly uttered to herself as she watched.

She continued to watch Kim Cuc Nguy approach the house.

Lisa then headed out from her kitchen and along the dimly lit hallway toward the front door and opened it before Kim Cuc Nguy was ushered inside.

"What the hell has been going on?" Moore immediately asked.

The Vietnamese teenager could hear that Moore's tone was agitated.

Kim Cuc Nguy reached into the pocket of her red duffle coat and removed a sealed envelope that contained a hand written note just as she always did.

The sole purpose for her being here was to pass on the hand written communications so that none of the usual traceable lines of communication needed to be used.

This from Kim Cuc Nguy to Lisa Moore was a normal procedure.

Moore tore open the envelope and read the hand written note inside it.

*'We need to urgently talk in person and inside her coat pocket is an unregistered phone that you can call me as soon as you get this note.'*

Lisa Moore then held out her hand and eventually Kim Cuc Nguy reached back into the same pocket and removed David Stringer's modified Taser phone and handed it to her.

When she studied the phone Lisa saw that inside the directory was listed just one contact number and it had no name attached just the number.

She immediately figured that Chapman wouldn't leave anything as traceable as her name inside the device.

From his office room at Tranton road David Stringer again listened to the one sided conversation via the mole that was discretely hidden behind the top button of Kim Cuc Nguy's red duffle coat.

David took a swig straight from the bottle of orange fizzy pop before he spoke.

"Here we go Richard." He announced.

Lisa Moore placed the phone to her right ear as she continued to stare into the brown eyes of Kim Cuc Nguy and waited for Chapman to pick up at the other end.

Of course Chapman would never pick up.

Kim Cuc Nguy nervously glanced down at the floor and waited for what she had already experienced once already but at least this time she knew what was coming unlike before.

She instinctively wanted to take a short step backward but knew that she couldn't.

Suddenly she heard that same electronic "snap!' as from Tranton road David pressed the third button and sent 20,000 volts through Lisa Moore's eardrum.

She made a similar single squeal as Chapman and then she slumped to the floor where her entire body uncontrollably shook.

Kim Cuc Nguy somehow managed to control her emotions this time and she immediately walked past Moore slumped on the floor and made her way back toward the closed front door.

When she opened it Richard and Jade immediately entered and it was this time a calmer Jade that closed it behind her.

"Let's do it the same way as before." Richard told her.

"I'll deal with the garage door and you deal with the woman." He continued.

"Only this time let's try it without you battering the crap out of her."

Jade mocked a sarcastic smile back at him before she walked toward Lisa Moore's still trembling body armed with the same roll of shiny grey duct tape.

"We're in Dave." Richard announced as he walked into the garage.

Soon he would open the large garage door from the inside.

Lisa Moore's eyes flickered as Jade again bit with her teeth a short single strip of duct tape from the roll and firmly pressed it vertically from just beneath Moore's nostrils to just beneath her chin.

A longer strip was then firmly pressed vertically over it to ensure that Moore couldn't open her mouth.

"So you're the little bitch that called the cops and told them that I was a ring leader of this little set up?" Jade quietly and calmly asked her.

She only hoped that Lisa Moore could hear and understand her.

Kim Cuc Nguy watched down with horror when she saw what happened the last time.

Jade placed a third strip over Moore's nostrils cutting off all of her oxygen before she rolled her over and onto her front where her wrists were tightly bound together.

Now Jade used more duct tape to tightly bind Moore's ankles together before she rolled her back over and onto her back.

Eventually she slowly peeled away the tape from Moore's nose and she didn't know if what she had done had produced the desired effect but she sincerely hoped that it had.

She hoped that for those two minutes Lisa Moore believed that she was being purposely killed while she could do nothing to prevent it.

Jade stared down at Moore's flickering eyes before she slowly leaned down and whispered something into her ear.

When she resumed her more upright position Jade smiled down back at her.

"I so hope you heard what I just told you." She quietly uttered.

Kim Cuc Nguy stared down at Jade and for a few brief moments the terrified teenager believed that Jade was actually more terrifying than Chapman, Moore and Davies combined.

**Level Thirty Seven**
**Monday February 5th 2001**

At the same time that Lisa Moore was being loaded into the back of Richard's Van Detective Inspector Nicola Garwood pressed on the doorbell outside Carmen's flat at the King's road Chelsea.

"Where are you hiding you little bitch?" She quietly uttered to herself.

Of course she still believed that she referred to Jade Harris and not Jasmine Stiles.

She stepped back and stared up at the windows of the flat for signs of movement but there was nothing at all and she immediately instinctively knew that nobody was home.

Nicola today had more questions for Jade Harris than she had three days ago prior to the discovery of the warehouse and auction room at unit 4F at the Stanley industrial estate at Woolwich.

Eventually she walked back to the silver Ford car where she climbed into the passenger seat and closed the door behind her.

"Jacob let's try her warehouse at Woolwich to see if she's there." She said with a sigh.

Jacob glanced across at her.

"But guv the Stanley industrial estate is closed off to the public at least until the forensic teams finish there." He reminded her.

Garwood glanced back at him.

"Like that would make any difference to Jade Harris." She sarcastically replied.

Jacob sighed before he turned the key and started the engine of the car.

"Every time we take a step forward that little bitch provides more questions." Garwood uttered.

She fastened her safety belt as Jacob began to drive the car.

"But guv if she purposely gave you that warehouse doesn't it mean that she's actually one of the good guys?" He asked.

"Or at least doesn't it show that she isn't one of the bad ones?"

Nicola stared across at Jacob with disbelief.

"So it doesn't matter to you that she knew where they were the entire time?" She asked him.

"Jacob, how can she be innocent if she always knew where their hideout was?" She asked.

"And why has everybody seemingly forgotten about the blood and fragments of human skull inside her flat at Walworth?"


Around an hour later the car pulled up outside the closed front gates that led into the Stanley industrial estate at Woolwich east London where they were met by three guarding uniformed police officers.

They confirmed that nobody other than the forensic teams SOCO (Scene of crime officers) had entered the estate.

Garwood sighed.

"Where the hell is she?" She quietly asked herself.

She turned to Jacob again.

"If Jade Harris is so innocent Jacob why is she hiding from us now?" She asked.

Jacob shrugged his shoulders as he restarted the car engine.

"In her defence guv she isn't answerable to us." He reminded her.

"She can pretty much go wherever she likes and she doesn't need our permission." He added.

Nicola shook her head with another deep sigh.

"I have no idea why on earth you would want to act in her defence!" She snapped.

There was a pause while Nicola regathered her thoughts and composure.

"Let's go back to headquarters." She sighed.

"I'm going to help out with interviewing all of those new prisoners." She added.

"Let's see if just one of them knows who Jade Harris is."

Nicola and Jacob headed back to the task force headquarters without a clue as to the whereabouts of Jade Harris.

**Level Thirty Eight**
**Tuesday February 6th 2001**

It was a day later when David Stringer stared down at the live image of the Candlelit Queen as she anchored out at sea in the Thames Estuary just eight miles east from the coastal town of Broadstairs Kent.

"I just went through her shipping logs and due to the tides she'll be anchored there for at least three more hours." He informed Richard.

"We need the third bargaining chip to absolutely convince them to hand over Sasha." He added.

"Like I heard you tell Carmen once Richard, they're traders so we trade with them and Miguel Sanchez can have his friends Chapman Moore and Davies back in exchange for your sister."

"The ship is going to moor just east of north Woolwich pier at about midday tomorrow." He added.

Richard responded and confirmed that he understood everything that David had just explained but his mind was understandably elsewhere.

*'Sasha's actually in British waters right now.'* David thought to himself as it suddenly dawned on him.

This time he didn't say it out loud but Richard was already thinking the exact same thing.

Even the usually unshakable David Stringer was beginning to feel the tension now that they were so close.

Now that she, Sasha was so close.

After a short while he latched onto another overhead satellite and looked down at the vast Spanish vessel *the Indigo* now anchored in the Mediterranean Sea just off the coast of Syria.

David's next task was to check over the maisonette at Pitcairn road where he knew were Richard Willows, April Marsh, Carmen Richardson, Jade Harris, Jasmine Stiles, Huy Nguy and his sister Kim Cuc Nguy.

There was no activity outside there and that was good because David knew that bound and gagged in the spare bedroom were Jane Chapman and now Lisa Moore.

He then turned his attention to the house that was owned by Debbie Davies at Amersham north east of Watford Hertfordshire.

"You have to do the last one today Richard." He uttered.

There was a silent pause before the former British army captain responded again.

"I know mate we're getting ready to go right now." He replied.

**Level Thirty Nine**
**Tuesday February 6<sup>th</sup> 2001**

Thirty one year old Debbie Davies after the assassination of her three Turkish friends kept a very low profile.

She also continued to wait for word from Jane Chapman via their sixteen year old message carrier Kim Cuc Nguy.

Unlike Lisa Moore she naturally presumed that Jane Chapman was also keeping a very low profile.

She knew however that forty seven year old Barak Yazici, thirty nine year old Atif Rahman and forty two year old Firat Alican well enough to know that they would never have done this to each other.

Even during the most heated of arguments none would have even considered drawing a gun on another.

Somebody did this to them and her biggest fear was that she was now a target because Davies herself was far from innocent.

She played a somewhat pivotal part in more than a few 'accidental deaths' and she was just as responsible for the abduction sale and profit of what was now over a thousand people.

Davies had every reason to feel paranoid and she genuinely believed that whoever assassinated her three Turkish colleagues was also fully aware of her existence and probably her whereabouts.

She was however more than astute but her single mistake was that she believed that the person or people responsible for killing the three Turkish men only knew about the activities that were carried out from the house at Larchwood drive at Sidcup.

She, just like Jane Chapman and Lisa Moore believed that nobody could possibly know about the larger picture.

That was almost impossible.

Today the Vietnamese teenager would arrive to hand deliver a sealed envelope just like she did every time that she visited.

She would also be one of a very few people that Davies would never ever suspect.

The timid Kim Cuc Nguy had no form of contact to the outside world.

She was after all essentially at sixteen years of age a child as far as Davies was concerned but of course that didn't stop her Jane Chapman or Lisa Moore using her as their personal message carrier.

However Kim Cuc Nguy herself was now thinking along those lines too.

She was sixteen years of age from a deprived country and even more deprived village but she was far from stupid.

Today she feared Jade Harris more than Davies Chapman or Moore.

David Stringer watched from above as Kim Cuc Nguy walked up the long gravelled driveway toward Davies's almost palatial home at Amersham just north west of Watford three days later than she was due and expected.

Unlike Lisa Moore, Davies put this fact down to Jane Chapman and not the Vietnamese teenager herself because it was Chapman that decided and controlled when Kim Cuc Nguy travelled and when she didn't.

David Stringer continued to watch from some sixty miles above as Kim Cuc Nguy approached the large solid oak front door.

He could also see the roof of Richard's dark blue van that was parked behind small dense woodlands at the edge of the vast grounds that came with her property.

David had already fully briefed Richard and Jade Harris regarding this situation.

Because of what he already knew of Davies and her activities he explained that if there was a person in his opinion worse than Jane Chapman in the entire world, it was without a shadow of doubt this woman.

"We should have taken her out with the Turks." David told Richard.

Debbie Davies opened the huge oak front door and she was dressed in a thin black cotton sleeveless vest and a short blue denim skirt with white designer training shoes.

"What's been going on?" She asked the Vietnamese teenager.

Debbie ushered her inside and closed the large wooden door behind her.

As they both stood in the large reception hall Kim Cuc Nguy reached into the pocket of her red duffle coat and removed another vanilla sealed envelope.

Davies stared into her brown eyes as she took it and tore it open before she removed the single sheet of paper and read it.

*'Debbie, Kim has a phone in her pocket that I bought for you to safely call me.'*

Davies glanced up at Kim Cuc Nguy before she returned her gaze to the hand written note that she wholeheartedly believed was from Chapman.

*'We're going silent for a few months because some of them from the warehouse are now in custody so give me a call as soon as you read this and then give the phone back to her.'*

Davies glanced back up at Kim Cuc Nguy.

"You've got a phone with you?" She asked.

Kim Cuc Nguy nodded her head and then removed David's phone from her other pocket and handed it to Davies.

Davies then opened the contact list inside the phone to see that just one number was saved and she naturally assumed it to be Jane Chapman's.

What appeared to be a telephone number was in fact a code that would transmit a signal back to David Stringer to show him that she had just pressed the green button and it also immediately activated the electronic device.

From his office bedroom David continued to stare down at the rooftops of the vast property.

"Ok, she has activated it so five, four, three, two, one, and..."

"Goodnight Miss Davies." He said into Richard's ear.

He pressed the third button on the small black box that immediately sent a signal back to the phone and along with it 20,000 volts straight through Debbie Davies's skull.

Just like Chapman and Moore she squealed as the device electronically 'snapped' into her ear before she slumped to the floor.

Kim Cuc Nguy this time had different instructions.

She immediately opened the front door and saw the dark blue van as it turned the corner and made its way down the long gravelled drive as Debbie Davies lay on the floor convulsing behind her.

"Jade?" David said into the tiny mole inside her ear.

"Could you go out of your way to try not to kill this one please?" He sarcastically asked.

Jade stared out of the passenger side window of the van.

"You're a comical little twat aren't you?" She asked in response.

The blue van pulled up outside the opened front door.

From inside the maisonette at Pitcairn road Jasmine Stiles giggled at her sister's response to David.

**Level Forty**
**Tuesday February 6th 2001**

While Debbie Davies was being bound with duct tape inside her own home by Jade Harris, at task force headquarters Sam Henning sat inside the ground floor office opposite Chief Inspector Keith Curtis.

It was Curtis that arranged this somewhat private meeting with Sam and it wasn't because they now had several members of the human trafficking ring in police custody.

This very private and personal meeting between the two old friends was with regard to what Curtis believed was rapidly becoming Detective Inspector Nicola Garwood's personal obsession with Jade Harris.

Sam then explained to Curtis that he recently visited Carmen Richardson.

He explained again that he knew Carmen from old and that he respected her.

Sam was absolutely positive that there was no way that Carmen would be involved with the human trafficking ring or with Jade Harris if she was involved.

They now understood that Jade had recently returned from the Greek island of Kefalonia where she was working for Carmen.

Although Sam was certain that Jade knew something about the incident that occurred at her flat on or around the night of Wednesday 8th November of last year it didn't actually link to the perfectly timed anonymous telephone call that named her as the ring leader of the group.

"Actually Sam I think they link up a little too perfectly." Curtis responded.

Sam nodded his head with full agreement of that statement.

"The problem is that at the time that one telephone call made perfect sense to Nik and remember that none of you had a single lead or clue as to the identity of anybody connected to the trafficking ring." Curtis reminded Sam.

He sat back in his office chair and stared out of the window to his right and Sam could see that he was deep in thought.

Eventually he returned his gaze toward Sam.

"How many of them do we have in custody right now?" He asked.

Sam informed him that there were now eleven men in police custody including the former head of the task force Martin Roberts.

"And they're all saying roughly the same thing?" Curtis asked.

"All of them except Roberts." Sam replied.

"Most of them are refusing to answer questions but one, a Romanian is beginning to open up." He continued to explain to the chief.

"He's a thirty six year old former Romanian army Captain called Abel Barbu." Sam added.

Curtis glanced back at Sam.

"And has this Romanian army Captain ever mentioned the name of Jade Harris?" He asked.

Sam shook his head.

"Her name has been purposely brought up during the interviews and he doesn't have a clue about her." He replied.

Curtis took in a long deep breath and then sighed.

"Ok Sam I want you to play Devil's advocate for me." He began again.

Sam nodded.

"Jade Harris killed somebody on or around the eighth of November last year." He continued.

"Show me the dead body." Sam immediately replied.

Curtis nodded his head.

"There were an unknown blood sample and fragments of human skull that match the blood sample on her new carpet." He then added.

Now Sam nodded his head.

"I'm still waiting for you to show me the body guv." He replied.

Curtis chuckled.

"I hate this game." He uttered.

"Jade Harris vanished at the same time that blood was spilled at her flat." He began again.

"Prove to me that she was even there at her flat when whatever happened there did because there's no DNA evidence to support or suggest it." Sam responded.

Curtis sighed.

"An anonymous telephone call was received by this task force that claimed that Harris was the ring leader of the human traffickers." He said.

Sam pondered for a few moments.

"Santa Claus deliver's six billion presents in one night every single year." He chuckled.

"Martin Roberts has named her." Curtis continued.

"See previous answer." Sam retorted.

Now Curtis chuckled.

There was a momentary pause.

"Ok try this one on for size." He started again.

"She lied about how she went from this country to a Greek island and doesn't know the name of the person that took her there."

Sam pondered again for a few moments before he finally responded.

"That's the one guv." He finally conceded.

"That's the one."

Curtis nodded his head.

"That lie is what Garwood can't get past." He replied.

"So do we bring her in on obstruction charges?" He asked.

"Let's face it Nik's right about that one, Harris is definitely lying." He added.

Sam again nodded his head in agreement.

"But if we bring her in what happens to the rest of this case?" He asked.

Curtis sat back in his chair again and seemed to study that same window before he took in yet another long deep breath.

"I honestly couldn't tell you Sam." He eventually replied.

"What I do know is that nobody but Roberts is claiming her as their ring leader and Roberts is the only bastard here playing for time."

There was another pause as Curtis returned his attention to the same window.

"If we pull Jade Harris in on any charge and involve her in this case as a suspect..." He began again.

"Because Roberts has named her and nobody else has the entire thing could swing in his favour." He sighed.

Sam raised his eyebrows.

"How the hell does that work?" He asked.

Curtis shrugged his shoulders.

"Roberts looks like he's the only suspect in custody that's telling the truth if we have Harris and he also claims that this was from his part a complete misunderstanding." He continued.

Curtis returned his stare toward Sam.

"A sympathetic Jury can't decide if he's guilty of not and suddenly Roberts walks free." He suggested.

Sam raised his eyebrows again and then dismissively shook his head.

"He was monitored handing over a suicide pill to the original fella that still won't talk." He pointed out.

"According to Roberts he believed that the prisoner claimed that he had a headache and Roberts is still saying that he has no idea how it ended up as a replacement pill in his pocket." Curtis reminded him.

Now it was Sam's turn to take in a long deep breath and sigh before he eventually spoke again.

"So do we bring in Harris on obstruction charges?" He asked.

This time Curtis immediately shook his head.

"I genuinely don't believe that she's involved with the trafficking ring." He replied.

"If we bring her in we add her to it and completely change the shape of the investigation." He added.

"And in the process we'd make Roberts look to be the only one telling the truth."

"And remember that he's the only one out of the eleven that wasn't caught red handed inside a holding pen or in the middle of an abduction attempt at Ilford."

Sam nodded his head.

"So do we now tell Nik to stop chasing her?" He asked.

Curtis shook his head again.

"If Nik is as obsessed with Harris as you think she is she could end up interrogating the prisoners and try to implicate Harris into the story." He explained.

"Leave her to chase Harris around London for now." He continued.

"Keep her out of the interrogation procedure."

Sam sighed and then climbed to his feet.

"You never know Sam she might by some miracle of fate turn up something that links Harris to the eleven in custody."

**Level Forty One**
**Wednesday February 7th 2001**

David Stringer watched from high in the sky as the British cargo feeder ship the Candlelit Queen moored at a quayside about five hundred feet east from the north Woolwich ferry crossing point on the river Thames.

Just as he predicted yesterday it was now around midday.

From the exact same screenshot on the monitor he could also see the police officers at the Stanley industrial estate that was still closed to members of the public and it would remain so until several forensic teams finished their work.

"They're a little too close for comfort." He quietly uttered to himself.

He then informed Richard that the huge vessel had just moored at the quayside.

"And a black range rover car has already pulled up right beside the ship." He added.

Richard confirmed that he received the information.

At the maisonette at Pitcairn road Richard turned first to Jasmine Stiles.

"It's time for you to let the lovely Detective Inspector Garwood find you again." He told her.

Jasmine nodded and climbed to her feet.

"Where should I go?" She asked.

Richard appeared to ponder for a few moments.

"The surveillance teams are due to change over soon at the King's road so you'll be better off being seen outside the warehouse at the Stanley Industrial estate." He advised.

"She won't get into unit 2B because the whole place is crawling with coppers." David interjected in his ear.

Richard nodded his head.

"And they'll tell Garwood that she's there." He replied to David.

Jasmine left the maisonette and headed for Carmen's black Saab convertible car.

"There are two very big men that just climbed out from the black range rover Richard." David informed him.

Richard then turned his attention to Carmen.

"Miguel Sanchez knows that we have the three women here and that Jane Chapman has information including his contact details which is why I wanted them taken as an insurance policy." He informed her.

Carmen nodded her head and forced a smile.

"So what do we do now?" She asked.

"We bring them down here for him to take when he leaves." Richard replied.

He then glanced down at the sofa where nineteen year old Huy Nguy and his sixteen year old sister Kim Cuc Nguy sat and stared up at him.

"You've met Miguel Sanchez?" He asked Huy Nguy.

The nineteen year old medical student nodded and so did his sixteen year old sister.

"So when we get Chapman Moore and Davies down here, you two need to go and wait upstairs." Richard said.

Again they both nodded.

Richard then smiled down at Huy Nguy.

"Can you help me to carry them down here?" He asked.

Huy Nguy nervously smiled back up at him and climbed to his feet.

The intense anticipation of what could, might and should happen had just suddenly notched up by a couple of levels.

That time was now rapidly approaching.

**Level Forty Two**
**Wednesday 7th February 2001**

Around forty minutes later inside the cubicle office at task force headquarters Detective Inspectors Sam Henning and Nicola Garwood sat at their respective desks in silence.

That silence was broken when Nicola's mobile phone rang and she pressed the green button and listened to the caller.

"Ok keep her talking and keep her there." She replied into her phone.

Nicola hung up the call and then climbed to her feet.

Sam Henning glanced up at her from a file that he was reading.

"Keep who, where?" He asked.

Nicola looked back down at him as she headed toward the door.

"Jade Harris is at the front gates of the Stanley industrial estate trying to get into her warehouse." She replied.

"If she knew what was going on inside unit 4F for all of that time she withheld information and I can finally nick her." She added.

Sam sighed and slowly climbed to his feet too.

"Nik, do you understand the implications that are involved if you now add Harris to the case?" He asked.

Nicola continued to stare at him.

"What are you saying Sam?" She asked.

She continued to stare at him in silence for a few moments.

"That little bitch knew that there was a human trafficking warehouse just down from her own facility and even though she did and said nothing you still think she's innocent?" She eventually asked.

"Is that what you're telling me Sam?"

There was a momentary pause and an immediate air of discomfort in the office.

Eventually Sam explained the real situation that was Roberts was the only person that had mentioned the name of Jade Harris.

Nobody else held in custody knew who she was.

If Jade Harris was now brought in as a suspect Roberts could be viewed as possibly telling the truth because he alone had mentioned her name and Harris would be in custody to validate his claim.

"I'm urging you not to arrest her Nik." Sam said with a near plea in his tone.

"I said before that she needs to be questioned because she does know something but nicking her would be counter-productive to the case as a whole right now." He added.

"When this is all under control we can bring her in at a later date to discover everything that she knows."

Sam pulled on his long black overcoat.

"Where are you going?" Nicola asked.

"Are you popping down for another cosy chat with your friend Curtis to snitch me out?"

Sam took in a deep breath and sighed.

"No Nik I'm coming with you!" He eventually replied.

"To make sure that you don't nick Jade Harris." He added.

**Level Forty Three**
**Wednesday February 7th 2001**

It was thirty five minutes after Detective Inspectors Nicola Garwood and Sam Henning left the task force headquarters building at commercial Street Whitechapel central London.

From sixty two miles high in the sky David Stringer stared down at a quite bizarre situation that was unfolding outside the closed green steel gates at the Stanley industrial estate at north Woolwich.

Three uniformed guarding police officers stood in front of Jasmine Stiles as she leaned on Carmen Richardson's black Saab.

The silver Ford that was driven by Detective Inspector Nicola Garwood pulled up beside it.

David Stringer glanced to the far right on the exact same monitor.

He could clearly see Miguel Sanchez, Theresa Sanchez and the young blonde girl as they all climbed into the back of the black range rover with the two *'heavies'* as he referred to them seated at the front.

He stared back across at Garwood Henning and Jasmine at the far left side of the monitor again and then back at the black range rover.

"If the warehouse buildings weren't where they are this lot would all bloody see each other!" He uttered to himself.

Everybody that had been issued with transmitting and receiving moles however heard his statement.

"Oh by the way Richard I have two things to tell you." He began again.

"Well one and I think another one." He said.

"The black range rover is just turning now and will start heading toward you and they'll be there in about thirty minutes." He continued.

"Ok and what's the second thing?" Richard nervously asked.

David continued to stare at the monitor in silence but this time it had nothing to do with his somewhat blinkered vision.

In truth he understood that he often missed the point with regard to what to inform Richard of and what not to depending on the time and the situation and this in his opinion was one of those moments.

"Dave, what's the second thing?" Richard eventually asked again.

*'Definite information is better than no information at all.'* David thought to himself.

"It's about the young girl that's with Miguel and Theresa." He finally replied.

There was a lengthy pause before he finally spoke again.

"It's definitely Sasha." He finally revealed.

In front of the closed green gates that led into the Stanley industrial estate Jasmine Stiles continued to lean on Carmen's black Saab convertible with her arms folded in front of her.

As soon as Detective Inspector Nicola Garwood stood in front of her Sam Henning turned to the guarding uniformed police officers and nodded his head and they immediately dispersed.

He then also turned his attention to Jade Harris.

"I can finally arrest you on charges of perverting the course of justice and obstruction." Garwood informed Jasmine with a victorious grin.

"Take no notice." David said in her ear.

"I just read her personal log and in it she's complaining that she isn't allowed to arrest you." He added.

Jasmine grinned.

"Do you really want to do that Nicola?" She asked.

"Walk to the gates and then turn to face them again." David told Jasmine.

"And do it quickly!" He urged.

"Like right now!"

Nicola Garwood took in a long deep breath before she continued as Jasmine slowly walked toward the closed green gates and then turned to face them both again.

Nicola and Sam both walked toward her.

"Jade, could I have a word?" Sam Henning asked.

Just then Jasmine watched a shiny black range rover drive past directly behind Garwood and Henning.

It was the only reason for her movement in order to turn their backs to the main road.

She smiled again but this time with relief.

"Shit that was close, good job Jaz!" David Stringer uttered in her ear.

Jasmine's smile broadened at David's remark.

The broad frame of Sam Henning stepped a little closer to her.

"You and I met some years ago when you first started out on the game do you remember me?" He asked in a calm and quiet tone.

Jasmine stared up into his eyes and studied them for a few moments.

She slowly shook her head after she had thought of the most plausible response.

After all he could be playing her and may have never actually met her sister at all.

"You all look the same to me." She eventually replied.

She continued to stare back up at him.

"Listen to me for just a few moments." He began again.

"Thanks to you we have almost broken this case." He continued.

"Carmen and I go back many, many years and because you're associated to her I knew that all of this just didn't sit right."

Jasmine still stared up into his eyes and she appeared to be so calm although her heart was absolutely pounding.

*'Hurry up before I throw up all over you!'* She thought.

She continued to stare up at Sam.

"All I really want to know is what actually happened to you." Sam assured her.

"How and when did you know that the traffickers were inside unit 4F?"

As she continued to stare up into his eyes Jasmine broke into another wry grin.

"Would you like me to show you just how I knew?" She asked.

"It would be so much easier to show you then to tell you." She added.

Suddenly Nicola Garwood stepped forward and stood beside Sam.

"If you know something else I swear I'll arrest you right now on obstruction charges!" She snapped.

Jasmine turned her attention to Nicola but the same wry grin remained.

"Nicola, if you do that I swear that you'll never see what I want to show you but you will meet Mr Alcott again." She retorted.

"Neither of us want that now, do we?"

Sam Henning promptly interjected.

"Ok Jade, what do you want to show us?" He asked.

Jasmine returned her gaze to Henning.

"You have to follow me in your car." She told him.

Nicola Garwood shook her head with a sigh and Jasmine returned her attention to her.

"Don't you want to see what I have to show you Nicola?" She asked.

Garwood stared back at her.

"Why don't I come with you in your car?" She asked.

Jasmine immediately giggled.

"Shut up you'll never be able to keep your hands to yourself!" She replied.

Jasmine walked back to the driver side of the Saab convertible where she turned to face them both.

"Do you want to see it or not?" She asked.

Garwood and Henning looked at each other before they both eventually walked toward the silver Ford.

"You'll need to become expert detectives afterward though." Jasmine quietly uttered to herself.

David Stringer chuckled in her ear.

"I swear I'm nicking that little bitch as soon as this is over Sam." Nicola quietly uttered.

*'I swear you're not.'* Sam thought to himself.

**Level Forty Four**
**Wednesday February 7<sup>th</sup> 2001**

Twenty eight minutes later David Stringer watched as the black range rover slowly reversed into the opened wooden drive in parking bay at the rear of the maisonette at Pitcairn road Tooting.

Within a few minutes there was an air of electrified tension as the forty two year old Spaniard Miguel Sanchez calmly stepped inside the living room.

He was followed by Theresa Sanchez and one of the two large men from the front seats of the range rover.

Already standing inside the living room were Richard Willows, Carmen Richardson, April Marsh and Jade Harris.

Lying bound and gagged on the floor were Jane Chapman, Lisa Moore and Debbie Davies.

Richard immediately stared into the thin brown eyes of Miguel Sanchez.

"Where is she?" He asked.

Today was the day that Richard was willing to die for this cause.

Miguel Sanchez slowly turned and the second large man entered behind Richard's twenty two year old battered and bruised younger sister.

Richard and Sasha stared at each other for what seemed like an eternity.

He could clearly see just how much Sasha had been physically abused.

Jade Harris stared straight at Theresa Sanchez.

*'I remember you.'* She thought to herself.

Richard reached out his hand to his sister.

Slowly, very slowly Sasha physically trembled as she edged toward the only man in the entire world that she trusted.

Suddenly Richard reached out and grabbed her before he pulled her toward him and tightly held her in his left arm.

Jade slowly strolled toward Theresa Sanchez where they finally made eye contact.

"Do you remember me?" Jade calmly asked her.

Theresa stared back at her and there was some vague recollection but not much.

Jade's smile broadened before she reached behind her back with her right hand.

Theresa smiled as Jade reached into the back pocket of her blue denim jeans and discretely removed a small handful of coins.

It was something that her dad taught her.

Suddenly and without any warning Jade swung with all of her might with a closed fist full of small change.

She connected directly onto Theresa's jaw with a loud crack!

Theresa Sanchez made no sound at all and continued to stare into Jade's green eyes.

Suddenly her Spanish brown eyes started to flicker as she swayed on her feet.

Jade stared straight back at her.

Theresa slowly closed her eyes and then unconsciously slumped to the floor.

"Now you fucking remember me." Jade quietly uttered.

Suddenly Miguel Sanchez pulled a short black pistol that he immediately pressed against the centre of Jade's forehead.

"You never touch my wife." He calmly informed her.

"You never touch my wife!" He repeated but this time he screamed loudly.

The two heavies immediately withdraw firearms.

Just as suddenly Miguel Sanchez felt something that was pressed against his left temple and his thin brown eyes glanced in the same direction.

Richard Willows stared down the short black barrel of his own pistol and he used it to gently nudge Miguel's head.

"You shoot I shoot and we all die, your choice." He very calmly informed Sanchez.

"I'm ready, are you?" He asked.

"Now take your wife and your three friends down on the floor and leave while I still let you."

Eventually Miguel slowly removed his pistol from Jade's forehead and turned to the heavies.

He shook his head before they finally re-holstered their firearms.

Miguel then nodded in the direction of the four women on the floor.

"Take them all to the car and untie them." He uttered.

Richard held Sasha in his arms while the two large men first carried the still unconscious Theresa Sanchez out to the car before they returned and removed Miguel's first partner in crime Jane Chapman.

"We will take them to their homes when we are finished here." Miguel informed his two Italian bodyguards but he spoke in English.

Debbie Davies was removed next and she was eventually followed by Lisa Moore.

Suddenly it was all over as quickly as it begun.

They were gone.

Richard then headed with Sasha toward the door that led out to the kitchen.

"Richard, we have to go." Carmen quietly reminded him.

He stopped and turned to face her.

"Just give me three minutes." He replied with a tremble in his tone.

Carmen could see that his eyes were filled with tears.

Just then Jade heard a familiar voice in her ear.

"David, can you tell my bitch of an ugly sister to get her arse moving please?" Jasmine asked.

Jade shook her head with a chuckle.

"Tell me yourself you old witch I can hear you, remember?" She replied on David's behalf.

Carmen then walked toward Jade and handed her the keys to her precious pale green Aston Martin DB9.

She stared into Jade's eyes.

"Are you ok now that you somehow managed to twat all of them?" She asked.

Jade immediately nodded with a smile.

"Good." Carmen replied.

"But you won't be if I find a single scratch on my car."  She assured Jade.

She said it with the same warm smile that she once showed Theresa Sanchez herself.

**Level Forty Five**
**Wednesday February 7th 2001**

Jasmine Stiles drove west on the A13 road and neared Aldgate east underground railway station and she knew that it would be around ten minutes before she headed south and crossed Tower bridge.

"When you cross the bridge head for the Elephant and Castle and if I need to divert you in circles for a few minutes before Jade gets there I will." David informed her.

"There are manic road works at Borough road in north Lambeth where you're going to meet so we can hold you up there too." He added.

Sixteen minutes later Detective Inspectors Nicola Garwood and Sam Henning continued to follow who they still believed to be Jade Harris.

They were now travelling on the A201 road toward the vast roundabout just north of The Elephant and Castle underground railway station.

Jasmine drove around it and took the third exit and headed north onto Newington causeway and they followed her.

Six minutes later the real Jade Harris passed the same underground station and onto the same vast roundabout where she took the second exit onto London road heading north-west.

After another four minutes Jade turned right onto the western end of Borough road and headed toward a set of temporary traffic lights due to the manic road works that David informed Jasmine of just twenty minutes ago.

Jasmine in Carmen's second car took a left on Newington causeway onto the same Borough road as her sister but from the opposite eastern end.

"I can now see you both on the same monitor." David informed them.

Inside Carmen's Saab convertible Jasmine glanced into her rear view mirror and saw the two senior police officers directly behind her and she beamed a grin before she waved her hand particularly at Nicola.

"She's a smug little bitch." Nicola uttered.

Sam and Nicola stared directly ahead as Jasmine in the car directly in front of them stopped right in front of temporary traffic lights when they turned red.

"Where the hell is she taking us?" Nicola asked with a sigh.

With the red light showing on the left side of the road the traffic from the right side started to flow toward them again.

"Here we go." David Stringer uttered with a grin.

Garwood watched as Jade Harris turned in her driver seat and smiled again with another wave of her hand.

"This is bloody ridiculous." Nicola uttered.

"She's just taking the piss out of us Sam."

Just then Sam and Nicola both heard a car horn that came from the other side of the temporary single lane street.

They both instinctively glanced across at a car that Sam immediately recognised.

"That's Carmen Richardson's Aston Martin." He uttered.

He stared at the unmistakable pale green prestige Aston Martin DB9.

Garwood and Henning continued to stare as Jade Harris stared straight back at them.

She suddenly blew a playful kiss that was directed toward Nicola.

"Who the..." Nicola quietly blurted.

Both Sam and Nicola turned in their seats and watched the back of Carmen's car as it continued to travel eastbound toward Newington causeway where they had just come from.

Nicola shot a glanced straight into Sam's eyes.

"How the hell can she be in that car?" She yelled.

When they both returned their gaze to the front the black Saab convertible was gone too.

The traffic lights were still showing red.

"What the…" Nicola quietly uttered.

"Nik, let's go back to Whitechapel." Sam insisted.

"We've been done."

**Level Forty Six**
**Wednesday February 7<sup>th</sup> 2001**

It was fifty minutes later when Jade Harris and her half-sister Jasmine Stiles stepped back inside the maisonette at Pitcairn road together at Tooting and they were both still laughing almost hysterically.

Richard Willows and his sister Sasha, Carmen Richardson, April Marsh, Vietnamese Huy Nguy and his sister Kim Cuc Nguy were all now headed toward Lydd airport Kent.

The same privately hired Leer jet that carried Jasmine to the Greek island at the beginning of last month awaited to return there.

"I bet she's having an absolute fit!" Jasmine laughed.

She was of course referring to the Jade Harris obsessed Detective Inspector Nicola Garwood.

"Can you imagine sitting in a car behind me when at the same time I drive past you on the other side of the road in a completely different car?" Jade asked in a fit of giggles.

David Stringer then informed them both that Carmen and the group were travelling on the M20 motorway and would arrive at Lydd airport within the hour.

He also informed then that Nicola Garwood and Sam Henning had returned to task force headquarters.

"I'd love to be a fly on the wall in her office right now." Jasmine giggled.

"You two are also booked onto a six o'clock flight in the morning." David reminded them.

"We're close to wrapping this up so I think you should both get an early night tonight." He added.

Jasmine and Jade stared at each other in a silent pause for a few moments.

"You're not my dad." They suddenly replied together.

At task force headquarters at Whitechapel Detective Inspector Nicola Garwood stared at the police photograph of Jade Harris on her computer screen but she still saw nothing that would provide her with a clue.

She re-checked Jade's personal file and saw that she was an only child so a twin sister was out of the question.

*'Who the hell was the second one?'* She wondered.

She glanced across at Sam Henning.

"You're absolutely sure that was Carmen Richardson's car?" She asked.

Sam glanced back across at her but before he had a chance to reply the office door opened and their boss Chief Inspector Keith Curtis entered.

Curtis stared at Sam.

Somehow Henning knew to leave the office and he immediately did.

He closed the door behind him leaving Curtis alone with Nicola.

"So Jade Harris threw you another curve ball then?" He asked.

Of course he already knew everything.

Nicola climbed to her feet and leaned against the wall on her right with her arms folded in front of her.

"How can you still seriously claim that she knows nothing?" She asked in response.

Nicola had if nothing else learned that she could at least speak her mind in front of Curtis.

Curtis sighed and sat down behind Sam's desk.

"Whether you like it or not her name was mentioned last year during an anonymous call and that resulted in us discovering blood samples and fragments of human skull inside her flat." Nicola continued.

"Then Oliver Alcott from the Old Bailey suddenly appears at Gatwick to rescue her." She reminded him.

"That alone means that she or even *they* knew that we wanted her." She pointed out.

"Then she alone conveniently gives us the warehouse at the Stanley industrial estate where she very conveniently rents one herself four bloody buildings away." She continued.

There was a momentary pause.

"And now she shows us that she can be in two cars at the same time!"

Curtis nodded during another momentary pause.

"If you continue to pursue Jade Harris there's a possibility that you also allow Roberts to walk free." He finally told her.

"She has something to answer for!" Nicola snapped in retaliation.

There was yet another silent pause that lasted for a few moments.

"Is this all about nailing Roberts or seeking the truth?" She eventually asked in a much quieter tone.

They stared into each other's eyes for a few moments.

"I know it's a slim chance but are you really willing to jeopardise losing Roberts just to find out what Harris actually knows?" Curtis retorted.

There was another air of silence before the conversation continued and it was Curtis that spoke again.

"Sir Christopher Dwyer and I both think that you need some time off." He informed her.

Nicola raised her eyebrows.

"You mean you need me out of the way!" She retorted.

Curtis folded his arms in front of him and stared down at the floor.

"You take three weeks leave so that I don't have to suspend you Nik." He quietly uttered.

Nicola's eyes widened again.

"What can you suspend me for?" She asked.

Curtis looked back up and straight at her.

"You're suffering from stress." He replied.

"You can't see it but you're completely obsessed with this whole Jade Harris theory." He continued.

"Take it from an old hand that you can't see the woods for the trees." He added.

"And this same old hand is standing outside of the woods watching you chase your own tail."

There was one last silent pause.

"You take three weeks voluntary leave or three weeks enforced leave it's your choice."

Garwood continued to stare at him.

"I want you to take the voluntary leave Nik." Curtis genuinely informed her.

**Level Forty Seven**
**Thursday February 8th 2001**

It was around three o'clock the next cold black morning when twenty nine year old Jasmine and her older sister by three months Jade took a taxi cab from the maisonette at Pitcairn road to Gatwick International airport.

At around five thirty that morning they stood side by side in a queue of around forty people as they prepared to board a flight for the Greek island of Kefalonia and they looked like identical twins.

"Oh bugger I almost forgot." Jade uttered.

She reached into her dark brown leather shoulder bag and removed Jasmine's passport and handed it to her.

"Can you imagine getting caught out now?" She asked with a giggle.

Jasmine chuckled too and reached into the back pocket of her tight faded blue denim jeans and handed Jade back her own passport.

"That would be quite funny." She replied.

"I can see it now both of us sitting in that same room in front of your friend Nicola Garwood." Jade chuckled.

There was a pause before she spoke again.

"I hope that she's ok." She said.

"David said that in her personal log it reads that she took voluntary leave but in the boss of the task force's log it says that he sent her home." She added.

"I do feel a bit guilty." Jasmine replied.

"But our needs were greater than her career." She added.

Jasmine and Jade had absolutely no idea that they were now being watched from a short distance.

"I haven't heard a peep out of David today." Jade pondered.

She then turned to her sister.

"Nope I haven't either." Jasmine replied.

Eleven people behind them in the same queue, was a slightly plump thirty year old man that stood at around five feet eight inches tall.

He had short light brown hair and he wore large heavily magnified glasses that made his eyes appear far too large for his head.

Today would be the first time that he had ever left the shores of the United Kingdom.

Of course Jade Harris had never met him in person and Jasmine never once looked back.

But as usual even although nobody knew about it there he was watching in plain sight.

**Level Forty Eight**
**Friday February 16th 2001**

It was a little more than a week after Jasmine and Jade boarded their flight back to Kefalonia.

At her home at west Dulwich south London Nicola Garwood sat on her brown leather sofa and watched daytime TV.

Her long straight blonde hair was down and she wore no makeup whatsoever.

She was dressed in a long pale pink towelling dressing gown with white slippers.

Her feet rested on top of her rectangular smoked glass coffee table as she sipped coffee and continued to watch nothing in particular on the television in front of her.

Beside her left foot was an opened vanilla envelope and the contents were placed on top of it.

A pre-paid return flight ticket rested on top of a hand written note.


*Nicola,*

*I know that everything seems difficult to understand right now but if you come to visit me in a week's time I promise to tell you absolutely everything with no tricks involved.*

*I couldn't tell you everything before.*

*Just get onto the plane.*

*Jade*

Nicola sipped her coffee and continued to watch TV after reading the letter.

In truth she no longer knew if she wanted the truth.

In fact she didn't even know if she wanted to continue working as a police officer.

**Level Forty Nine**
**Saturday February 24th 2001**

It was just over a week after Nicola Garwood opened the letter from Jade Harris at her home at west Dulwich and discovered the open return flight ticket.

Nobody at the Greek island of Kefalonia knew if she would accept the invitation or not.

In fact at that time even Nicola didn't know if she would take the opportunity to learn the absolute truth about her obsession that was twenty nine year old Jade Harris.

It was surprisingly warm for the time of year even on the Ionian Greek island of Kefalonia.

As promised nineteen year old medical student Huy Nguy and his sixteen year old sister Kim Cuc Nguy were returned to their small village on the southern coast of Vietnam.

They flew out three days ago and were now at home with their family.

Twenty two year old Sasha Willows stood at the bottom of the front garden at Carmen's eight bedroom home with her arms folded in front of her and she stared out at the Ionian Sea in silence.

Most of her time was spent alone and in silence but she was very slowly recovering.

Her older brother Richard would be with her and there for her for the foreseeable future.

Lying on a sun lounger at the far end of Carmen's pool was the short plump figure of thirty five year old April Marsh.

On another sun lounger at the opposite end of the pool and in front of the main entrance door of Carmen's house twenty nine year old Jade

Harris wore a small orange two-piece bikini and she also wore her sister's large dark sunglasses.

Twenty nine year old Jasmine Stiles swam in the heated pool from one side to the other dressed in a similar design two-piece dark blue bikini.

Jasmine swam toward her half-sister where she eventually rested her elbows onto the poolside and stared down toward the bottom of the garden.

"Do you think she's going to be ok?" She asked.

Jade lowered her sunglasses to glance at Jasmine to see the direction that she nodded.

She then turned on the sun lounger to see Sasha staring out to sea again.

She turned again to face Jasmine.

"She's been to hell and back." She reminded her sister.

"But she has Richard and she'll get through it in time." She added.

Jasmine continued to stare at Sasha.

"And she's got us." She eventually replied.

Jade then raised her eyebrows as she returned her sunglasses to their original position on the tip of her nose.

"So are you going back to Ashford when we go back home?" She asked.

Jasmine shook her head with a grin.

"I'm moving in with you and you're giving me a well-paid job in your shop." She replied.

Jade raised her eyebrows again.

"Oh is that right?" She asked.

Jasmine rigorously nodded her head.

"Whenever I leave you alone for more than a week you get abducted." She replied.

"It happened once!" Jade retorted with a giggle.

Again Jasmine nodded her head.

"It happened once so far you mean!" She playfully snapped back.

"It could be the start of a trend!"

Jade giggled again.

"You're so not living with me." She informed Jasmine.

"I so am." Her half-sister assured her.

Just then Carmen Richardson stepped out from the large main entrance door and stared toward the girls.

She was dressed in a long white loose fitting denim shirt and a pair of white denim jeans with beige leather sandals.

"She just boarded her flight at Gatwick so you two need to go and get ready." She informed Jasmine and Jade.

"She'll be standing here in four hours from now."

Jasmine and Jade stared at each other for a few moments before Jade spoke again.

"Hopefully we'll go to jail so that I don't have to let you live with me." She uttered.

She then slowly climbed off the sun lounger.

Jasmine chuckled again as she climbed out of the pool and snatched Jade's pale blue towel.

"They'll make you share a cell with me." She retorted.

Jade immediately nodded her head.

"I generally get that lucky." She sighed.

## Level Fifty
## Saturday February 24<sup>th</sup> 2001

Four hours and thirty seven minutes later twenty nine year old Nicola Garwood stepped out through the opened glass doors from the airport building on the Greek island of Kefalonia.

Ironically it was Dennis Christos that checked her passport and flight ticket.

He had also met Jasmine Stiles and believed her to be Jade Harris.

As she stepped outside with her light blue suitcase on wheels she immediately caught a scent of natural lemon in the air.

She slowly glanced around at her new warmer Mediterranean surroundings.

*'I'm guessing that you'll be watching me from somewhere.'* She thought to herself.

She was of course referring to Jade Harris.

Nicola saw a line of five private taxis just ahead and she casually walked across the narrow concrete road toward them with the belief that out in the open she would easily be spotted.

As she approached the taxi cabs she saw that the driver that stood in front of a silver Mercedes at the very front of the line held a small white card.

As she neared him she could see that her own name was written on it with bold black marker.

It was in the same handwriting that was displayed on her personalised plain white cup back at the Stanley industrial estate at north Woolwich.

She shook her head with a sigh as she stood in front of the driver and then stared into his brown eyes.

"I'm Nicola Garwood." She announced.

Marinos Georgas displayed a somewhat nervous warm smile.

"Do you know where to take me to?" She asked.

He immediately nodded his head with the same smile.

He then opened the boot at the back of the car and took her blue case and placed it inside before he closed it again.

"From what I've seen so far this looks like a lovely island." Nicola said.

She was attempting to make small talk in this completely new environment.

Marinos opened the back door of the car for her to climb inside.

"I hope that you will wish to see much more of it during your visit." He eventually replied.

"There is much to see here." He added.

Nicola climbed into the back seat and Marinos closed the door behind her before he walked around to the driver side where he climbed in and closed his door behind him.

"So do you know Jade Harris?" Nicola enquired.

Marinos and Nicola made eye contact via his rear view mirror.

"Jade is my good friend." He replied.

Marinos started the engine and the silver Mercedes pulled away.

Nicola placed a pair of large dark sunglasses onto her nose.

"How long will this drive take?" She asked.

Again he glanced at her via his rear view mirror and smiled.

"We will arrive in around half an hour." He replied.

Nicola turned her head and stared out of the right side of the car at the electric blue Ionian Sea and she took in a long deep breath and then closed her eyes before she exhaled it.

*'Stay focussed.'* She reminded herself.


A little more than half an hour later, Carmen Richardson walked from the narrow hall at the front of her vast house and into the spacious white kitchen.

She then stepped through it and out to the back of the house with Richard Willows behind her.

Marinos Georgas raised his eyebrows as he glanced at Carmen through the car windscreen and switched off the engine.

Both he and Nicola climbed out of the car at the same time.

Carmen immediately walked toward Nicola and reached out her hand to shake.

"Good afternoon Detective Inspector Garwood, I'm..." Carmen began.

Nicola interjected.

"I know who you are Miss Richardson." She said.

"I've seen your picture on your quite impressive arrest sheet." She added.

Carmen and Nicola stared at each other for a few moments and it allowed Nicola to re-stabilise her composure.

*'Stay focussed.'* She reminded herself for the second time.

Carmen then formerly introduced the man that stood beside her.

"This is Richard Willows." She began.

"You won't know him by the way." She sarcastically added.

Richard nodded his head toward Nicola but her attention promptly returned to Carmen.

"Where's Jade Harris?" She asked.

Carmen slowly shook her head with a sigh.

"The ball today Detective Inspector Garwood is in my court taking into account that I happen to know that you're unofficially suspended from duty." She began again.

"You'll see Jade when I'm good and ready and not before."

There was a silent pause as the two women stared into each other's eyes once again.

"And how the hell could you possibly know that I'm suspended?" Nicola eventually asked.

Carmen stared straight back into her eyes for a few moments before she responded.

"If you stop with the bullying tactics for a little while we have much to show you today." She replied.

"Including how I know everything about you." She added.

"Perhaps you'd like coffee before we begin?" Carmen suggested.

A short while later Nicola was ushered inside the house where she followed Carmen through the kitchen and out to the hall at the front of the house with Richard and Marinos Georgas behind them.

Carmen then opened a brown wooden panelled door on the right side before she invited Nicola through it.

Nicola had no way of knowing that behind the door directly behind her on the left side sat the real Jade Harris and her half-sister Jasmine Stiles.

She was ushered inside Carmen's study and was followed by Richard Willows, Marinos Georgas and Carmen herself before she quietly closed the door behind them.

Nicola stared across the room at David Stringer.

He sat behind a multitude of computer monitors on Carmen's polished desk and nervously stared back at her.

His over magnified eyes blinked and to Garwood it looked like they did so in slow motion.

She slowly walked toward him.

"Who are you?" She asked.

She then habitually folded her arms in front of her.

David suddenly broke into a grin as he continued to stare up at her.

"My name's David but the chicks call me big Dave." He nervously replied.

Richard Willows stood behind Nicola where he stared down at the floor and shook his head with a quiet chuckle.

Carmen then stood next to Nicola and stared at David too.

"He's about to become your best friend when he's finished being a twat!" She informed Nicola without removing her stare from David.

Nicola turned to Carmen.

"I somehow doubt that if he's associated to you." She replied.

Carmen then turned to face her.

"Within an hour I promise you're going to love him." She assured her.

"I somehow doubt that too." Nicola Immediately replied.

She was eventually ushered around to the other side of the desk where David sat and stared at four working monitors.

"So what's all of this?" She asked.

David glanced up at her.

"Before I show you some things can I just tell you that he forced me to do everything?" He asked.

His right forefinger was pointed directly at Richard Willows.

David eventually started his show and tell for Nicola and he began with a bland looking green and brown dating website.

He then logged into the still running human trafficking auction site that was buried within it.

"What the bloody hell…" Nicola gasped.

"Take a seat." David said as he watched her stare into monitor number one.

"We'll be here for a while."

In the next fifteen minutes Nicola would learn that the auction website buried inside a fake dating website was created owned and run by thirty six year old Jane Chapman from Watford.

David then loaded a disk into the computer and monitor number two flickered into life and she watched recorded footage because from Carmen's Greek mansion he had no satellite capability.

"I know that place." She said as she pointed at the screen.

David turned to face her.

"This is Mr Vladimir Kolov leaving his house in his hired car that I know you have the details of." He informed her.

"This was recorded as you can see on Wednesday November the twenty third last year" He added.

He pointed his finger toward a digital dated clock at the bottom right hand corner of the screen for Nicola to see.

"This is him driving to Jane Chapman's house at Watford." He informed her.

"But when you watch this entire footage for over two hours you'll see that Vladimir Kolov Meets with your old boss Chief Inspector Martin Roberts." He continued.

"And this was when Roberts was handed the suicide pill that Roberts later gave to your very first prisoner."

Garwood turned her attention toward David.

"Can you validate all of this?" She asked.

There was a short pause as Nicola stared into David's enormous slow blinking eyes.

Suddenly it all registered.

"Hang on how do you even know about that pill?" She asked.

David broke into a wry grin.

"I'm sure that at the end of this recording you'll recognise Roberts when he climbs from his car outside your task force building and then walks inside it." He replied.

"I tracked him all the way back to find out who he was." He added.

"I already knew who Kolov was." He continued.

"And then of course your new boss nicked your old boss."

Nicola then stood upright and walked around to the front of the desk but turned to face David again.

"Who the bloody hell are you?" She asked in a blunt tone.

"You're not civilian."

Richard Willows now stepped forward.

"That would take some time to explain but the short version is that he pretty much doesn't exist." He informed her.

"He was completely erased from the grid about five years ago." He added.

There was a momentary pause before Richard continued.

"And the same authorities that govern you govern him Detective Inspector." He informed her.

"You more often than not work indirectly from his part, for the same department heads."

Garwood then pointed her finger toward the back of the computer monitors.

"So this is all admissible as evidence?" She asked.

"And who exactly are you?"

Richard flashed one of his smiles.

"I often work with him." He replied.

"And yes it can be made admissible."

Nicola stared into Richard's blue eyes for a few moments.

*If he's telling me the truth I've got Roberts!'* She thought to herself.

"Shall we break for coffee and allow Detective Inspector Garwood to digest everything so far?" Carmen suggested.

Nicola glanced at Carmen.

"You've seen just the tip of a Titanic sized iceberg Detective Inspector." Carmen assured her.

During that break for refreshments Nicola also heard about the roles of Jane Chapman's close accomplices the photographer Lisa Moore and the human trafficker prior to this case thirty one year old Debbie Davies.

"Chapman lives at Watford, Moore at Pinner and Davies lives at Amersham." David informed her.

"I have all of their addresses so that you can pay them a visit."

The affiliation between Davies and the four Turkish men Barak Yazici, Atif Rahman, Firat Alican and also the earlier deceased Doruk Gezmen was never mentioned.

That would become essential to a later part of the story that was finally unfolding in front of Nicola Garwood's eyes.

After the coffee break she also learned of the Indigo, the British vessel the Candlelit Queen, Miguel and Theresa Sanchez, and also the story regarding Sasha Willows.

"So where is Sasha Willows now?" Nicola asked.

"I remember reading her case file." She added.

Richard smiled.

"She's here and never leaving my sight again." He replied.

Nicola nodded her head with acknowledgement.

"I'm going to need to talk to her at some point." She informed him.

Again Richard nodded.

"I know and she knows too." He replied.

There was another short pause before Nicola returned her full attention to Carmen.

"So where is Jade Harris?"


Jasmine and Jade sat in the lounge and very quietly talked before the door opened and Carmen stepped inside before she closed it again behind her.

"Ok she's actually taking it all quite well and the good news is that she isn't anywhere near as pissed as she was when she first arrived." She informed them both.

Jasmine and Jade glanced at each other and showed Carmen the same smile.

"We'll have Jade in first." Carmen said.

She then headed toward the door and placed her hand onto the handle before she turned to face them again.

"Which one of you is Jade?" She asked.

The real Jade Harris beamed a grin back at Carmen.

"You're really crap at this Car." She said with a nervous giggle.

Carmen smiled back at her.

"No I'm just secretly crapping myself actually." She replied.

"As soon as I find the time to pass out I intend to."

Nicola Garwood sat in front of David Stringer on the edge of Carmen's desk when Carmen opened the door and stepped inside.

She was followed by real Jade Harris before Carmen closed the door behind her.

Nicola slowly stood up and walked toward Jade.

Jade was five feet nine inches tall and she had straight shoulder length reddish brown bobbed hair and blue eyes.

She was dressed in a pale blue t shirt and a pair of tight fitting blue denim jeans with white designer training shoes.

Nicola stood right in front of her where she intently stared into Jade's blue eyes.

"So are you going to tell me the truth this time?" She eventually asked.

Jade half smiled back at her before she shrugged her shoulders.

"I've never told you a lie before." She replied.

Jade then slowly turned and looked toward the closed study door.

"You can come in now." She called out.

Nicola now stared at the door too.

It slowly opened and a second Jade Harris stepped inside and closed it behind her.

Nicola immediately walked toward her and just as intently studied her.

This Jade was also around five feet eight or five feet nine inches tall with straight shoulder length reddish brown bobbed hair but she had green eyes and a small dark brown mole just above her upper lip on the right side.

She was also dressed in a pale blue t shirt and tight fitting blue denim jeans with identical white designer training shoes on her feet.

*'I've read her file a thousand bloody times.'* Nicola told herself.

*'She's an only child!'*

She glanced down at the small mole and then back up into green eyed Jade's green eyes.

*'Green eyes, distinguishing marks, small mole above right upper lip.'* She reminded herself as she recited Jade's criminal record by heart.

She then turned to blue eyed Jade.

The *real* Jade Harris.

"So who exactly are you?" She asked.

The blue eyed Jade displayed a wry smile.

"My real name's Jade Harris." She replied.

Garwood shook her head and walked toward her and as she did green eyed Jade, Jasmine Stiles from behind her removed the dark brown mole and then began to remove the green contact lenses that covered her natural blue eyes.

Nicola stared into the real Jade Harris's fake blue eyes and this time when she stared down she could see the very faint outline of her dark brown mole.

Jade then lowered her head and very carefully removed the blue contact lenses before she showed Nicola her natural green eyes.

"You see, it's me." She said.

Nicola then spun around to see that Jade's sister Jasmine now had blue eyes and no mole in sight.

She slowly stepped back so that she could see both of them in the same line of sight.

Carmen and Richard glanced at each other as they watched in silence.

Eventually Nicola pointed to the real Jade.

"So you're Jade Harris?" She asked.

Jade nodded with a smile.

Nicola then turned her attention to Jasmine.

"So who are you?" She asked.

"Bloody hell Nicola I bought you your own cup!" Jasmine replied with mock disappointment.

Nicola's head spun back to Jade.

"So you're Jade Harris?" She asked again.

Again Jade nodded her head.

"Please tell me that this isn't the first time that we've ever bloody met?" Nicola almost pleaded.

Jade broke into a stifled giggle.

"I did blow you a kiss at Lambeth." She replied.

"So we have sort of met before today."

Nicola's head was now spinning and she started to feel physically quite sick.

Eventually she walked back to the desk where she once again sat down in front of David's monitors and placed her head in her own hands.

Nicola already knew what had been done and for what reasons.

*'I've never met Jade Harris before today.'* She told herself.

Suddenly she looked up again.

"Which one of you did I interview at Gatwick?" She asked.

Unfortunately Jasmine Stiles held up her hand.

She stared at one and then the other as it all started to register.

*'I could never have obtained a slip up or confession from Jade Harris because I never interviewed her.'* She considered.

*'Jade Harris has never obstructed me in my line of enquiries!'*

She stared up at one and then the other again before she finally turned her attention to Carmen.

"I need some air." She uttered with a sigh.

She stood upright again and eventually left the room and closed the door behind her.


Around twenty five minutes later Jasmine stepped outside to the pool where she found Nicola sitting on an old sawn down tree stump.

Nicola glanced up at her.

"If it's any consolation you bloody terrified the life out of me the entire time." Jasmine told her.

Nicola placed her head back into her hands.

"I can't believe that I've been so blinded." She replied.

Just then Jade also stepped outside and eventually the two girls sat down on the grass in front of Nicola and her stare turned initially to Jade and then back to Jasmine.

"Explain to me first, what was all of this about?" She asked referring to their almost identical appearance.

Jade explained that in order to do what they did without prosecution it was necessary that Nicola always chased a shadow.

If and when the time arrived that they would appear in court the case would have to be thrown out due to the fact that Nicola had only ever pursued Jasmine Stiles and not the real Jade Harris.

"And to prove it I actually stood right in front of a CCTV camera at Gatwick for about five minutes as myself after you interviewed her and she was no longer there."

"What's really scary is that you and I apparently passed each other without knowing it."

Nicola sighed and slowly shook her head before she once again stared into Jade's green eyes.

"Who died inside your flat at Walworth?"

Jade first told Nicola the story of when she watched the abduction across the street from her flat that consequently led to her own abduction on November the fifth of last year.

"I watched their van turn up outside the flat."

"It was the same van that took the other girl the week before." Jade informed her.

"Kelly George." Nicola interjected.

Jade raised her eyebrows.

"There's a missing person report from across the street from your shop at New Kent road." Nicola explained.

"Her name's Kelly George." She added.

There was a pause.

"She's just seventeen."

Jade covered her own mouth with her hand as a single tear rolled down her cheek.

After a short while she sat and recalled the night that she watched the pretty young blonde girl being loaded into the back of the security van and her eyes continued to well up.

She eventually glanced back up at Nicola.

"When they came for me I waited behind the living room door with a baseball bat." She informed her.

"I hit one of them but I don't know much about the rest of it." She added.

Jasmine now interjected.

"I was never told about the death so that when you asked me about it at Gatwick you'd clearly see that I never had a clue just by my reaction." She said.

"It was actually something that I was never allowed to know about until you personally told me." She added.

There was another pause but there was still something that Nicola needed to understand.

"If you all knew all of this beforehand why didn't you just bring what you had to us?" She asked.

Both Jasmine and Jade turned and stared toward the bottom of the garden where twenty two year old Sasha Willows still stood and stared out at the ocean.

"We had to get her back first." Jade quietly replied.

Nicola stared down at her too.

"Is that Sasha Willows?" She asked.

Both girls nodded as all three of them continued to stare at Sasha.

Jasmine and Jade watched as Nicola climbed to her feet.

She slowly walked to the bottom of the garden where she eventually placed an arm around the thin shoulders of Sasha Willows and held her.

"See I told you she had an almost human side to her." Jasmine whispered to her sister.

Jade nodded as she wiped her tear filled eyes.

What neither of them could see was the continuous stream of tears that rolled down Nicola Garwood's face as she held Sasha Willows in her arms.

**Level Fifty One**
**Saturday February 24th 2001**

At around seven that same evening David Stringer stood very, very nervously inside Carmen's spacious kitchen.

His short mousy brown hair was combed into the usual centre parting and he was dressed in the black suit that hung in his wardrobe for the past few years.

He also wore a white cotton shirt and a burgundy tie that he borrowed from Richard along with his also never worn before today shiny black leather shoes.

In his hand David nervously clutched a single red flower.

Richard Willows stood in front of him and adjusted his tie.

"You're all set then String?" He asked.

David usually had plenty to say about dating conquests but today would be different because he was about to go on a very first real date with an actual tangible woman.

Carmen Richardson strolled into the kitchen dressed in the same long white denim blouse and white denim jeans and she beamed a grin.

April Marsh followed Carmen into the kitchen and she was dressed in a thin black knitted pullover and a pair of blue denim jeans.

Detective Inspector Nicola Garwood followed close behind.

Carmen quietly chuckled just due to the look of sheer terror that was displayed on David's face.

She then glanced down at his hand.

"David, did you steal that rose from my garden?" She asked.

Stringer glanced down at it and then very nervously back up into Carmen's eyes.

"You're only asking me that because you're standing next to a police woman." He nervously uttered.

"I'll put it back after."

Richard, Carmen, April and Nicola laughed all at his response.

"Are you excited?" Carmen asked.

She could clearly see that he was actually more terrified than excited.

Suddenly Jade Harris casually strolled into the kitchen.

She was dressed in a shimmering deep red satin sleeveless knee length dress with glossy black patent leather high heeled shoes on her feet and as she entered she fitted her left droplet earring.

Carmen leaned across.

"This is the king of online dating sites very first date with a woman that actually breathes oxygen." She whispered into Nicola's ear with a giggle.

David promptly handed the red rose to his date Jade Harris and she accepted it with a beaming smile.

Suddenly Jasmine Stiles walked into the kitchen wearing a similar dress to her sister and she also adjusted her left earring.

"Oh god no he asked both of them out at the same time." Richard very quietly uttered to himself.

Jasmine suddenly stopped because everybody stared at her.

"What?" She asked.

Her eyes slowly travelled around and glanced at everybody else that stood in the kitchen.

"She'll be fine." Carmen quietly told her with a reassuring smile.

Jasmine nodded her head with acknowledgement.

"I'm not going to protect her." She replied.

"I'm going to protect him." She added.

"One wrong move and she'll punch his lights out!"

"And you know he's going to make a wrong move."

David slowly turned to look at Carmen.

"Can I borrow another flower please?" He asked.

Suddenly everybody in the kitchen burst into laughter with the exception of David.

Eventually Marinos appeared from outside and he was dressed in a white cotton open necked shirt and smart black trousers with shiny black leather shoes.

"I must protect him from both of them." He chuckled.

"Bugger he's a bloody real Greek smoothie." David whispered to Richard.

Marinos Georgas was in fact Jasmine's date for the night.

After a short while Marinos, Jasmine, Jade and David left the kitchen and made their way to the silver Mercedes that was parked at the rear of the house.

As Carmen watched she suddenly realised something.

They had done it.

It was over.

Richard's somewhat sophisticated plan had somehow worked.

"Get your hand off my arse or I'll break it David." She heard Jade say from outside.

Garwood watched with a half-smile.

"I could do with his help every now and then when I go home." She quietly uttered.

Richard Willows glanced across at her and smiled.

"We'll work something out." He assured her.

"He wants to help you."

**Level Fifty Two**
**Sunday February 25<sup>th</sup> 2001**

It was again unusually warm the next morning and at around ten o'clock Nicola Garwood and Jasmine Stiles casually strolled along the golden sandy Lourdatta beach.

Nicola's long straight blonde hair was for once down and she was dressed in a thin beige knitted pullover and a pair of faded blue denim jeans with white training shoes.

"So how was the double date last night?" She asked with a chuckle.

"Did David behave himself?"

Jasmine laughed.

"After all of the crap he comes out with when he's hiding behind his PC." She began.

She stopped talking for a few moments to stifle another chuckle of amusement.

"He sat silently terrified of Jade all night." She eventually added.

Nicola glanced out toward the Ionian Sea.

"He told me this morning that they're going to wind down the task force within the next two weeks and I'm going to be left to manage the unsolved cases." She informed Jasmine.

"Sam Henning and Keith Curtis are retiring but Jacob Saunders will stay with me." She added.

Nicola turned to Jasmine again.

"Jacob's the Detective Sergeant that was with me during your farcical bloody interview at Gatwick." She added.

"Oh the one that waved to me when I was on my way out for breakfast?" Jasmine asked.

Nicola sighed.

"That's the idiot." She replied.

There was a pause before Jasmine asked the all-important question.

"So what happens with the case about Jade Harris?" She asked.

Nicola glanced back at her.

"There's no case involving Jade Harris." She replied.

"I would have hit him with the bat too."

She turned her head to stare back out at the gently swaying blue ocean.

"Isn't it insane that I get told what I'll be doing in two weeks from now by a chubby little shit that spends most of his life in his spare bedroom?" She asked with a chuckle.

She looked back toward Jasmine and watched as she stifled another giggle.

"Yes but he's not your average chubby little shit is he?" Jasmine asked in response.

Nicola shook her head with full agreement.

They walked in silence for another few moments before she stopped and turned to Jasmine again.

"So you're not actually gay are you?" She asked.

Jasmine stared down at the golden sand and pondered on the right use of words to respond to Nicola's question.

"That's dangerous ground to walk on Detective Inspector Garwood." She eventually replied.

She then stared up into Nicola's eyes.

"Taking into account that I happen to know how obsessed you've with my sister." She added.

She giggled again.

Nicola saw the funny side to Jasmine's statement and laughed too and then they continued to walk.

"How long are you going to stay here for?" Jasmine enquired.

Once again Nicola stared out at the ocean.

"Carmen told me to stay for as long as I like." She replied.

"A week maybe two before I get officially called back into work."

Jasmine stared back down at the sand and nodded her head with a genuine smile.

"Good, I'm glad." She replied.

Nicola stopped again and turned to face Jasmine.

"Talking of work when I do go back I'd like to get my hands on Jane Chapman, Lisa Moore and particularly Debbie Davies." She said.

It was now Jasmine that stared out at the blue ocean before she fixed her gaze upon Nicola.

"Miguel Sanchez took them all back to their houses after the deal was made at Tooting." She replied.

"David has all of their addresses so they're not difficult to find." She added.

Nicola smiled back at her and considered what a refreshing change it was to have this woman in front of her actually telling the truth for once.

**Around Four Months later...**

## One
## Saturday July 7th 2001

Saturday July 7th 2001 would prove just like yesterday to be the hottest day of the year for more than two decades on the Indonesian island of Sulawesi.

At 3:10pm the temperature reached its scorching peak as a battered old green former Serbian military truck very slowly trundled into the deserted looking village of Tapalang on the island's north-west coast.

Forty three year old Spaniard Miguel Sanchez peered through the bug smeared windscreen and appeared to be searching for signs of life, but none of the local villagers were naive enough to even attempt to work outside in this ridiculously hot and incredibly humid climate.

Miguel was a thin man who stood at five feet seven inches and he had a mop of black curly hair and sported a thick black bushy moustache that had just begun to creep over his upper lip and he had narrow dark brown eyes that gave the impression that he was always squinting.

He wore a dirty white short sleeved cotton shirt that showed darkened soaked patches of sweat beneath his armpits and across his chest and he also wore dark brown corduroy slacks and filthy old white training shoes.

It was difficult to comprehend that over the years Miguel had become an incredibly wealthy man.

As his battered old truck slowly rolled to about halfway through the village, Miguel continued to search the area in front of him with both windows of the rusty pale green steel cab lowered in a pointless attempt to get some much needed cooler air inside.

He shook his head when he heard children playing somewhere in the distance, probably down on the beach to his left but then a wry grin appeared because he knew that at their age he would have ignored warnings from his parents and would have been outside with his friends too.

As he neared the northern end of the dirt track road, Miguel slowed the truck down to an almost dead stop and stared out to the left of his driver side window.

He knew that what he was searching for was around here somewhere.

His eyes scanned for a narrow discrete fork in the dirt track road that he knew was here because he had made this trip in the past, but for some reason he always missed this hidden turning.

The discrete turning passed under trees on both sides and would lead him toward the perilous cliffs edge but then the dirt track road would bank to the right so that he could begin the even more perilous journey over a mountainous region.

This dangerous road was only ever used by the Indonesian military because it led to just one place but Miguel Sanchez was no soldier and he had never been one.

He bought his beloved truck from a man who knew a man who knew another man and there were of course no questions asked.

Suddenly his foot slammed down hard onto the brake as he stared at the darkened narrow dirt track beneath the trees on his left where he could see very faint tyre tracks embedded into the earth and a wry grin suddenly appeared.

"Ahí está" He quietly uttered to himself in his native Spanish tongue.

*'There you are.'*

Beneath the faded green canvas awning at the back of the truck, Miguel's thirty eight year old wife Theresa Sanchez sat on the wooden bench that ran the entire length on the right side.

Theresa was a large woman these days thanks to a near fatal illness that was followed by a lengthy medicated recovery with a heavy and consistent use of steroids.

She was five feet six inches tall and had long straight jet black hair that was pulled back into a ponytail and her beautiful brown eyes were the only remaining evidence that she had once been an incredibly beautiful woman.

Theresa was dressed in a khaki military style short sleeved shirt that was far too tight just like her almost matching lighter khaki knee length shorts.

On her feet she wore beige desert boots and her outfit showed that what were once long and slender tanned legs now displayed large clusters of black and blue varicose veins.

The couple had been childhood sweethearts until twenty years ago when Theresa grabbed her opportunity and moved to the bustling Spanish city of Madrid to become a fashion clothing catalogue model until she was struck down by her sudden illness three years later.

Back then Miguel walked his own path too, and he created, with his cousin Louis, what would become a thriving export business.

He didn't see Theresa again until ten years ago when he returned to his sleepy home town to attend the funeral of his mother and it was then that he discovered that his beloved Theresa was back at her family home and stricken with illness.

The romance was immediately re-ignited and as Theresa slowly recovered she involved herself in Miguel's business with his cousin and these days she was responsible for monitoring the cargo prior to its delivery, just as she was doing today.

In their native Spanish tongue the cargo was known as El Ganaderia.

Translated into English it means *The Livestock*.

Lying on the scorching hot steel floor of the truck were three women from the United Kingdom.

The woman furthest from Theresa lay slumped against Miguel's rusty green cab.

She was around five feet six inches tall and had long matted blonde hair and she was dressed in a filthy black sleeveless cotton vest and a just as filthy short faded blue denim skirt.

There were no shoes on her feet and her ankles had been very tightly tied together with stiff bright blue nylon rope that caused bloody red sores despite the fact that she hadn't moved for the entire trip.

Her wrists were chained behind her back with solid steel handcuffs and strapped over her face was a filthy white paper industrial face mask that had been lightly doused with chloroform to keep her completely subdued for the journey.

Lying in front of her was a woman with shoulder length reddish brown hair and she was dressed in a ripped filthy white cotton blouse and a pair of tight fitting light grey pinstriped slacks.

Her ankles were just as tightly tied together with the same stiff blue nylon rope and her hands had also been chained together behind her back and she too wore a white paper mask that kept her completely unconscious.

Just like the blonde travelling companion behind her, she had in fact been rendered and kept unconscious for what was now the better part of three months.

These women just like all of the others were only ever partially woken in order to be given just enough food and water to survive before they were returned to unconsciousness.

It was the simplest way to manage them all on such a grand scale.

The two women could in some way consider themselves fortunate that they knew nothing of this trip or where they were headed, but the same couldn't be said for the third captive woman.

On the burning hot steel floor in front of Theresa's beige desert boots was another blonde woman and she was in her early to mid-thirties.

Her shoulder length blonde hair was also matted because she had spent so long in captivity and of course most of it unconscious.

Theresa stared down into her pale blue eyes and saw that they were still full of anger and frustration and they glared straight back up at her.

She was dressed in a filthy black sleeveless vest and a pair of beige denim shorts with no shoes on her feet.

Theresa Sanchez had taken a liking to her beige leather sandals and concluded that this woman most certainly no longer needed them just like her two unconscious travelling companions no longer needed theirs.

Before this woman was revived to a semi-conscious state, a large dirty brown rag had been pushed into her mouth and shiny black duct tape was then firmly pressed over it and the extra strong black tape was then very tightly wrapped over her mouth and around her head three times to ensure that she couldn't speak.

Theresa Sanchez liked to talk during these longer journeys but she saw no reason to debate.

Her hands, like the two unconscious women behind her were tightly chained behind her back and the same stiff blue nylon rope caused the same red and bloody sores around her ankles, but hers were more defined and incredibly painful because occasionally she would attempt to kick out at Theresa's sadistic taunts.

Her bare thighs showed redden marks that were provided by the scorching hot steel floor and all because she had intentionally been given the ability to move, albeit just a little.

Like Miguel, this conscious blonde woman had just heard the sounds of children playing somewhere in the distance but they were too far away for her to hear single defined words so that she could try to work out where she had been brought to.

She was absolutely certain of only one thing.

This was without a doubt, far, far too hot to be London.

Printed in Great Britain
by Amazon